THE INSTITUTE

'Aren't you ashamed?' the Prefect mocked wickedly. 'You've made yourself wet girl. Aren't you a slut?'

'Yes, Mistress,' Chantel whispered, hiding her face against the books on the shelves.

'Tell your sister what you are,' the Prefect ordered.

'I'm a slut,' Chantel whimpered, crushed by the shame of having her guilty secret revealed to all.

'You deserve to be punished more severely,' the Prefect told her, unwilling to let the opportunity to degrade and punish her pass so quickly.

'Yes, Mistress,' Chantel repeated. She tried to squeeze her legs together, trying to hide the telltale signs of her arousal, but she could feel the dewdrops of love juice start to trickle down her thigh.

T0314674

A NEXUS CLASSIC

THE
INSTITUTE

Maria del Rey

This book is a work of fiction.
In real life, make sure you practise safe, sane and consensual sex.

First published in 1992 by
Nexus
Thames Wharf Studios
Rainville Road
London W6 9HA

This Nexus Classic edition 2004

Copyright © Maria del Rey 1992

The right of Maria del Rey to be identified as the Author of this Work has been asserted by her in accordance with the Copyright, Designs and Patents Act 1988.

Typeset by TW Typesetting, Plymouth, Devon

Printed and bound in Great Britain by Clays Ltd, St Ives PLC

ISBN 0 352 33352 9

All characters in this publication are fictitious and any resemblance to real persons, living or dead, is purely coincidental.

This book is sold subject to the condition that it shall not, by way of trade or otherwise, be lent, resold, hired out or otherwise circulated without the publisher's prior written consent in any form of binding or cover other than that in which it is published and without a similar condition including this condition being imposed on the subsequent purchaser.

The Random House Group Limited supports The Forest Stewardship Council (FSC®), the leading international forest certification organisation. Our books carrying the FSC label are printed on FSC® certified paper. FSC is the only forest certification scheme endorsed by the leading environmental organisations, including Greenpeace. Our paper procurement policy can be found at www.randomhouse.co.uk/environment

One

Lucy sat with her head in her hands and listened vaguely to the muffled sounds around her. The bare cell was cold and dark, lit only by a single bare bulb that flickered irregularly, ready to give up the fight. The mattress was hard, a thin sheet of foam rubber placed over a wooden frame, and every so often Lucy shifted her weight uncomfortably to stop the numbness.

It wasn't a bad place to be locked up, Lucy reflected. The cell was fairly large, with an old china toilet in the corner and a table and chair near to the door. It had been home to her for almost a week and she wondered how much better her new place was to be. She felt certain that this was to be her last night in a cell; after all that she had been through she could not imagine that the Institute was a place of cells and padded rooms.

She looked up at the sound of footsteps approaching. Somehow the cavernous maze of cells under the court seemed both to deaden sound and to amplify and echo it. There was a pause for a second and the peephole in the door opened with a sharp metallic clang. Lucy smiled when she saw that it was Dave, the youngest and friendliest of the guards.

'I've got a visitor for you,' he said, smiling. His thin pale face was framed by the black peephole in the door, but even the dim weak light couldn't conceal the light in his eyes, and his lop-sided grin.

1

'Another social worker?' Lucy asked wearily, standing up and taking a step towards the door. She liked Dave and hoped that he would spend at least some time chatting to her. He made her laugh and they had flirted harmlessly, though now that she knew she was destined to spend the next six months in a women-only establishment she wanted him to go much further.

'Too well dressed to be a social worker.' Dave laughed. 'She looks more like a lawyer or the police.'

'Do I have to see her?' Lucy asked. She stood right up against the door and stooped down slightly so that she was face to face with him. She was tempted to reach out and stroke the contours of his face, to feel the rough masculine texture of his skin beneath her fingers.

'You don't have to do anything, love.' Dave broadened his smile, breathing in the faint scent that Lucy wore. 'But see this lady and I'll come in for a chat later,' he promised.

'If I don't have to . . .' Lucy waited coyly, then pursed her lips and swept back her long golden hair.

'Good,' Dave laughed. 'She'll be along in a second.'

'I didn't say yes . . .' Lucy protested innocently, but her eyes shone and she smiled eagerly. Dave winked at her and slammed the peephole shut with a satisfyingly sharp retort.

Lucy returned to the bed. She searched through her bag and found a mirror and the last of her make-up, then quickly checked her face. Carefully she applied the last of the lip gloss and brushed her long straight hair. In the dim unnatural light she felt that her hair looked dead, and she missed the sunshine that imparted a luxurious golden sheen to her flowing locks.

She could hear the sharp echoes of feminine heels on the cold stone floor and the heavy clodding of an escort. She sighed impatiently. Lucy had seen dozens of people in the previous few days: social workers, psychologists, educationalists. They had questioned and prodded her,

2

asking anything and everything they could think of. She had hoped, now that sentence had been passed, that all of this would cease. She was sick to death of answering the same questions, of peering into the same cold and uncaring eyes.

The door creaked open and the cell was flooded by a harsh electric glare that seemed to carve out an angular niche in the faltering light. She noted immediately, and with a little disappointment, that the guard was not Dave. The guard was partially hidden by the steel door, and the centre of the light was occupied by a tall blonde woman, dressed in a simple red suit.

'Hello, Lucy.' The woman stepped into the cell confidently. The guard withdrew, locking the door and leaving Lucy and the woman alone. 'My name is Anne Young, and I'm not a social worker.' She smiled disarmingly and offered her hand to Lucy.

Lucy was intrigued. She stood and shook hands. She could feel at once that Anne was not of the same breed as the legions of caring professionals that had plagued her existence since childhood. Anne had a poise and confidence that was striking. Lucy noted, with the professional eye of the petty thief, that the simple red suit was well cut and obviously well made. The clothes fitted the woman – elegant, attractive and expensive.

'May I?' Anne asked, taking the only chair. She sat down at once, not waiting for Lucy's assent. 'If I'm not a social worker then what am I doing here?'

Lucy sat down on the edge of the bed. She nodded and smiled, finding Anne's chic style a refreshing change from the dowdy people, and their depressing manner, that haunted the court.

'I'm a journalist.' Anne announced. 'In fact, I head a team of investigative journalists for a national television company. You'll see my name when the credits roll at least once a week.'

'Do you appear in the programmes?' Lucy

interrupted, trying to remember if she had ever seen Anne's striking face on television.

Anne shook her head. 'I leave that to other people; I'm not interested in that particular game. Would you like to appear on television?'

'I suppose so,' Lucy admitted, though she had never even considered the idea before. She could hardly believe that such a thing could be possible. jealously she looked at Anne, who seemed to embody the cool glamour of television, and then at herself, a small-time petty thief on the road to nowhere. The contrast was unsettling and not a little depressing.

'It could be arranged. You're certainly pretty enough, and I'm told that you're quite a smart girl in your way.' Anne paused to let the suggestion sink in. 'I have a little job on at the moment, and if you help me out I'll see what can be arranged.'

'What sort of job?' Lucy froze. She recognised that the enticing picture being painted was intended to lull her into a false sense of security. She knew that nothing in the world was free.

'What do you know about the Institute?' Anne asked her, sensing that Lucy's natural suspicions had been aroused.

'Not a lot,' Lucy admitted. 'I know it's an alternative to prison for women between the ages of eighteen and twenty-one. I know it's hard to get into. That's about all.'

'Aren't you surprised that you've had to sign the Official Secrets Act? Aren't you just a little bit suspicious about all the secrecy?'

'I've had to sign a whole load of papers; that's nothing new.'

'But the Official Secrets Act?' Anne leant forward conspiratorially. 'There is something fishy going on. I deal with the government all the time, and I know a lot of people. But I get nothing when I ask about this place.'

'So?' Lucy pulled away. She sat further back, unwilling to be pulled into the cosy atmosphere that Anne was so obviously trying to build.

'We know where it is. We even know one or two people who work there. But we can't get any further. I can sense that this is a big story, I can feel it,' Anne pressed her hand against her chest to emphasise the point. 'All I need is a way in.'

'What's in it for me?' Lucy demanded, finally understanding what Anne wanted. She felt a bit more at ease, and could understand Anne perfectly now that she knew what she wanted. It meant that the air was clearer and they were conversing in a single tongue with no place for ambiguity or misplaced dreams.

'I like you.' Anne smiled. 'You're very direct. I like that. I think you are just the person we need. You're going to the Institute tomorrow. All you have to do is tell me what's going on. It's that simple.'

'What if nothing's going on?'

'But something is going on. Have you ever heard of a correctional establishment run without public scrutiny of any kind? This place doesn't even exist officially.'

'But what if nothing is going on?' Lucy persisted.

'I'll still pay you. Five thousand pounds when the story is delivered.' Anne sat back and studied the look of shock on Lucy's young face. She had seriously underestimated Lucy. The story about appearing on TV might have worked on someone less astute or more gullible. But Anne now saw that Lucy was very sharp indeed. She was pleased. If the Institute really was suspect then it would take guts and a good deal of ingenuity to get the truth out into the open.

'Five thousand? Cash?' Lucy whispered, trying to regain her composure. She had never had that sort of money before, and the thought of it made her head spin.

'In cash. And I meant it about television. You're smart, and attractive. I could get you a job if you wanted. Perhaps not appearing on the screen, but then not in the typing pool either.'

'How will I get the story to you?' Lucy wanted to know. She had already started to think through the consequences of the agreement.

'Is that a yes?' Anne laughed enthusiastically.

'It's a maybe. If the place is so difficult to crack how can you get the story from me?'

'I'm working on that. I have a couple of possible leads. All you have to do is get the story ready. Write it down or use a cassette tape. Make sure you get all the details. Include names and dates. I'll make sure we can get it from you, don't worry.'

'When?'

'I'll give you a few weeks to settle in. I imagine we'll have our communication link sorted out in a month or so.' Anne stood up to go, bent down to straighten her skirt and saw Lucy watching her closely.

'If this place is so secret what do you think will happen if I get caught?' Lucy asked, suddenly remembering the Official Secrets Act and the shroud of mystery that Anne claimed surrounded the Institute.

'Your contact will have a password. Don't worry. I've done this sort of thing many times in the past. A journalist does not reveal sources, unless she wants to stop being a journalist, and I've no intention of doing that. Don't worry, just be sensible.'

'What's the password?' Lucy also stood up. She felt uncertain and wanted Anne to stay a little longer. She had never done anything like this before; her life had been a long catalogue of mundane disasters. The uncertainty was tinged with a little elation; her life had just taken a pivotal leap into the unknown and, she hoped, for the better.

'The password is "Conrad",' Anne decided after a pause. 'You know, *The Secret Agent* and all that.'

'Conrad,' Lucy repeated. She didn't know what Anne

was talking about, and the word had a strange and exotic ring about it.

Anne stepped forward and tentatively planted a soft kiss on Lucy's gently pursed and glossy lips.

Lucy was dumbstruck. She breathed Anne's sexy perfume. The gentle peck on the mouth was soft and sweet, and totally unexpected. Lucy felt a wave of confusion and she took a faltering step backwards.

Anne saw the look of horror etched on Lucy's face and knew that she had made the second gross error of the day. Lucy had looked so sweetly innocent that Anne had been attracted immediately. She had seen the way that Lucy had been eyeing her closely and had assumed that the attraction was mutual.

'Conrad, don't forget,' Anne said quietly, hoping that Lucy would not be so repelled by the pass that the deal was off. She knocked on the cell door loudly and waited for the guard to let her out.

'Five thousand. But you can stick your job. Lucy glared angrily. She watched Anne leave and then flopped down on to the hard bed, feeling tired and bewildered.

The kiss had been so sudden that Lucy had been caught off-guard She felt disgusted and repulsed by the idea of letting another woman touch her or make love to her. Other women had tried it on before, and Lucy had always felt the same sick reaction. It was only the thought of the money that had stopped her from slapping Anne in the mouth.

Minutes later Dave returned. 'Are you OK?' he asked, shutting the heavy steel door behind him.

'Fine,' Lucy muttered. She had been lost in her thoughts and had not heard him entering the cool cell. She sat up smartly and smiled, glad for the company, especially glad that it was male company.

'Not bad news, I hope,' he continued easily.

'No, I'm all right, thanks. Just a bit nervous about

7

tomorrow.' She sat back on the bed, curling her feet under her.

'Scared of all those lessies eh?' he laughed, sitting casually on the edge of the bed.

'What do you mean?' Lucy demanded anxiously. 'What do you know about the Institute?'

'Only joking, girl,' he calmed her, surprised that his joke should provoke such an intense and frightened response. He inched closer to her, and squeezed her hand reassuringly.

'Are you sure?' she asked, gazing into his eyes imploringly. She already felt better, realising that Dave's protective instincts had been aroused.

'I know a girl like you needs a man to look after her,' he smiled, mocking himself gently. He pulled her close and as she snuggled up, he could feel her naked breasts under her thin T-shirt.

'Are you a real man?' she teased. She allowed him to take her in his arms. She was drawn to him almost magnetically, and their lips were joined into a single long passionate embrace. The memory of Anne's lips on hers was effaced by the cool feel of Dave's mouth.

Dave began to pull away slowly, so that she was forced to lift herself higher and higher. At last he pulled away completely and he saw that her face was slightly flushed. He liked the slightly demure look about her eyes, the soft brown colour and the large oval shape that gave her a fleetingly oriental look. He paused for a second then took her under the chin and pulled her up to meet his mouth again. She felt soft and responsive against the taut hardness of his body.

Very deliberately he began to outline the gentle curve of her body with the flat of his hand. He rubbed his fingers up from her thighs and on towards her heavy round breasts. He took each breast in his hands and squeezed gently, massaging the softly malleable globes, all the time using his tongue to explore her mouth and breathing in her soft scent.

8

Her responses became more urgent as he rubbed his thumbs teasingly over her nipples, so that the sensitive points of flesh puckered temptingly. They parted for a second and he pulled the T-shirt over her head. She smiled shyly and he admired the full, firm white breasts and the small round nipples, dark and enticing. She shivered with pleasure when he went down, taking each cherry in turn and gently biting and pulling. From the soft moans of pleasure that escaped from her mouth, and the way she half closed her eyes and parted her full red lips, he knew that she was one of those women with acutely sensitive nipples. He concentrated his attack on her breasts, sucking hard and long on the erect objects of arousal.

She searched for his hardness blindly, brushing his body with her hands, seeking his prick eagerly. But he pushed her hands away repeatedly. He carefully laid her back on the bed, and eased her light cotton leggings down. She lifted herself up and he pulled her panties down to her knees, brushing her mound with his mouth. 'Let me touch you . . .' she gasped, but he refused, keeping her hands away from the hardness that she only managed to touch for an instant.

He slipped a finger into her crack, and found that she was already moist. He liked the warmth and honeylike feel of her pussy, and very gently he began to use his fingers to explore her there. He slid his fingers in and out slowly, first one finger then a second. She moved under him, easing his entry and accepting the waves of pleasure that he produced. He moved faster and faster, probing first here and then there,' he knew where to press and where to let his fingers rest. He let himself be guided by her sighing song of pleasure, and by the electric dance under his fingers.

She started to buck under the rapid thrusts of his fingers – one, two, three. She felt as if a symphony were being played in the deepest places in her wet vagina. She cried out urgently and seized him tightly in her arms, clinging to him desperately as she was taken by the storm of orgasm that engulfed her and smothered all consciousness.

She seemed to wake from a hazy dream. She was naked in his arms, and he was planting soft tender kisses on her neck. She again tried to seek out his hardness, wanting to feel the rigid flesh in her hand, in her mouth, deep inside her cunt. But he took her hand and forced it over her head.

'Do you want me to fuck you?' he whispered, pressing himself down on her. She could smell the faint masculine odour on him, his hot breath on her face. Her breasts were still tender as she pressed herself against his muscular chest.

'Please, let's make love now,' she whispered. She wanted to undress him, to rid him of the dark blue uniform that smothered his individuality.

'I'm not sure you deserve it,' he teased, pressing his pulsing prick against her thigh.

'Please, don't do this,' she said weakly. The rub of his prick on her thigh was maddening. It felt hard and powerful, even underneath the thick uniform.

He began again to suck her nipples. He knew that she would respond, unable to resist the powerful impulses that his mouth could work on her.

Dimly Lucy heard a sound outside the cell, but she was overwhelmed by the hungry mouth on her nipples, and the expert fingers that were tracing a long slow path from the mouth of her sex to the entrance of her arsehole. Suddenly she was aware that there was another person in the room. She jumped up and out of Dave's embrace.

'What the fuck's going on?' she demanded furiously. She tried to cover herself with her T-shirt, but was aware that this was only causing Dave and another guard amusement.

10

'Relax, girl,' Dave smiled serenely. 'This is my mate Andy. We're like brothers; we share everything.'

'Hello Luce,' Andy smiled. 'Dave told me you was a looker and he weren't joking.'

'Wouldn't you want two of these?' Dave asked. He undid his fly and pulled out his stiff white prick. He held it proudly in his hand, squeezing the base gently and affectionately.

Lucy knew now why Dave had deliberately aroused her, but the sight of his thick hard prick took the edge off her anger at Andy's unwelcome intrusion. She looked on silently as the two guards undressed in front of her, piling their clothes in an untidy bundle on the table and chair. The two men were completely relaxed, and showed off their taut muscular bodies unselfconsciously.

Dave stepped forward and pulled the T-shirt away from Lucy. She knelt forward on all fours and her firm round breasts moved slightly, her nipples erect dark bullets swaying in unison. She reached out and took Dave's extended prick in her hand. She closed her grip around the base of the hardness, marvelling at the smooth solid feel of it in her hand. Very slowly she stroked it, passing her fingers over the entire length, enjoying the silky smoothness of it, the spiky brush of dense hair at the base, and the softly sensitive head.

Dave began to kiss Lucy on the back of the neck, as with his hands he explored her body, feeling his way down her back and over her buttocks. He parted her arse cheeks slightly and leant forward, admiring the glorious view of her arse crack with the enticing picture of her tight round arsehole and the soft pink flesh that peeped through the folds of her pussy lips.

Lucy explored Dave's body with both hands. She playfully milked his prick, feeling it become even harder under the skilful play of her fingers. She slipped her fingers under his balls, weighing the cool heavy sac in

11

her hand, as if measuring his vitality. Bending her head lower, she started to plant tender kisses on the inside of his thigh. She passed her tongue through the tight curls of hair, moving gradually upward and inward.

Andy watched Dave and Lucy moving together, positioning themselves for mutual pleasure. He knew what to expect. He and Dave had shared many women together, working in partnership to give, and to derive, the maximum of pleasure from any encounter.

Dave had parted Lucy's arse cheeks and was pressing his fingers into her pussy, stimulating her sex into a heightened state of arousal. When he judged that Lucy was ready he turned to Andy and nodded his assent.

Andy padded across the cold floor, climbed on to the bed and positioned himself behind Lucy. He took her soft white buttocks in his hands and regarded the exposed sex with a look of adoration, then swooped down and unhesitatingly speared her sweetness with his tongue, pressing his mouth deep inside. She moaned softly and moved her arse backward, allowing him to gain deeper access into her sex.

With Andy sucking and licking her pussy, Lucy felt a wave of delirium pass over her. She was kissing Dave's thick hard prick with ever-increasing urgency. She was wildly licking and biting, from the base to the tip in a single mad movement of desire. Dave swivelled to one side so that he could reach down to begin to torment her inordinately sensitive nipples. Unable to contain herself any longer she opened her mouth fully and drew in Dave's manhood. She sucked deeply, swallowing the silver drop of fluid that she had drawn earlier with her lips and fingers.

Dave released her tits and took her head in his hands. He brushed her hair back, away from her face, so that he could see her taking his prick deep into her warm inviting mouth. He watched her move up and down, playing her tongue over the full length, almost letting

12

go then drawing back down in a sweeping blissful motion.

Andy sucked deeper and deeper, letting her hot sticky juices fill his mouth with her deep feminine taste. He found her golden place and lashed it with his tongue, gratified to hear her moan with pleasure and wriggle with a rush of satisfaction. He worked her patiently, lapping up her sex juices and propelling her to the edge of orgasm. He judged the moment right and withdrew. He could feel the dampness on his face, and on licking his lips he found her taste smeared all over him.

She closed her eyes and urged Dave on with her hands. She was taking his wide deep thrusts fully into her mouth, so that the thick purple head was working right into the back of her throat. She drew her cheeks in with each thrust, forming a slippery wet pussy with her mouth. She had the faint taste of semen in her mouth already, and from the pulsing and throbbing of his flesh she knew that he was fast approaching release.

She sighed with a ripple of pleasure when she felt Andy thrust his hardness deep into her sex. He had used his mouth to prepare the way, and she was wet and aching for his prick to burst into her. The wet slippery warmth of her cunt enveloped his hardness, and he closed his eyes and gave himself to the blissful sensation.

She had never been fucked like this before. The feel of two rock-hard pricks working into her was overwhelming. Dave and Andy were pounding in unison, thrusting their pricks with a single ecstatic rhythm, the rush of elation coming from both ends in a single joyful motion. She could hardly breathe, hardly move, but she ached for more. The tension building up within had its own momentum and Lucy felt unable to resist.

Suddenly all motion ceased. The three bodies froze, seized by the tidal wave that swept them into a single mutual orgasm. They clutched each other tightly, their

13

bodies contorted and their faces ablaze. Lucy took the pumping pricks, swallowing the spunk that was pumped into her hungry mouth and pussy. She felt herself to be on fire, her pussy pulsating around Andy's draining prick. All three felt as one, falling through space, transcending the narrow walls and sterile atmosphere of the cell and finding the only true escape possible.

Lucy picked her T-shirt up from the floor and covered herself when they sat back on the bed. It was a strangely coy gesture given what had just happened, but neither Andy nor Dave made any comment. They sat in silence, not even looking at each other, but wrapped in the same aura of satisfaction and exhaustion.

Lucy tingled; her tired body seemed somehow more alive than it had ever been. She felt safe and secure wedged between the two naked men. Though they hardly knew each other they had shared each other's bodies unselfishly and each had received as much pleasure as had been given.

'We've got to go,' Dave said, eventually breaking the silence. His normally cocky voice was soft and tender, and he squeezed Lucy's hand gently.

'Please stay a bit longer,' Lucy said, taking Dave's hand and pulling him closer. She didn't want to be left alone again. Anne's visit had unsettled her, and all her illusions about the institute had been shattered, only to be replaced by a black shadow of unknowing and trepidation.

'I'm sorry, Luce,' Andy told her quietly, 'but if we don't get back we'll be missed.'

Lucy bent down and kissed Dave's flaccid cock delicately. She saw the last few drops of fluid twinkling in the dim light and so took the prick into her mouth to suck it clean. The warmth of her mouth, and the softness of her tongue, soon had the desired effect. She could feel the prick harden and lengthen in her mouth, twitching back to life in seconds. When it was hard and virile again she released it.

'You as well,' she said, turning to Andy.

But the sight of her sucking Dave's prick had been enough to rouse Andy's massive penis back to life. She took it into her mouth at once, and suddenly found her mouth full of the taste of her own pussy. The strange reaction lasted only an instant and was replaced with the pleasurable sensation of hard prick rubbing firmly on the inside of her cheek.

Keeping her mouth firmly on Andy's prick, she managed to move him off the bed and got him to stand in front of her. Dave soon understood and also got off the bed and stood next to Andy.

Lucy smiled. She looked up at the two men and pouted alluringly. They turned in towards each other, so that their pricks were two poles pointing at each other. From her position she could see that the two pricks were equally large, yet different. She edged forward and kissed each in turn, paying homage to the two instruments that had brought her such rapture.

Very carefully she took the pricks in her hand and squeezed them together. She sensed the reluctance of the two friends to get too close but she managed to get them to edge just a bit nearer to each other. She admired the two thicknesses now joined together, a massive fusing of male sex flesh. Gradually she began to take them into her mouth. She had to stretch her mouth over the full width of the combined pricks, but the lubrication that she applied with her tongue and the natural flexibility of her mouth ensured that it didn't take very long to have both deep inside her.

She began to ride the two pricks, working her tongue between them, over the two sensitive glans, under the heads. Unable to resist the ecstatic feel, she soon had Andy and Dave making short tentative thrusts deeper into her mouth. The pressure of her lips against the glossy wet flesh of the pricks caused little pulses of pleasure to well up deep in their balls. Without wanting to they began to ride her mouth together. The rhythm was nervous and unsteady at first, but soon they began to get used to the feeling of their pricks massaging against each other.

Lucy relaxed a little as the two men began to pump together, driving their pricks simultaneously back and forth, a dual dance of elation into her tightly packed and delicious mouth. She sensed their orgasms building up, and could feel the pricks flexing and pulsing as they thrust back and forth. The taste of their pricks, each slightly different, was soon merged so that she closed her eyes and could imagine that it was one giant penis, a ramrod of fierce power expertly fucking her mouth.

When the explosion came she could feel the two men experiencing each other's pleasure. The spurting come filled her mouth and she could hardly swallow it all.

Both Dave and Andy looked a little embarrassed when they withdrew. Their pricks were smeared with thick globules of creamy sperm and glistened sexily in the dim flickering light. Lucy smiled and used her tongue to lick clean each of the pricks in turn, swallowing every last drop of sperm with evident relish.

'We really have got to go now,' Dave apologised. His body glistened with a thin layer of sweat, and his sharp angular face was a little flushed.

'It's OK,' Lucy told them sadly. She sat back on the bed and watched them getting dressed, a wistful look on her tired face. It was, she realised, the last time for six months that she would be able to have sex, and she was glad that it had been so enjoyable.

Andy gave her one last lingering kiss before departing, the door clanging behind him with an ugly finality. Lucy watched him go and turned to Dave, who straightened his uniform and brushed back his hair with his hand.

'Don't worry, love,' he whispered. 'I'm going to try to wangle my way on to your escort for tomorrow.'

'Do you know anything about this place they're sending me to?' she asked, suddenly becoming aware of the cold that was creeping into the cell as night fell.

'Never even heard of it before,' he admitted, shaking his head. 'But anything's got to be better than a real nick, hasn't it?'

'I suppose so,' Lucy agreed, feeling a little encouraged by the thought that she had managed to avoid prison again.

'Don't worry. You can look after yourself, I know you can,' Dave told her sympathetically. He gave her a last full kiss on the lips, playfully brushing her nipples with his fingertips.

When she was alone Lucy got into bed. Her head was filled with apprehension and worry. The most favourable eventuality, she realised, would be to find that there was nothing wrong with the Institute and to get five thousand pounds for saying so. But she knew that the one precluded the other. There was no way that a woman like Anne Young would pay that kind of money for a non-story.

She drifted off to sleep, dreaming of the money she would get and the pricks she had just enjoyed.

Two

The cramped van rocked gently as the driver turned off from the main road and on to a leafy country lane. Lucy stared out of the windows without enthusiasm. She was unmoved by the gently rolling hills of Surrey and the pleasant views of the countryside illuminated by the bright sunshine. Only half an hour from London and already she pined for the grey cramped streets of the city.

'Now remember,' Mary began, lighting up another cigarette nervously, 'don't mess this up.'

Lucy pretended not to hear and turned away, unwilling to be subjected to another moralising sermon from the plump and dowdy social worker.

'Listen to me,' Mary insisted, though the dull tone of voice testified to her sense of defeat.

'Leave me alone for fuck's sake,' Lucy responded testily. She was sick to death of being told how lucky she was, how she should avoid screwing things up, how she should be all sweetness and light to the world. She wasn't interested.

'That's just the sort of attitude,' Mary retorted, 'that's going to fuck you up. Goodness knows, we've all done our best. You just don't know how lucky you are to get into this place. The judge was going to give you a proper stretch this time.'

'Give me a stretch?' Lucy repeated sarcastically.

'What are you, some kind of old lag?' she sneered at Mary's futile attempt to strike the right note of toughness and severity.

Mary ignored the smirking guard that sat between her and Lucy. She felt frustrated by Lucy's wilful and dismissive attitude. 'Please,' she appealed, changing tack, 'try just a little to keep out of trouble.'

Lucy stared resolutely out of the window, inured to any appeals to her better nature. She knew that Mary was right, but she would not allow Mary the privilege of knowing that fact. It had been difficult to convince the judge that prison was not her just reward for the numerous charges of petty theft and of handling stolen goods. It had taken five days, and an exhausting battery of psychological tests and personality profiles, to convince him that she deserved to spend six months at an experimental correctional establishment.

At first Lucy had no wish to go; she had spent a large portion of her life passing from one institution to another. She saw no reason to believe that the Institute offered anything different than the neglected and squalid places she had already tried. It was only when she realised entry was restricted that her attitude changed. The Institute was a very difficult place to get into, unlike the other places where entry was easy and only exit difficult.

She was unsure who had first selected her as a potential candidate. However, once her name had gone forward, it had been down to her to prove that she was the right type of person. She qualified on all the obvious factors: between the age of eighteen and twenty-one, female, unstable background, a petty criminal, extensive institutional experience. It had taken five days to qualify on the other factors: intelligence, aptitude, personality, emotional stability and so on.

Passing the tests, and hence qualifying for admission to the Institute, was the first time Lucy had passed anything. She felt a rare glow of pride that she kept to herself, a secret and personal feeling that she was unwilling to share with anyone. After the judge's reluctant approval she had been obliged to sign a number of documents setting out her agreement to the plan. She felt it odd to have to sign documents stating that she went to the Institute voluntarily, or a contract of nondisclosure, but it was explained that the Institute was both highly experimental and, more saliently, secret.

The van abandoned the twisting country lane for a shaded bumpy track. Lucy looked back, but the road they had travelled was already obscured by a dense forest of trees. Minutes later the track opened out and they all turned to look at their first view of the Institute.

It was a large square building, six storeys high. The brickwork was dark brown and slightly shabby. Every floor was identical, with rows of tall rectangular windows functionally decorated with thin, greying net curtains. The slanting roof projected regularly spaced dormers with long, thin, shuttered windows.

Lucy felt deflated by the view. She had expected a grand Georgian mansion set in expansive, well-tended grounds. There was nothing about this building that hinted at exclusivity; it looked more like a rather down-at-heel provincial college than anything else.

The van pulled to a halt in front of the entrance.

'Now, remember what I told you,' Mary stressed, unable to resist a final admonishment as the guard opened the rear doors of the van.

The large black front door of the building opened and a woman emerged. Lucy judged her to be in her late thirties. She was dressed in a sober grey jacket and matching pleated skirt.

'That's Mrs Schafer,' Mary explained. 'She's very well known in her field. She's in charge, so make a good impression, OK?' She got out of the van, clutching her paperwork in one hand, and strode towards the woman waiting at the top of the stone steps that led up to the entrance.

Dave gave Lucy a friendly open smile as she jumped down from the van. 'Don't worry, Luce,' he said quietly, 'this'll be a doddle compared to inside.'

'Yeah, I know,' Lucy replied confidently. She brushed past him slowly, affectionately pressing her hand against his crotch.

'Soon as you're out,' he whispered, 'you look me up. I mean it, girl.'

'I know you do,' she replied. She felt his prick stir, and harden quickly, and squeezed it longingly. She knew it would be a long time before she would have the opportunity of making love with someone as young and as virile as him. Reluctantly she gave him a quick peck on the cheek, inhaling his clean masculine aroma for the last time, and then walked with casual assurance towards Mary and Mrs Schafer.

Mary signed the last few forms and turned to face Lucy. 'I hope you enjoy your stay here, Luce,' she said pleasantly.

'Don't call me Luce, you ain't my friend and never will be,' Lucy replied cruelly, more for the benefit of Mrs Schafer than for anything else.

Mary stared at her stony-faced, then, without a word, turned and headed disconsolately back to the van. Lucy watched her go. She felt a pang of regret, but was eager to see how Mrs Schafer responded to the little scene. It was a game that Lucy had played often; she could always read a person from their reactions to such little set pieces.

'Follow me,' Mrs Schafer ordered, seemingly oblivious of all that had just occurred.

Lucy followed her through the quiet lobby of the building and up a long curving flight of stone stairs to the left. There was the cool atmosphere of a library about the place, and she wondered what she had let herself in for. It occurred to her that the Institute might be some sort of private school; the word education had certainly been mentioned to her several times in conversation. She followed Mrs Schafer along a short corridor lined with numbered doors, one of which they passed through into a small anteroom. The walls were bare apart from a single dark painting, a geometric abstract done in oils. A desk occupied one part of the room, and a row of padded chairs sat opposite. As they entered, a young woman, who had been seated behind the desk, immediately stood to attention, her eyes averted respectfully. Mrs Schafer nodded curtly and the woman, dressed in a simple uniform of white shirt and blue skirt, returned to her position behind the desk. Mrs Schafer swept through the anteroom and into the office with Lucy following closely behind.

'Stand there,' Mrs Schafer said sternly, and pointed to a spot a foot from the large mahogany desk in front of the window.

Nonchalantly Lucy stepped into place and peered sceptically at Mrs Schafer, who had walked to the window to watch the van depart. The office was light and airy, the sun streaming in making it a little stuffy but not uncomfortable. Apart from the desk there were two black armchairs in one corner, which, with a glass coffee table, formed a restful alcove in an otherwise functionally furnished room.

'You will never speak to anyone in that manner again,' Mrs Schafer declared, turning back from the window. Her tone carried a threatening undercurrent which Lucy caught at once. She stared at Lucy with icy coolness, awaiting a response. Lucy stared back, then turned away from the clear blue eyes, unwilling to take up the unspoken challenge that had been made.

Mrs Schafer visibly relaxed. 'The premise,' she began,

22

taking her seat behind the desk, 'on which this Institute is founded is that young people like you have lost all sense of the hierarchy implicit in the society around you. It's not that you cannot distinguish between right and wrong.' She paused and studied Lucy, as if to confirm this. 'I don't think it was ever that simple. We live in a society more complex than at any other time in history, more complicated than many people can easily comprehend. You, and others like you, cannot see the fine layers into which society is stratified; you see all power relationships as a blur. You make up for this weakness by reducing everything to a basic us and them relationship.'

Lucy was unimpressed with the explanation. It sounded like the sort of stuff middle-class professionals had been dishing out to her for years. 'I think . . .' she started to say.

'Our task here,' Mrs Schafer interrupted, 'is to give you the ability to distinguish between the different strata that exist all around us. When you can see the fine detail, you will also understand that the cleavage of society into different social groupings results in a natural division of authority. We will eradicate the "us and them" syndrome completely.' She glanced at Lucy, who was staring out of the window, wearing an exaggerated expression of boredom on her plain young face. 'Here at the Institute the hierarchy is explicit. You will know the position of everyone. And you will know what authority and what power each individual carries according to her place. For now all that you need know is that everyone else is above you.'

She stopped and looked at Lucy. 'Did you,' she asked, 'understand anything of what I was trying to say?'

'Yes I do!' Lucy retorted angrily. 'You reckon you're going to teach me my place, don't you? Teach me to be happy at the bottom of the shit-heap.'

Mrs Schafer smiled. 'Defiance, good, I like that,' she said, impressed also by Lucy's brightness.

Lucy was surprised by the smile. She had expected, with mounting excitement, an angry confrontation. Instead she listened with astonishment as Mrs Schafer outlined the strict taxonomy of power at the Institute. She was the ultimate authority, the very apex of the pyramid. Her authority was shared with her members of staff. Below the staff was the appointed head girl, who in turn shared power with the prefect leaders, and they with the prefects. At the very bottom were Lucy and the other ordinary young women.

'But even among the girls,' Mrs Schafer continued, 'there is a natural unimposed order, one that you will learn to navigate yourself. As a new girl I think you will find that you are at the bottom, even among your nominal peers.'

Silently Lucy listened as she began to explain, with self-evident relish, the division of power between the different classes in the Institute. Any transgression of the rules would be punished. Any individual could be disciplined by any other individual of a higher class. Lucy suddenly realised that almost the entire population of the Institute would be able to punish her. It was not a good feeling.

'Membership of each class carries different privileges and different powers. The rules here are many and deliberately complex. New girls are given only the first rule, which is that you will address every individual of a class higher than yours as Mistress. You will address me as Mistress Schafer. Failure to abide by this rule will mean that you will be punished. I hope,' she grinned, 'to see you again after you have succumbed. It's always the defiant ones that give me most pleasure. You are dismissed,' she announced, flicking her wrist in the direction of the door.

Lucy felt a little stunned by all that she had heard.

There was an odd feel to what she had been told; she was sure that she was missing something. The word 'punishment' had carried a strange connotation, though nothing untoward had been said. She imagined that the punishment consisted in some kind of school-like sanction; doing lines, extra lessons, or maybe having to do menial cleaning-up jobs.

'Thank me before you leave,' Mistress Schafer ordered, just as Lucy opened the door.

'For what?' Lucy asked innocently, genuinely perplexed by the request.

'Because I am a Mistress,' Mrs Schafer replied simply.

'Thank you,' Lucy said. Noting the look of expectation on Mrs Schafer's stern face she added, '. . . Mistress Schafer.'

She shut the door behind her and faced two young women in the anteroom. She glared at them momentarily, anxious to assert herself as she had done in every other establishment. However the two women stood with the casual self-assurance that comes only with the wielding of authority, and which Lucy recognised immediately. Reluctantly she averted her gaze, suddenly nervous at being alone in the new and unknown environment.

'Follow Mistress Julie; she'll take you to your room where you can change,' the woman behind the desk ordered, evidently accustomed to the giving of directions.

The other woman stared at Lucy with tightly pursed lips. She had noted the insolent glare Lucy had briefly shot them and, unlike the woman behind the desk, was unwilling to let it go.

'She's only just got here,' the one behind the desk warned Mistress Julie, catching the hostile look that passed between her and Lucy.

'Yes, Mistress Christine,' Julie replied, chastened by the unexpected rebuke. She blushed slightly.

'In future you show your Mistresses respect. Any insolence, even if it's only a look, will get you punished,' Mistress Christine explained severely to Lucy, who listened wide-eyed with mounting disbelief.

'Yes, Mistress,' Lucy found herself saying, her instinct for self-preservation stronger than her reluctance to address the woman as anything but an equal. It was all so confusing; she had never been to a place where the girls conformed to the petty rules when staff were absent. It seemed an unnatural way to act.

'After she's changed take her to Mistress Shirer's class. She should catch the last lesson of the morning session,' Christine told Julie, who listened silently. She stood with her legs a few inches apart, her shoulders pulled back, pressing her small pointed breasts forward. The flared blue skirt was cut short and ribbed with tight pleats. 'You can go now,' Christine bluntly dismissed Lucy and Julie, and turned to the paperwork that littered her desk.

'Thank you, Mistress Christine,' Julie responded at once.

Lucy also repeated the strange incantation, though she still didn't understand what the thanks were for, just as she didn't understand why she had had to thank Mistress Schafer for a five-minute lecture.

Lucy was aware that the two young Mistresses were watching her and averted her gaze, hoping that she hadn't given them the wrong kind of look. But that didn't do the trick. She racked her brain, afraid that she was breaking some strange rule when it occurred to her that she had to open the door. She strode forward with relief and opened the door for Julie. She received no thanks, nor was she given any indication that she had acted correctly; instead Christine appeared to have forgotten that she even existed and Julie simply stepped out into the corridor.

Lucy followed Julie down the long quiet corridor,

keeping a respectful distance just in case. It gave her a chance to study the girl in front of her. Julie was tall and slim, and the short skirt flapped gently over her round bottom with every step.

'Excuse me, Mistress Julie,' Lucy ventured, unable to contain her ardent curiosity any longer.

'You speak to a Mistress only when spoken to,' Julie replied firmly without glancing over her shoulder or slowing down.

Lucy fell silent, angry that she had to speak, and be spoken to, in such a demeaning manner. She felt that in the absence of the rules, or more precisely in the absence of the will to obey the rules, she would have been more than equal to Julie.

The building was a honeycomb of long door-lined corridors, winding stone steps and short connecting passages. The doors were numbered and coloured differently, but Lucy could not discern any pattern. She followed obediently, lost and without bearings in more ways than one.

Eventually they climbed a flight of narrow cold steps that led to six doorways. Julie opened the door to room 4C and entered.

The room was small and spartan, badly lit; only a stream of light from a high window provided any brightness. There were two beds, one on either side of the door, each of which had a small bedside locker. The only other furniture was a compact desk below the window and a chest of drawers, topped with a large square mirror, next to it.

Lucy had been in worse places, and found the room quite acceptable. She remembered laughing at girls who had been shocked to see the squalid little rooms at some of the other institutions she had been in. One of the beds had a neatly folded uniform on the pillow, and she guessed it was hers.

'I'm the landing prefect in charge of these six rooms,'

Julie explained as Lucy explored her part of the room. 'That means,' she continued, 'that you are mine. If you fuck up, I get punished. Do you know what that means?' Lucy shook her head. 'It means that you don't fuck up. And to make sure you don't I have the power to punish you every time you break a rule.'

'But what are the rules?' Lucy asked forlornly.

'One of the rules is that you address me properly.'

'OK,' Lucy sighed, 'what are the rules, Mistress Julie?'

'You find out what the rules are when you break them and get punished. Eventually you get to know what sort of thing you can and can't do.'

'Do you know the rules, Mistress Julie?' Lucy asked, still finding it difficult to phrase her remarks in the stilted and archaic form that was demanded.

'I know some of the rules,' Julie smiled gleefully. 'It's a painful process, finding them out. I'm going to enjoy teaching you, but you won't enjoy learning,' she added maliciously.

'Mistress, how are we punished?' Lucy asked. The question was uppermost in her confused and anxious mind.

'That depends. A prefect can punish by putting a girl to work, to act as a skivvy, or if she wants she can spank a girl on the arse, but only with the hand and only six strokes.' She paused to smirk at the look of absolute horror that fell on Lucy's face. 'A prefect leader can do all that, but can spank a girl as many times as she likes, and in public as well. The head girl can beat a girl on the arse with a cane or strap if she wants to, and in public of course. A member of staff can do anything she likes, within reason I suppose.'

'This is some sort of madhouse,' Lucy muttered. Her mind was reeling, her face went pale and she felt dizzy.

'That's why they've brought you here,' Julie laughed, forgetting that she had been incorrectly addressed.

'It's not right. Don't people run away?'

'Run away?' Julie snorted with derision. 'You poor stupid cow, you've got no idea, have you? Why do you think you did all those bloody tests? What did you think, that this was some sort of posh finishing school for people like you?'

Lucy sat back on the bed. She felt as if the world was slipping from under her. Almost absently, it occurred to her that Anne Young had been right.

'You'll never run away, I didn't when I was new. We've been specially selected – we're just the sort of people who love it here. We're built for this place.'

'No, it can't be right,' Lucy repeated, shaking her head.

'And what about all those papers you signed?' Julie pointed out. 'You've signed your life away; there is nothing else for you but this.'

'What about you?' Lucy demanded.

'Address me properly,' Julie snapped petulantly, 'unless you want your education to start now.'

'I'm sorry, Mistress,' Lucy mumbled, frightened by the clear menace in the other's voice. She could tell at once that it was not an idle threat.

'Now, change into your uniform.'

Lucy got up and began to change. She dropped her green bomber jacket on to the bed and pulled off her trainers and socks. Looking up she saw Julie eyeing her closely. She stood to unzip her jeans and seeing that Julie was still studying her closely, turned around. She unzipped her jeans but did not pull them down immediately; she felt very conscious of the eyes burning into her back. Instead she pulled her sweatshirt up and over her head. For a second she enjoyed the feeling of the sun beating down on her large firm breasts, then she reached for the white uniform shirt.

Julie came up behind her and reached around under the arms and took hold of the naked, well-shaped breasts. Lucy froze as Julie squeezed the two globes of soft milky white flesh. Expertly she weighed them in her hands, brushing her thumbs playfully over the nipples.

Julie was delighted when Lucy began to redden with embarrassment. She let go of the breasts and took hold of the top of Lucy's jeans and slowly began to pull them down, tugging gently so that they began to drop, revealing a pair of white cotton panties. Lucy just stood stock still, her mind completely blank, overcome with horror. Julie left the denim trousers at knee level.

'You'll look so much better in your uniform,' she leered, sliding her hand up the inside of Lucy's thigh. She thrilled to the softness of the skin, the way it resisted the firmness of her touch. Eagerly she pressed her fingers up towards the soft folds of skin that the tight-fitting panties barely covered.

Finally all the anger and frustration boiled over. Sick to her stomach with revulsion, Lucy swung around and struck Julie as hard as she could.

The blow was unexpected and Julie was flung back into the centre of the room. She was dumbfounded, her look of shock absolute. She had never been rejected by any of the girls under her charge, and this eventuality now caught her off guard. 'I'll have you later, you little bitch,' she hissed venomously. 'You've broken every fucking rule in the book. If I took you to one of the staff you'd be flogged till you fainted.'

Lucy pulled her jeans up, let her breasts remain bare and faced Julie. 'Well, if them tests were any good they would've known that I don't deal in that shit.'

'I'm going to enjoy you.' Julie glared back. 'I'm going to punish you day in, day out for what you've done.'

'Just try me,' Lucy urged, her old self-confidence returning. Defiance had always been at the core of her being, and now it gave her a centre of gravity, something to grip on to in an effort to stay afloat. She looked at the whole business of Mistresses and punishments with nothing but scorn and contempt.

'Get changed,' Mistress Julie told her. She felt a little afraid of the new girl's aggressive determination. She had been a prefect for only a matter of weeks and had yet to acquire the bearing and the confidence of the others. She knew that it was her task to inform the prefect leader and the head girl of what had happened, but she was afraid to lose face. For a moment she longed to return to the simplicities of being one of the girls, to live without the responsibilities or the burden of command.

Lucy changed quickly, keeping her eyes on Julie, who stared back. Both were still testing each other, unsure who had the strongest will. Lucy had been a little intimidated earlier, but now she sensed that it was the Mistress who felt threatened.

'Follow me,' Julie ordered when Lucy had dressed. She tried, and almost succeeded, in investing her voice with the same tone of authority that had come naturally to Mistress Christine.

'Where are we going?' Lucy asked suspiciously, hands on hips, unwilling to yield an inch.

'Address me properly!' Julie demanded stridently. The two girls faced each other squarely. 'Don't forget that you're alone here,' she reminded Lucy. 'I'm the only person you know. You do as you're told or you'll be in deep shit.'

Lucy realised, with a profound sense of relief, that she and Julie were finally talking the same language. 'Yes, Mistress,' Lucy replied, though the words were rendered meaningless by the mocking tone of her voice.

'You'll be begging to get a lick of my pussy by the end of the month,' Julie warned, regaining her composure slightly.

'Yes, Mistress,' Lucy sneered.

'You've got to go to class,' Julie reminded her. 'Just try some of that crap in there and see what you get.'

'Yes, Mistress.'

'Open the door,' Julie demanded.

'Fuck you!'

Trying to ignore Lucy's triumphant laugh, Julie finally opened the door. She held the door open and waited for her to move. She waited until Lucy was passing through the door and then slammed into her, pressing her painfully against the door frame. Lucy struggled but Julie held her tightly, using the frame to trap Lucy's right arm and holding the other with her own.

'You'll regret this,' Lucy said threateningly, giving up the pointless struggle to get free. She was held firmly between the door frame and Julie, who was taller and stronger than she was.

'That's no way to talk to your Mistress,' Julie teased. She slipped her free hand under the short skirt and stroked Lucy's soft thighs.

'What's wrong, couldn't find a bloke to give it to you?' Lucy continued to mock.

Julie ignored her, slipping her fingers into the thin white uniform briefs. She grazed her hand through the tight curly bush of pubic hair, trying to press down to the soft folds of the pussy lips that she had tried to touch earlier. She switched target and began to rub Lucy's dark nipples over the white nylon shirt; she took each nipple in turn and squeezed it between thumb and forefinger, tugging at them lightly.

Lucy shut her eyes, realising with dawning horror that the play on her breasts was beginning to excite her.

'Nice responsive nipples,' Julie observed, her eyes shining with a frisson of sexual excitement. Lucy's nipples were erect and visibly poking against the uniform shirt. 'Just as I like them, nice hard nipples to bite and suck,' she continued, managing to unbutton part of the shirt and playing with the bare breasts, exploring the feel and shape of them, always returning to the hardened puckered nipples. She realised that Lucy's breasts were sensitive to the lightest of caresses.

Lucy kept her eyes clamped tightly shut. The constant playing with her nipples had aroused her, her pretty white panties becoming damp. She tried not to think of Julie; instead she remembered the last night she had spent with the two guards in the cell below the court. Desperately she tried to imagine that it was one of the men that was teasing her. She remembered how Dave had also used her breasts to excite her. But even the memory of two hard pricks pumping inside her could not entirely blot out the image of Julie artfully massaging the large round breasts.

Suddenly Julie stopped, releasing Lucy, and took a step back into the room.

Lucy opened her eyes slowly. Her heart was pounding wildly and a fire was burning in the pit of her belly, inflamed by the spasms of blissful sensation that had issued from her tight hard teats. Her shirt was half open and her firm young breasts were exposed, the nipples pointing away from each other.

'Dress yourself, girl,' Julie ordered, a satisfied grin on her long thin face.

Lucy began to button up, her face burning with an angry bitter shame. She was obeying an order without wanting to, aware that Julie had again reversed the positions. It was Julie who was now confident and brash, while she was the one who was confused again and on the defensive.

Julie brushed arrogantly past Lucy in the doorway, her fingers lightly touching Lucy's thighs. Lucy looked away, unable to make any response. She followed Julie through the maze of corridors and steps. Again her instinct for survival helped her identify landmarks to enable her to navigate back to room 4C. She forced herself to take note of numbers on doors and coloured arrows painted discreetly on some of the walls.

Without wanting to she also caught herself looking closely at Julie. She wondered what would have happened if Julie hadn't stopped. She knew that if Julie had pressed their mouths together she would have accepted the kiss urgently. As she walked, the wetness between her legs was a reminder of just how easily she had been aroused by the touch of another girl. The experience undermined her completely.

Julie stopped outside the first door in a corridor on the ground floor, near to the stairs that led to Mistress Schafer's office. She knocked and waited before entering, with Lucy following meekly.

The classroom was small and bright, the windows on the wall opposite looking out on to a small square courtyard. When Lucy saw the courtyard she understood the strange geography of the building. She had assumed that the building was a single massive monolith, whereas it was in fact shaped around the courtyard. The insight cheered her up slightly. Any gain in knowledge of her environment, no matter how trivial, was important to her survival.

The classroom consisted of four rows of single desks. Each row was divided into two pairs of desks close to each other, separated by a larger space, in effect leaving a long central aisle between the rows. There were a number of empty seats in the class, and Lucy quickly counted twelve young women present. Another solitary desk was placed in front of, and set at a diagonal to, the others.

The teacher, a black woman in her thirties, stood behind a large oak desk at the front of the class, on a raised platform several inches from the floor. She had soft chocolate-coloured skin; her thick glossy hair was swept back over her head and tied in a tight bun. She was dressed in a smart black jacket and short matching skirt, her long shapely thighs clad in sheer black stockings that made her dark skin appear lighter than it was. Her face was round with full heavy lips painted deep red and parted in an inviting pout.

'Why is the new girl late?' she demanded of Julie, in clear stern voice that immediately brought silence to the class.

'She was disobedient and insolent, Mistress Shirer,' Julie replied dutifully.

Mistress Shirer dismissed Julie disdainfully and turned her large bright eyes on Lucy, standing nervously by the door.

'Come forward, girl,' Mistress Shirer told her.

'Yes, Mistress Shirer,' Lucy replied obediently, avoiding the Mistress's penetrating gaze.

'Stand properly, girl,' she instructed, and Lucy straightened up and put her chest forward. Mistress Shirer noted the erect nipples pressing visibly against the uniform shirt. 'Tell the rest of the class your name.'

Lucy remembered to respond to the Mistress first, and then turned to face the rest of the young women. Her heart was pounding and she felt nervous. She looked at the girls, who stared back at her with undisguised interest. They were all dressed in the same minimal uniform of blue skirt and white shirt. Lucy told them her name and was told to sit at an empty seat in the third row.

She walked down the centre of the class and took her seat nearest the aisle. The desk to her left was empty. On the other side of the aisle both desks were occupied, the one nearest to her by a petite Indian girl, who looked much younger than the minimum age of eighteen, and next to her a plump plain girl who wore wire-framed spectacles and stared back blankly.

'The new girl,' Mistress Shirer began, leaning forward against the desk so that the tops of her breasts were visible, 'has arrived at a most opportune moment. The formal part of the class is ended for today.' She stood up and then walked around to the front of the desk and sat on the edge, crossing her legs.

Lucy felt drawn to the expanse of stockinged thigh that the Mistress displayed nonchalantly. She looked round at the other girls, and felt a little relieved to find them also staring at Mistress Shirer with varying degrees of admiration, an admiration tinged with a heavy dose of apprehension. She looked up and was startled to find the Mistress staring directly at her. She took the gaze for a second, staring back with darting eyes. But then, heart pounding, she turned away, intimidated by the forbidding expression on Mistress Shirer's face. She avoided the cold searching stare, and gazed down instead at Mistress Shirer's glossy black ankle boots, the sharp heel like an upturned pyramid, the steel tips aimed directly at the floor.

'This morning I instructed the prefects to conduct a search of your rooms,' Mistress Shirer announced. She silenced the eager buzz of expectation by jumping down from the desk, the crack of her heels a sharp report around the room. She stood, arms folded across her chest and long lithe legs placed apart, and stared at the girls. 'The thief among you will step forward now to receive her due punishment.'

Lucy looked around the room. She felt relief that stealing still took place; it was the first sign of outward normality that she had encountered in the Institute. She recognised the girl immediately. Lucy had been in the same situation herself on a number of occasions and was not fooled by the girl, who was looking around earnestly, searching with her quick blue eyes for the culprit. Lucy caught her eye and smiled to her, letting her know that she knew and didn't care if the girl was the thief. But the girl ignored Lucy, instead sneaking glances in the direction of Mistress Shirer.

'You will be punished whether you own up or not,' Mistress Shirer told the girls. 'But if you don't own up you will regret angering me.' She waited, deliberately letting the tension build up. Receiving no response she walked down the central aisle with a slow elegant stride, a hint of menace flowing around her. The girls eyed her with a mixture of fear and fascination.

'You girls are destined for punishment,' she continued slowly, prolonging the tension.

Lucy was gripped by a sudden and irrational fear that Mistress Shirer was talking about her, and felt a dense wave of panic rising within. Part of her rebelled against the fear, refusing to be intimidated by the severe presence of the lithe black Mistress. Still another part of her felt a fearful attraction, dazzled by the menacing sexual aura that emanated from the Mistress.

'No matter how hard you try,' she paused by Lucy, you return again and again to your old modes of behaviour. You find that doing wrong gives you pleasure, and that the fear of capture, and consequent punishment, is the spice that draws you.'

Lucy held her breath, but relaxed when Mistress Shirer took another couple of steps and stopped at the last row of desks. All the girls at the front were craning round excitedly, relieved that they had escaped. Lucy shared the feeling of relief, feeling almost light-headed. Again she caught herself being attracted to the Mistress sexually; her eyes followed the contours of the gently curving body. Mistress Shirer wore a skintight skirt and her firm round bottom was firmly impressed on the black material. Lucy noted that no panty-line was visible and that the tightness of the skirt had gently parted the arsecheeks, emphasising the deep rear valley between the firm globes of the buttocks.

Shocked by her thoughts, Lucy looked at some of the other girls. She saw them looking at the Mistress in the same way, the feeling of desire mixed with the same feeling of fear.

'Stand up, girl!' Mistress Shirer ordered the girl sitting in front of her.

'Please Mistress ...' the girl began to explain, her

37

small round face collapsing. Tears welled in her bright blue eyes and her pretty little mouth was trembling.

Mistress Shirer slapped the girl's face, and the retort echoed through the silent room. The girl clutched her reddened cheek, eyes wide with dreadful anticipation of what was to follow. She looked at Mistress Shirer imploringly, but the Mistress took her by the hair and pulled her out of her seat.

'I'm sorry, I'm sorry,' the girl whined. She managed to free herself of the Mistress's grip and fell to the floor. The rest of the girls watched her grovelling on hands and knees, kissing and licking the glossy ankle boots, pressing her mouth eagerly on the shiny black leather.

Lucy was horrified. She turned and looked at the other girls, but they were watching excitedly. Many were smiling gleefully, enjoying the sight of the girl degrading herself. She turned back to the girl, sickened by the lack of sympathy shown to her by the others.

Mistress Shirer pulled the girl up by the hair, clutching a tight handful of the long brown locks. She strode purposefully back to the head of the class, her backside wiggling slightly as she walked, pulling the sobbing girl behind her.

'This filthy little bitch is a thief,' she explained, standing the girl up to face her classmates. 'Like all bad girls she has to be punished again and again.'

'Please, I'm sorry ...'the girl whimpered, squirming nervously.

'Unbutton your shirt,' Mistress Shirer commanded brutally '

The girl started to undo the buttons, but her hands were shaking and unable to grip the buttons properly. Mistress Shirer pulled the shirt open impatiently, ripping the buttons away. The girl seemed to shrink back, trying to pull her naked breasts away. Mistress Shirer tugged the girl's hair to make her stand properly.

The girl winced and pressed her chest out, displaying the fullness of her firm breasts to the other girls.

Lucy eyed the creamy white globes with a mixture of self-disgust and unconcealed interest. Her mind was filled with the memory of Julie caressing her own breasts so expertly and, now that Julie was gone, she felt excited by the image. She had never felt this way before. It was an unexpected and peculiar emotion, and had an eroticism about it that she had never experienced before.

'Cup your breasts,' Mistress Shirer commanded the girl, and the girl obeyed, cupping her large breasts and raising them up, accentuating the swell of her flesh. The girl's face was blushing deep red with shame, her eyes fixed firmly on the ground.

The first blow startled Lucy, who had become lost in the contemplation of the beautifully raised breasts bathed in the bright sunlight that streamed through the windows. Mistress Shirer began to lay hard sharp slaps on the ripe fruit held up to her, the loud slap of flesh beating out a rhythm of painful punishment. The soft breast skin was flawed with a deep crimson tan, the impression of Mistress Shirer's fingers clearly marked for all to see. The girl closed her eyes and bit deep into her lip. Her chest was burning and stinging, the regular strokes on her breasts painfully sharp.

Mistress Shirer varied her stroke, ensuring that each breast was spanked in turn, and also spreading the strokes over each breast, so that the girl's flesh was an even colour throughout. She paid special attention to the nipples, landing several blows directly on each, so that they stood out sharply and glowed a deeper colour than the surrounding flesh.

'Thank you, Mistress,' the girl whispered when the breast spanking was finished. Her chest was patterned with deep red fingermarks on a carpet of a smooth pink tan. Her chest seemed to be aflame, the smarting concentrated in the tight sensitive buds of the nipples, sending confused messages to the rest of her body. The stinging aching pain had turned into a deep red heat, warming first her chest and then suffusing slowly down to her belly.

'Let the others see how you are marked,' Mistress Shirer ordered.

The girl uncupped the two punished fruit and put her hands on her head, elbows parallel to her shoulders which she pressed back, so that the breasts were fully displayed to their best advantage. The flesh on the underside was still milky white, but it merged gradually with the scarlet fingermarked flesh where Mistress Shirer's expert hand had chastised her. The dark red-brown nipples were hard little buttons that were provocatively erect, begging for relief from the smarting ache that covered them.

Lucy was excited now by the girl's vulnerable stance the blue skirt and torn shirt adding to the exposed look. She felt uncomfortable with the new feelings that had been aroused in her. Looking around the class, hoping somehow to find her bearings, she found instead that the other girls were also enjoying the spectacle, eyeing the punished girl with unconcealed lust. She knew the look, knew what it was like to feel hot desire raging and pulsing through her body, but she had only ever felt like that towards men. Now it was as if a whole new world had been opened up to her, and, like an explorer in a new world, she felt excited by the possibilities and yet gripped by the deepest of fears and a great disorientation.

The punished girl kept her eyes averted but held herself up, pressing her breasts higher. She glanced up at the other girls and tried to look defiant, but the blushes of embarrassment were clear to see.

'Bend over the punishment desk,' Mistress Shirer told the girl eventually. Disconsolately the girl turned away from the other girls and bent across the desk at the head of the class. She pressed herself low on its surface, so that her breasts were squashed flat, finding temporary solace in the coolness of the desk top.

Mistress Shirer unbuttoned the skirt and it fell around the girl's ankles. Slowly she pulled the white cotton panties down to the girl's knees. 'Part your legs,' she instructed and the girl obeyed.

The other girls craned forward in their seats, enjoying the view of the young naked backside so temptingly exhibited. The tight round arse-cheeks were pleasingly parted, hinting at the puckered arsehole within. A mat of brown curly hair indicated the entrance to her sex, and was clearly visible at the top of her thighs. As the girl turned her head back and looked at the class, her eyes welled with sorrowful tears, shamed by the terrible humiliations she had endured and was going to endure.

Mistress Shirer walked slowly round to her own desk, revelling in the sight of the girl exposed so deliciously on the punishment desk. The girl's breasts were still glowing with the afterburn of the spanking. From a drawer in her desk Mistress Shirer withdrew a long supple cane and she tested its mettle by swishing it through the air several times. The girl looked up beseechingly, terrified by the sight and sound of the wicked cane being played through the air.

Lucy stared at the girl, her eyes feasting on the beautiful pert backside and exploring the private places. It was as if she had only just discovered how beautiful and mysterious a feminine body is. The long silky thighs were stretched tight, every muscle extended and displayed for all to see.

Lucy was also stirred by the sight of the austere and attractive Mistress wielding and flexing the long bamboo cane. It was obvious that the Mistress was relishing the opportunity to degrade the recalcitrant girl.

'This is how I punish my naughty girls,' Mistress Shirer told the class, using one hand to position the unfortunate girl, pressing her down into the desk so that the arse-cheeks were raised temptingly higher.

The first blow whistled through the air and landed with a crack across the bare backside. The girl cried out as the stroke bit deeply into her flesh, a sharp spasm of pain seeming to connect up with the heat oozing from her punished breasts. A deep red line was etched across the white globes of her arse, a livid reward for her bad behaviour. Mistress Shirer paused deliberately before striking the next note of the painful litany.

The girls watched in awed silence, hearts pounding and minds racing. Lucy felt her head spinning; she was at once repelled by the painful public humiliation of the girl and attracted to it. Her eyes tried to take in the whole picture: the girl spread exposingly on the desk, her attractive young rear hoisted up, the stern black Mistress, brandishing the cane and administering a painful and deeply sexual punishment. Mistress Shirer raised the cane high so that her skirt rode up, exposing long supple thighs clad in sheer black stockings. The picture was dazzling, a blindingly intense erotic tableau that drew Lucy's eyes like a magnet.

Stroke followed stroke and the punished girl's arse soon bore several distinct red lines deep in the flesh. She ached and cried, tears falling down her young pretty face. The pain was churning her insides; she felt a little sick, and was trembling.

Lucy turned away, checking her own behaviour against that of the others around her. She looked at the two girls in the aisle opposite and was shocked to see them caressing each other secretly. The small Indian girl, who looked no older than sixteen, had pulled her skirt up high and parted her legs wide, and Lucy could see that the plump girl was rubbing slowly between the dusky uncovered thighs. The Indian girl reciprocated by gliding her delicate little hand along the plump girl's thigh.

The Indian girl, careful not to attract Mistress Shirer's attention, shifted in her seat. She pulled her knickers a little way down and guided the other girl's hand into place. When she saw that Lucy was watching she smiled. With her free hand she gently lifted her skirt so that Lucy could see the plump girl fingering deep into the dark puffy folds of her pussy. The shock on Lucy's face was evident, and the Indian girl beamed delightedly, turning slightly to give Lucy a better view, and blew her a kiss.

Lucy blushed. She was aroused intensely by the view of the two girls masturbating each other, but didn't know how to respond to the smiles and the affectionate kiss that had been blown to her. She turned back to the equally arousing sight of the girl being chastised by Mistress Shirer.

The girl's arse was on fire – the pain had become unbearable. The girl forgot everything; her whole life and was concentrated on her naked backside, and nothing else registered. Each stroke seemed to pump some strange sensation into her. The steady rhythm of correction assumed a singular importance, and without wanting to the girl began to raise her arse higher. The pain became pleasure-pain, her pussy wet and aching.

Her breathing came in short gasps, the muted sobbing replaced by the unwanted release of soft wordless moans. She lifted her arse higher still, trying to meet the downward stroke of the cane halfway. Her pussy was alive with pleasure, her tight bud a molten burning centre of sex energy.

'Hurt me, harder,' she moaned softly. Her cheeks were crossed with the impression of the cane. At last the girl could hold herself no longer – she arched her back and let out a cry. She was oblivious to the cane and the searing pain, overcome instead by a wild cataclysmic climax. She gripped the desk and lifted herself as high as she could, stretched almost on to the tips of her toes.

The girl dived into an almighty screaming orgasm. She lost control as the last of the heavy strokes found her reddened arse. The caning stopped and she was sobbing uncontrollably, holding on to the desk with all her strength to stop herself collapsing to the floor. Suddenly she seemed to wince, gasped audibly, and then let out a warm white jet of piss. She was too tired, or too overwhelmed to do anything, so she let the piss stream out until the flow stopped to a trickle that ran down her thighs and on to her skirt and panties.

Mistress Shirer had stepped back and had not been soiled by the girl's piss. She seemed pleased that the girl had lost all control and had abased herself completely and utterly.

'Jenny can clear her own mess now,' she said calmly. 'The rest of the class is dismissed.'

Jenny had not been given permission to stand, and so she remained bent over the desk, her painful arse on display to all, wallowing in her degrading condition. The other girls filed past her, eyes fixed on the alluring sight of her vulnerable backside.

Lucy followed the other girls silently, numbed by all that she had seen and felt. It was as if she had entered a new world where the perverse and obscene were considered normal. Every act and gesture was loaded with a sexual significance that she had previously been unaware of, or that had previously been absent altogether.

'I'm in room 2C,' the Indian girl told Lucy when they were outside the classroom. She smiled in a friendly, innocently open way, totally at odds with the wanton behaviour that she had displayed earlier. 'Why don't you come to visit me later?' she continued when Lucy made no reply.

Lucy turned and fled, unable to cope with the encounter, unsure whether the invitation was sexual or social. She headed vaguely in the direction of her room, her mind reeling. Nothing was right with the world; everything had been turned upside down. She had been at the Institute for only a few hours and already her personality had been stripped bare. The hard wall of defiance and arrogance that she had so carefully constructed to protect herself had been demolished, leaving nothing in its place but uncertainty and fear.

She walked blindly down the long corridors, up and down identical flights of stairs. She felt lost in more than the geographical sense. There was nothing for her to hold on to, no yardstick by which to measure herself. The other girls seemed totally corrupted by the erotic atmosphere of the place.

She felt enticed by the powerful sexual atmosphere that clung to the air like an early morning mist. For the first time she had found herself attracted by the possibilities of making love with other girls. The revulsion that she had felt for the idea before had vanished, and she wondered whether it had all been a massive negation of her true self. it occurred to her that she had previously denied the very thing that she was attracted to, simply because she had been unable to come to terms with it. It was a dangerous thought, she realised; her whole life was suddenly thrown open to question.

At last she found herself in familiar territory as she recognised the stairs leading up to her room. She bounded up gratefully, eager to find respite from the strange and cruel world around her. The room was empty and she flopped down on the bed with relief, tired by the enormous emotional strains of the day.

She closed her eyes tightly and tried to drown out the thoughts and images clamouring noisily in her mind. Repeatedly strong dreamlike images filled her with waves of disgust and desire. She saw Julie's hot mouth on hers, saw Jenny being beaten on her lovely tits, saw herself being touched by Julie, saw the elegant wiggle of

Mistress Shirer's walk – saw Jenny letting out a long stream of piss.

The silence of the small room closed about her. With an effort she slowed her breathing, seeking calmness. Gradually she relaxed, letting the flood of thoughts wash over her, cascading through her mind until everything was still. All that remained was the heat in the tightness of her sex.

She changed position on the bed, so that her feet rested on the pillow and her head was at the foot of the bed. She lovingly caressed her breasts over the thin material of the shirt, cupping the large round orbs and playing her thumbs gently over the sensitive erect nipples. Taking the nipples between her thumbs and index fingers she gently squeezed, sending spasms of pure pleasure piercing through her body. Lazily she massaged and rubbed her tits, the ripples of pleasure connecting with the heat in her belly.

Slowly she pulled her knees up and apart, carefully covering herself with the skirt in case someone entered the room. She felt the panties press deep into her, damp again from the ferment of anticipation in her belly. She moved one hand down and began stroking the inside of her thigh, her fingers delicately kneading the responsive flesh. She pressed her fingers over the damp panties, exploring the entrance to the delicate folds of her pussy lips. With her other hand she continued the play on her breasts, making more urgent attacks on the hardened nipples, rousing herself expertly.

She traced the contours of the panties deep between her thighs; she liked to feel the soft material pulled deep up into her rear crevice, emphasising the shape of her buttocks. She lifted her bum a little and slipped the panties down, quickly pulling them off and hiding them neatly under the pillow. All the years in homes and institutions had taught her the art of concealing all. She resumed her position so that anyone entering the room suddenly would be met with the demure and innocent sight of Lucy having a quiet sleepy rest on the bed.

She spread her thighs, carefully arranging her skirt to provide maximum concealment, and felt a cool breeze brush the entrance to her naked sex. She parted her cunny lips with her outer fingers and pressed the middle finger a little way in, finding the wet stickiness appealing. A surge of pleasure passed over her as her fingers began to tease and play with her excited pussy. She liked to make love to herself slowly, ensuring that every sensation was savoured, bringing herself to the edge of climax then drawing back a little to prolong the tension.

She began to dig her fingers deeper, pressing in and out rhythmically, ensuring that each thrust finished on her secret place. She swallowed the soft moans of pleasure, aware always of the possibility of capture. As she roused herself to higher levels of pleasure she began to writhe and lift herself up to meet the thrusting, grasping fingers. Her pussy was soaking wet, her fingers enveloped in the sex honey. She tightened her muscles against the greedy fingers, forcing herself to work harder.

Unable to contain herself any longer, she arched her back and pressed fingers from both hands into her crack. She let out a long gasp of satisfaction and fell headlong into climax.

Afterwards she lay back breathing deeply, feeling wonderfully relaxed after the orgasm. Her mind had been filled with the erotic images of the day, and the picture of Jenny was foremost in her mind. The sight of the girl being punished had excited her intensely, and she guessed that it had had a similar effect on the rest of the' class. Without wanting to she wondered what it had been like to be punished so publicly. The pain and the humiliation must have been unbearable, but Jenny had been driven to an intense orgasm by the experience.

Lucy couldn't understand the connection between pleasure and pain, yet it seemed that the entire Institute was based on the connection. She had never allowed anyone to punish her physically, and did not plan on it now. But still she was fascinated by all that she had seen.

Anne Young had been absolutely right – there was definitely something going on at the Institute. Belatedly she realised that all she had to do was report on the regime, even if only to list the incidents she had witnessed already, and she would get the money. The thought made her feel a little better; it gave her a link, however tenuous, with the outside world.

Sitting restlessly she stared around the room. There was nothing in it to betray a hint of personality; everything was boring and functional. Listening intently for the sound of anyone approaching she stole across the room and sat on the other bed. Satisfied that it was safe, she opened the bedside locker and quickly examined the contents. The contents were disappointingly bland, mainly books and stationery.

She guessed that half the chest of drawers was hers. The bottom two drawers were empty, the top two filled with clothes. The top drawer contained skirts and jeans and a pair of trainers. The second drawer was neatly filled with the neatly folded skirts, shirts and panties of the uniform.

Certain that the coast was clear, she carefully began to dig through the top drawer. She guessed that her roommate would keep all her private things there, safely isolated from the dour uniform and school things. She lifted the jeans and peered carefully underneath, then she pulled out a soft pink cardigan and checked through the pockets, which proved to be empty. She had almost given up when she felt something cold and hard right at the back of the drawer, buried deep behind the neat piles of clothes. It felt like a wallet and, very carefully, she prised it out.

It wasn't a wallet. It was a long thin strip of stiff black leather, about twelve inches long. One end was shaped like handle and the other was totally flat.

She held it by the handle curiously, trying to work out what it was for. Only after swinging it through the air did she realise that it was some kind of instrument for punishment. Her first reaction was to put it away but she held on to it, weighing it in her hand and plying it through the air several times.

She wondered what it would be like to have it across her backside and shivered. Cautiously she started to replace it in its carefully hidden position but then she stopped.

Half apologetically she smiled to herself in the mirror, but she was overcome with curiosity. It was as if she had no choice in the matter; she simply had to find out what it felt like. She turned her back and lifted her skirt over her waist. The sun fell across her bare buttocks, reflected in the mirror. She straightened up and studied herself critically. Her bottom was pert and rounded, her silky thighs long and smooth.

She held the skirt up with one hand and drew back the other, clutching tightly the leather strap. She let the strap whistle across and land squarely on her soft white arse-cheeks. She winced at the sharp sudden pain and let the strap fall to the floor. A thick red strip was etched on her backside, a perfect impression of the strap. The sudden pain was replaced with an aching stinging sensation, and then a hot golden glow seemed to spread over her bum-cheeks. It was not an unpleasant feeling in a strange sort of way.

She bent over to display her arse fully. The arse-cheeks were spread a little, offering a glimpse of the tight arsehole set in the darker rear cleft. She was a little surprised to find herself becoming excited again. She felt hot between the thighs, the damp heat merging imperceptibly with the glow from her behind. Bending a little more she used her free hand to rub the surface of her wound, feeling the raised weal like a message in braille inscribed on her flesh.

'What the fuck are you doing?'

Lucy was startled and jumped up immediately. She had become totally engrossed in her reflection and in masturbating herself once more. Burning a deep bright red with shame she brushed her skirt down, trying desperately to think of some excuse. Though she was freshly showered and clad in a short towelled robe, Lucy recognised the girl at the door as Jenny.

'Is this what you want?' Jenny sneered. She slammed the door shut and turned her back to Lucy, lifting the robe to display her reddened bottom.

'I wanted to see what it felt like . . .' Lucy admitted red-faced, her eyes fixed on the other girl's beautifully marked posterior.

'I'll show you what it feels like,' Jenny laughed menacingly. She stepped forward and picked up the leather strap from the floor.

Lucy watched silently, aware of what was going to happen and powerless to resist. She wanted it to happen, wanted to experience the feeling of being chastised; she simply had to see what it was like.

Jenny took Lucy by the arm and pulled her close. She pressed their mouths together and Lucy eagerly accepted a long searching kiss.

'Suck my tits,' Jenny ordered, stepping out of the robe and standing naked next to Lucy. She cupped her breasts and Lucy bent down to take the hardened nipples in her mouth, tasting each in turn, knowing instinctively how to give pleasure. She flicked her tongue over the extended buttons then bit them gently.

Jenny pulled Lucy up and kissed her lovingly on the neck and mouth. Then Lucy bent over submissively and allowed herself to be positioned by the other girl, legs apart, skirt pulled up, arse raised high.

She felt on the verge of orgasm even before the first stroke was applied to her vulnerable backside. The pain was much more intense than when she had smacked herself, but the heat between her legs was also more potent. She couldn't see herself in the mirror, but she imagined the sight of her arse-cheeks being tanned a deep crimson colour and was further inflamed.

Jenny raised the strap high and brought it down with a heavy smack. Her breasts, still pink after the beating earlier, jiggled enticingly. She was enjoying the stimulation of beating another girl, revelling in her rare position of dominance. Her hot bum-cheeks were painful reminders of her own recent humiliation and now she was experiencing the exquisite pleasure of punishment from the other end. She was already planning what to do to Lucy once the spanking was finished.

Lucy was woken by an urgent nudge. It had been a difficult night for her, her mind a ferment of doubts and images. She dreamed of money and sex, of pleasure and reward, and of the strange world that she had entered. Everything she had ever known was laid open to question; there was not an ounce of certainty left.

She opened her eyes and found Jenny standing by the bed.

'Turn over,' Jenny told her, smiling. Still half asleep, Lucy turned over on to her stomach. The covers had been drawn and she was naked.

The first stroke across the buttocks shattered the early morning quiet and shocked Lucy to wakefulness. A tight pain was impressed across her soft white arse-cheeks by the hard black strap. Lucy gasped and tried to get up, but Jenny pushed her back and inflicted a second stroke. A searing, aching pain suffused a raging lava of heat into her body. A third and fourth stroke were applied in turn, Jenny slowly gaining expertise in the use of the strap.

51

Lucy closed her eyes, trying to keep the pain out to no avail. She knew that if she tried she could fight back; she was bigger than Jenny and could certainly take the strap off her if she wanted. But the will and energy to do so were lacking. Instead she lay still and accepted her punishment, her arse-cheeks quivering under the repeated savage blows from the strap. She felt a wave of self-disgust rise up when she realised that she was becoming wet between the legs. Unable to resist the powerful desires, she raised her backside up, meeting the swift downward swing of the strap. Each blow sent a spasm of pure joy deep into her pussy, the red heat from her arse-cheeks spreading a golden glow inside her. She let out delirious gasps and moans, the pleasure and pain becoming indistinguishable.

Jenny studied the raised arse in front of her. She had inflicted a series of deep scarlet weals on the previously pure unblemished flesh. The buttocks were parted slightly and she could see that their crimson tan had spread down between the thighs and deep into the gaping sex, the rosebud just visible in all its feminine glory. She liked to feel the buttocks, tracing her fingers along the strap marks, following the contour of tight hot arse-flesh. She spread the buttocks and admired the puckered bumhole, noting that even here the strap had left its mark.

'Turn over,' Jenny ordered once more. Lucy obeyed, turning over on to her back. She flinched a little as her aching wounds touched the sheets. 'I want you to call me Mistress,' Jenny told her in a whisper. She bent down and seized Lucy's mouth, pressing her tongue deep in a passionate and affectionate kiss. 'Just when we're together,' Jenny continued, whispering between kisses. 'This'll be our secret, our game.'

'Yes, Mistress,' Lucy answered, enthralled by the idea.

'Does your backside hurt?'

52

'It stings . . .' Lucy smiled.

'It stings, Mistress,' Jenny corrected.

'It stings, Mistress,' Lucy repeated.

'That's how it should be.'

'Yes, Mistress.'

Jenny gave Lucy one last kiss and stood up; she was naked under her skirt. She smiled and then climbed on to the bed, standing without shame over Lucy's face. 'Now you have to suck me off,' she smiled. 'I'm going to come in your mouth.'

'Yes, Mistress,' Lucy smiled back nervously. Jenny squatted down over Lucy's mouth, squirming herself into position so that sex and mouth were locked tight.

Lucy could hardly breathe as the strong feminine smell of female sex enveloped her. She gingerly flicked her tongue over the velvety folds of Jenny's pussy lips, the soft curly hairs tickling her. Finding the entrance to the sex she pressed her tongue inside, tasting the salty taste of another pussy for the first time in her life.

Jenny began to wriggle, moving down hard on to the mouth clamped between her thighs. Lucy was searching with her tongue, lapping at the thick honey of the pussy juices, enjoying the cloying flavour of her Mistress.

As Jenny began to ride wildly, bucking her hips back and forth, Lucy suddenly saw herself. It was as if she had taken a step outside of herself. She could see herself urgently sucking deep into another girl's pussy, her bare backside crossed with lash marks, her cunt hot and wet with desire. Her head spun with bewilderment and disgust and sick fascination.

Jenny, panting wildly, clamped Lucy's head tightly with her thighs and cried out with release. Lucy came at the same time, arching her back, the fingers of one hand pressed deep into her quim, her face wet with a thin film of sweat and sex juices, her mouth drinking deeply from Jenny's sopping pussy.

As Jenny dismounted, Lucy opened her eyes and

stretched deliciously. She felt alive, her body, especially her rear, tingling with a new feeling of vitality. There was no thought of rebellion or escape any more. She realised that she had so much to learn, and that a new self was emerging from the ruins of the old.

And it was still only the start of her second day at the Institute.

Three

'Look,' Anne Young pointed out, her voice reasonable and persuasive over the phone, 'we can work together on this. We can both do well out of this story when it finally breaks.'

'I've told you already,' Simone Shirer repeated patiently, her rising irritation kept firmly in check. 'I have nothing to say to you.'

'I mean we're both independent career women – we need to support each other. If we don't no one else will.'

'The answer is still no,' Simone said emphatically.

'I'll get the story, but if you don't cooperate now I don't know how sympathetic I can be in the future.'

Simone shook her head in a private gesture of disbelief. It was difficult to believe that a person could switch from sweet reason to an appeal to solidarity and then to blackmail in the space of a single conversation. 'My answer is still no,' she said finally and put the phone down.

She sat pensively for a minute, wondering what to do about the journalist's sudden and wholly unexpected approach. The idea that the press might find out about the Institute had always been the nightmare scenario that was never fully addressed. Exposure would mean the end of the Institute and all its work, and, in consequence, professional ostracism and personal disgrace.

The fact that Anne Young had managed to find out both her name and telephone number was a great worry. It meant that the story had already progressed beyond casual curiosity and was now being actively pursued. She wondered whether any of the other members of staff had been similarly approached.

There was to be a staff meeting that afternoon and it was the obvious place to air the incident. She wanted to discuss the position with Fiona Schafer first, and to derive a common policy to deal with the situation before it progressed any further. The last thing that they needed was to ignore the problem, or to allow people to be panicked into talking. Mrs Schafer had very good links with the Ministry; if anyone could bring pressure to bear, she could.

It was, she realised with a sigh, another complication in her already hectic life.

J.K. looked up from his textbook and listened for a second; hearing nothing he turned back, realising that he had again forgotten all that he had been reading. He forced himself to read again, but the words trickled past his consciousness without making an impression. His concentration, or the little of it that was focused on the mechanical scanning of words from the book, was interrupted by the sharp sound of high heels on the stairs outside the room.

His heart was pounding as Miss Shirer left the house, as she did every morning, to work at the Institute. He waited anxiously for several minutes, afraid that she would suddenly return, having forgotten something.

He was Miss Shirer's tenant. She owned the large Victorian terraced house that they shared, he in a small self-contained flat on the ground floor and she in the other two storeys.

As an undergraduate he had found the rather cold atmosphere in the house quite conducive to concentrated study. The house was secluded, being a little way off a quiet road, and usually quiet. Miss Shirer did little to intrude beyond asking an occasional polite question about the progress of his studies. The two lives were lived quite separately and rarely collided.

The rent was quite substantial for a student, but this was offset both by the restrained atmosphere in the house and the chores that he had to carry out. On their first meeting he had been a little intimidated by her. She was tall and rather stern, and, in an austere sort of way, the most beautiful black woman he had ever seen. He judged her age to be around thirty-five, and she spoke crisply but with a faintly melodious Caribbean accent. He had liked the house almost immediately but blanched at the rent that she demanded.

From his reaction she realised that he couldn't afford to pay and so she outlined, quite precisely and in detail, a set of duties that he could carry out in return for a reduction in rent.

His primary task was to ensure that the house remained clean and tidy at all times. In particular he was to clean her rooms three times a week, wash and iron her clothes, do all small household repairs and do her weekly shopping. He agreed at once. They shook hands; she gripped firmly and smiled. It was the only physical contact between them. He still remembered how he had turned away from her eyes, looked nervously down at the ground. She still made him nervous in an ill-defined way. She was so sure of herself and seemed always in control, in contrast to his own general lack of confidence and uncertainty.

That had been three months ago. He had settled into a routine of study that occupied all his time. He had yet to make many friends at college, and so had no social life to take him away from his books. Of course his college work was excellent, but this only served to further alienate him from the other students, both male and female. The only respite from study lay in the household tasks.

He didn't notice it at first, but over the weeks he began to lose himself in the household chores. He could switch out all thoughts of reading and exams, and could relax from the strains of learning. Instead he would concentrate on the simple tasks of tidying up, or washing or pushing a trolley around the shops. Perhaps it was the absence of any greater responsibility, or the simple pleasure of jobs well done. Housework became his release.

Miss Shirer complimented him very early on; she smiled and told him that she had never had a maid as conscientious as he, then she laughed and climbed the stairs. He blushed, typically confused by her remark. Instead of responding he watched her walk upstairs, admiring her soft dark skin. He could remember clearly that she had worn a tight skirt well above her knee that day and he had stared at her firm thighs and well-rounded bottom pressing against the skirt, accentuating the shape of the arse-cheeks.

However, in the last few days he had found a new diversion in the routine tasks of the house.

Satisfied that she had gone he stood up, put his textbook away, promising himself that he would return to it later, and left the room. The sun was streaming in through the windows, shafts of light dissected the hall, and everything was still.

He climbed the stairs quickly and went first into her sitting room and glanced around cursorily. Some magazines were spread carelessly on the coffee table, a book lay on the floor next to the settee and beside it was an empty coffee cup. 'I'll come back to this,' he said to himself before climbing the second flight of stairs with mounting excitement.

He entered Miss Shirer's bedroom and took a deep breath, savouring the sweet scent of make-up and perfume. He drew the curtains and let the light flood into the room. The bed was unmade, and discarded clothes lay in a bundle on the floor beside a pair of slippers. The dressing table was not its usual ordered self.

He started by making the bed, then fixing the dressing table and putting away the slippers. He worked quickly and methodically to his routine. He picked up the discarded clothes. The skirt and blouse he put on a chair – these were to be washed. The other items were her silky black stockings and her black panties. He loved the silky feel of her lingerie on his skin. He rubbed the stockings on his cheek, revelling in the smooth cool feel of them. The panties he held to his face and rubbed softly over his mouth, sniffing the deep musky smell of the feminine sex.

Quickly he undressed. He slipped off his clothes and bathed naked in the bright yellow sunlight that warmed the room. He was already aroused, his prick erect, and he squeezed it gently, reassured by its silky smooth hardness. He sat on the edge of the bed and very slowly pulled on the black stockings, savouring the smooth coolness on his thighs. He stood and admired himself in the mirror on the dressing table. The thick black stocking tops made his skin look soft and milky. He turned and studied the contours of his backside, the firm white cheeks in contrast to the darkness of his stockinged thighs.

He pulled the panties on. His prick was rock hard and its glans glistened with the first sticky drops of seminal fluid. He pulled the panties up tight. The thin black material couldn't contain him, and the top of his hardness extended above the panties which bulged with the weight of his testicles and the base of his prick. Again he turned to admire his backside. The thin shiny panties were pulled up between his cheeks, emphasising both the roundness and the whiteness of his bottom.

He shivered with pleasure. He suddenly felt both beautiful and desirable. He posed provocatively in front of the mirror, arching his back, bending over stretching his long thighs. His prick quivered with excitement, and he caressed it gently as he moved this way and that. Stepping gracefully across the room he pulled open one of the drawers. Quickly he found the suspender belt that matched the panties and expertly put it on.

It was a good feeling. He felt free of all his insecurities and of his mundane everyday existence. He no longer felt like a boring student devoted to his work, no longer felt lonely and afraid of all around him.

He sat at the pretty pink vanity chair, crossed one leg over the other coquettishly and stared at his face in the mirror. He was clean shaven, not unattractive; his hair was blond and wavy and fell naturally across his face. Gingerly he poked through the make-up box, taking up and then discarding different shades of lipstick, mascara, eye shadow and face powder. At last he found a shade of lipstick that he fancied. It felt good to be frivolous, good to be able to do something simply because he liked to. Leaning in closer to the mirror he puckered his lips and gently applied the lipstick. It felt, and tasted, delicious.

The action of smoothing the lipstick across his lips brought unbidden memories of his childhood flooding back. He had a vivid memory of his sister. She was a few years older than he and liked to boss him about. He didn't mind – he had no other brothers or sisters, nor any other children to play with. She was good to him mostly, though she had a terrible temper that she would occasionally turn on him.

As she had entered her late teens she had begun to experiment with cosmetics, mostly their mother's. His sister had invented the game of dressing up. She had started by testing the cosmetics on herself, but very quickly hit on the idea of using J.K. She would sit him in front of the mirror and paint his face with lipstick and powder. She had often used a thick black pencil to paint his eyes and mascara to extend his eyelashes, even trying false lashes once.

He liked the game and had extended it by adding jewellery to the make-up. His sister had thought it a great idea. Soon his ears glittered with earrings, bracelets slipped from his wrists and his mother's long string of pearls dangled from his neck. One day his sister finished dressing him up and sat back to examine her creation. Suddenly she leaned forward and touched her rosy lips on his. She had held him under the chin and pressed her mouth against his, pulling him closer still.

He had known it was wrong, had instinctively felt he ought to pull away. Instead he had opened his mouth and accepted her cool kisses. She had pressed her tongue into him and sucked at his breath. His head seemed to be spinning; he had felt dizzy and confused and excited.

At last she had pulled away and stood up. Vividly he remembered looking up at her, unsure of what to do. 'Get that stuff off you . . .' she had told him coldly, and had left the room. He had been stunned, when he had stood up he realised that his prick was hard and bulging in his trousers. He locked the door and started to remove the jewellery. Halfway through he had stopped, unzipped his trousers and pressed his aching prick. Standing in front of the mirror, still made-up like a pretty girl, he had masturbated for the first time in his life. He had been fourteen years old at the time. His sister had never played that game again. It had been a turning point in his life, a pivotal event that he replayed often in his mind.

Putting the lipstick away, he began to look for a complementary shade of mascara. He was so engrossed with the make-up that he didn't hear the door to the bedroom open. However, when he sat up straight to look at his new face he was startled to see the reflection of Miss Shirer in the mirror.

She had been thoroughly unnerved by the early morning phone call and in her rush to get to work she had forgotten to pick up her briefcase. Luckily she had time to turn the car back before she hit the main rushhour traffic.

Climbing the stairs she had heard him in her bedroom and decided to have a word with him about his work. She stood now, in the doorway, leaning against the door frame, arms folded, her long legs slightly apart, watching silently with a faint look of surprise on her face.

He jumped up, knocking the vanity chair over in panic. His heart was pounding, and his face had become deep red with shame. He couldn't face her, and turned away nervously.

'I did suspect something of this sort,' she declared. 'Don't think that I hadn't noticed that my make-up was disappearing, nor that the standard of the housework has declined.'

He tried to stutter a reply but couldn't. He was suddenly aware of his near-nakedness and covered his prick with his hands.

She strode across the room and dealt him a sharp slap against the face. He cried out and clutched at his face, and when he pulled his hands away he turned into the mirror and saw the impression of her fingers scarlet on his cheek. The bright red lipstick was smeared across his face so that it too seemed part of the sharp pain.

'I'm sorry . . .' he muttered quietly, his eyes filled with tears. He wanted to run away, to disappear back into his little room, back into his anonymous normality.

She took his chin and turned his face to examine the redness. Gently she wiped away the smeared lipstick. The resounding slap was only the second time they had ever touched. She rubbed his cheek gently now, soothing away the pain with her fingertips.

She pulled him forward slightly and kissed him. Her mouth was cool and her tongue searched for his. He closed his eyes and seemed to float on air. They seemed to kiss for ages, her beautiful dark lips pressed firmly against his. She let go and he pulled away. When she looked at him and smiled, again he averted his gaze shyly.

She reached out and touched his prick which was hard again. Its head was smeared with sticky fluid. She rubbed along its length, pulling the panties down towards the stocking tops. The feel of her fingers on his flesh was ecstasy. She began to rub slowly up and down the full hard length of his prick.

He stood awkwardly, arms at his side, afraid to embrace her in any way. She pushed him back on to the bed with one hand, the other still caressing his cock. He slid back on to the bed, propping himself up on his elbows, watching as she expertly wanked his prick.

He could feel his juices swelling in the base of his belly. Hesitantly he stretched an arm to caress her on the nape of the neck, but she brushed his arm away impatiently. The sight of the beautiful black woman, her breasts heaving in the tightness of her jacket, wanking him, and of himself clad in her underwear excited him as much as the touch of her fingers on his hardness.

He glanced at the mirror across the room, caught the image in his mind, closed his eyes and gasped as his sperm jetted out. She continued to play with his prick until every last drop of spunk had been drawn. The glistening white cream was smeared over his belly and on to the stockings and suspenders. He lay back with his eyes shut and breathed deeply, his mind still full of the images that he had just experienced.

'I want everything cleared up – properly. You will wash my things most thoroughly, do you understand?'

He opened his eyes and saw her standing over him. She had resumed her normal persona, commanding, severe but still infinitely more beautiful than any other woman he had ever seen. Her chocolate skin was smooth and flawless, her dark glittering eyes set in a long oval face. The mouth was long with pouting full lips, which when parted in a smile revealed perfect white teeth.

'You mean I don't have to leave?' he asked quietly, a little surprised.

'You have still so much to learn,' she replied softly. She turned and left.

He listened to her descend the stairs and leave the house, then waited until he was certain that she had gone before he flopped down on the bed, totally stunned by what had happened. Already his prick began to harden again, fired by the images that danced in his head.

Simone felt much better. She had always known that J.K. had been intimidated by her sexually, and was always aware of the way his eyes would follow her, looking on with a faintly childish look of awe. She had never been inclined to build on his submissive feelings, but the revelation of his secret cross-dressing opened up a number of possibilities she wanted to explore.

Sex always helped to put things in perspective. It gave her the mental space to step back and look at the bigger picture. The fact that a journalist had finally begun to snoop around need not necessarily be bad. It would force them to concentrate fully on the future direction of the Institute. If it was to retain its unique position of secrecy, proper procedures for handling the press and media were required. On the other hand, if the high-security mantle was to be replaced, a fully thought-out and well-balanced public image needed to he created. In either case the Institute would not be open to smart operators like Anne Young.

'You as well?' Fiona asked, as soon as Simone entered her office.

'This morning. And you?'

'Last night. In that case it's just the two of us so far.'

'Are you sure?' Simone asked, taking a seat by Fiona's desk.

'I've dropped discreet hints, but so far no other staff have mentioned it.' Fiona leaned back in her seat and studied Simone carefully. 'What do you suggest?'

'The obvious thing is not to panic. I think we ought to come clean this afternoon, let the rest know that the press has started looking into us.'

'That sounds reasonable enough. Do you know Anne Young?'

Simone shook her head. 'No, but she tried to convince me that she's not some junior reporter.'

'That's right,' Fiona smiled nervously. 'She heads the best investigative team on television. I've met her on a couple of occasions. She's smart, very determined and totally, totally manipulative.'

'Sounds as if she ought to be working for us,' Simone laughed.

'Do we get on to the Ministry or not?' Fiona asked.

'How do you think Anne Young would react to that?'

'Probably only make her more determined. The first hint of direct political involvement and she'll double her efforts to get into us. Scandal is what she wants.'

'And if we don't tell the politicians and the thing blows up without their knowing?'

'You're right, an informal chat with the Ministry is probably our first step.'

Simone stood up to leave. 'And this afternoon?'

'We tell the staff to be alert, and not to allow themselves to be panicked into being indiscreet.'

'What about us? Could we get at Anne Young in any way?'

'What do you mean?' Fiona looked a little shocked. 'You don't mean blackmail?'

'Yes, you're right,' Simone smiled. 'We are psychologists after all, not journalists.'

'We don't want to descend to her level.'

Simone stopped by the door, and looked at Fiona. 'You have told me everything, haven't you?'

'Pardon?' Fiona looked up nervously.

'It's just that I get the feeling that I've missed something.'

'There is one thing,' Fiona paused for a second. 'Anne Young and I have been fairly close in the past.'

'Oh yes?' Simone had felt that Fiona was holding back.

'We were both very young. I was still doing research for my thesis; I was delivering a paper at a big conference in London. She was a journalist on a local newspaper.'

'And?'

'We had sex several times. That's all.'

'That's all?' Simone asked sceptically.

'That's all. But I'm worried that it'll look bad if it gets out to the people from the Ministry.'

'You've never made any secret of your sexuality,' Simone pointed out coolly, 'so there's no avenue for blackmail. Is there?'

'No, I suppose you're right. But Anne Young does make me very nervous.'

'I'm sure we can handle this whole incident,' Simone said confidently. 'There is just one more thing.'

'Yes?'

'Is her sexuality as open?'

'Her sexuality,' Fiona laughed, 'is legendary.'

Simone laughed too. She flashed a reassuring smile and left, leaving Fiona Schafer to make the first of her calls to the Ministry.

J.K. had been unable to return to his textbooks. The events of the previous day had shattered his entire mode of existence. Nothing could ever be quite the same again.

After Miss Shirer had left he had showered and then cleaned the house meticulously. He had returned to his room and nervously awaited her return; he felt excited by the sexual tension that had suddenly overtaken them.

On her return, early that evening, Miss Shirer had gone straight to her rooms, just as she did every evening. He had waited anxiously for her to give him some indication of what to do next, but there had been none. He debated making the next move himself but felt intimidated by her presence, and he feared rejection more than anything else. He had wanked himself to sleep and awoke early that morning with the picture of her luscious lips still fresh in his mind.

When he heard her coming downstairs the next morning, he realised that she was on her way to the Institute and not to him. In a fit of dejected panic he rushed from his room and caught her as she was half way down the last flight of stairs. He looked up at her imploringly, noting the dark grey business suit, the short skirt, the stockings, the shiny black high heels.

She continued down the stairs and stopped a few steps from him. He had looked quite attractive in her lingerie, and she had liked the feel of his hardness clothed so delicately in the silkiness of female underwear. She smiled, unable to decide whether the plans she had for him were a private dalliance or a professional experiment. As he came closer she reached out and brushed her hand lovingly through his hair.

'I thought you were leaving . . .' he said softly. It was neither a question nor a complaint, but simply an observation.

She pulled him softly towards her, and kissed him fully on the mouth, her cool breath breathing life into him, her hand still entwined in his hair. Suddenly she tightened her grip and pulled him away.

He looked at her wide-eyed as she pulled him down. She had gripped a handful of hair tightly. It hurt as she steered him down on to the steps. He sat down in silence, her hand still gripping tightly, his eyes longingly on her glossily painted lips.

'Today you begin to learn, and believe me, you have much to learn,' she said sternly. 'Luckily I am used to dealing with naughty girls; it is after all what I do at the Institute. There are rules to be learned, and the first rule is that I am your Mistress. Do you understand?'

He failed to respond and she tugged sharply at his hair. He let out a cry of pain and his eyes filled with tears.

'You will address me always as Mistress, and you will do all that your Mistress tells you. Do you understand?'

'Yes,' he replied after another sharp tug at his hair.

'Yes what?' she demanded, taking more of his hair in her grip.

'Yes, Mistress,' he replied.

'Good. You will find your new clothes upstairs in my bedroom. You will wear these all the time that you are in my part of the house. You will continue to do the maid's work as before. In your part of the house you will dress as you do now. Understood?'

'Yes, Mistress.'

'You need a new name,' she said, pausing to think. 'When in my part of the house and in uniform your name will be Jaki,' Mistress decided. 'I like that. Jaki. Now, thank me.'

'Thank you, Mistress,' he said quietly. Mistress had relaxed her grip on him slightly. He felt elated and excited by what he had been told, but still afraid and more confused than ever.

'That is not how you thank your Mistress,' she said angrily and slapped his face forcefully. She tightened her grip on his hair once more and forced him down on his hands and knees, head down towards the steps. 'Kiss my shoes,' she demanded.

He began by gently kissing the shiny black leather shoes at the pointed toes. The leather was cold against his mouth and tongue. He started to work around the length of the shoe, pressing ever more urgent kisses against the unyielding material. At the base of the heel he began to lick and suck, and closed his eyes to give himself fully to the sensation. The heel was hard and sharp, but still he worked passionately with his mouth. His prick was hard and he felt on the verge of spurting thick wads of come.

She pulled him up sharply, knowing full well that he felt lost in a new world of sensuality. 'Good,' she said, evidently satisfied with the response. She pulled him up higher and kissed him gently on the lips, then released him, almost casting him aside.

Mistress left the house and he was alone, on the stairs, overwhelmed by the erotic experience of paying homage to his Mistress. The taste of the shoe was still strong and tingling in his mouth. His prick had been hard from the moment she had touched him, and was now throbbing powerfully, aching for relief. The pain and the humiliation she had inflicted on him were mingled with a strange kind of pleasure that filled his entire soul.

He stood up and quickly made his way up to her bedroom, remembering what she had told him. He stripped immediately and found a neatly folded bundle of clothes on the vanity chair. He took each item in turn and studied it, eyes wide with amazement. There was a simple white blouse which buttoned up from the front and had a small tight collar, much like a man's shirt. He held the skirt to his hips and measured it against his legs. It was very short, dark navy blue and slightly flared, with a white apron that tied up at the back. In addition there were black stockings with a tight fishnet pattern, matching black lace suspenders and panties. The panties were cut high at front and rear and had a shiny, silky sheen. On the floor beside the vanity chair was a pair of navy shoes with heels only about an inch high, but nicely pointed at the toes.

With slow languid movements he dressed in his maid's uniform. First the stockings, then the suspenders and panties. The panties were sufficiently high cut to cover his enlarged penis, and at the back the thin sliver of material was pulled tightly into his anal cleft. As he dressed he posed in the mirror, delighting in the touch of the clothes on his skin, appreciating the contrast between pale skin and dark lingerie. He put the blouse on and then the skirt, glad that it was so short. The shoes were uncomfortably tight but roughly the right size for his feet.

At last he was fully dressed. He felt that something was not quite right; his outfit didn't feel complete. He realised that he had no make-up on; Mistress had not left any on the vanity chair. He wobbled unsteadily to the dressing table and searched for his favourite shade of lipstick. He found it and hesitated. He knew that she would be angry if he used her cosmetics, and the thought sent a wave of excitement and trepidation pulsing through him. He pursed his lips and applied the lipstick carefully.

'Hello, Jaki,' he said quietly. He looked at himself in the mirror. He felt as if a great weight had been lifted from his shoulders – he felt free. He practised walking up and down the room, eager to perfect a feminine gait. It wasn't easy, and he swayed unsteadily at first, unused to the heels and the shape of a woman's shoe, but gradually he gained control.

He kept glancing at his reflection. He went from room to room, gliding like a princess on a bed of roses. He slipped easily into his new persona.

Jaki felt deliciously alive. Men can't be attractive and desirable in the way a woman can, and Jaki wanted to be loved and desired more than anything else in the world. Now at last she had succeeded, and she felt attractive and alluring in her sexy maid's uniform.

Carefully and meticulously, she began to do the housework.

The days seemed to fly past. Incredibly J.K. had managed to return to his studies. He had settled into a routine that left him both the time and the energy to concentrate on his work.

For one part of the day he was J.K. He lived quietly in his flat, he studied and read, he cooked and cleaned his flat, he slept alone, an untroubled peaceful sleep, free of the unspoken tensions and dire dreams that had kept him awake before.

At other times he was Jaki. She would flit about the house cleaning the upstairs rooms, washing clothes, and generally looking after things. She still found the time to parade herself in front of the mirror, to surreptitiously try on the clothes that Mistress discarded. She usually ended each session lying on the bed, her skirt pulled up around her waist, eyes closed and masturbating. She imagined it was Mistress playing with the hard prick, caressing it with an expert play that always ended with a forceful sigh as the spunk squirted out in long delicious spurts.

In one way things continued as before. J.K. seldom saw Mistress. Once or twice he had deliberately met Mistress at the front door and on the stairs, but she ignored him with ill-concealed contempt. Jaki had yet to meet Mistress.

Jaki had finished all her chores for the day. She felt a little tired but pleased with all that she had done. She had decided to hoover the carpet that day and had taken great delight in doing the bedroom. She had positioned herself in front of the dressing-table mirror, so that if she bent down she could see up her own skirt. She had adopted different postures to see which was most revealing, and had been aroused at the sight of her panties pressing deep into her arse, the skirt

71

riding up slightly so that the bum-cheeks were almost exposed.

She put away the vacuum cleaner and now stood in the same position, bent over almost double, her arse visible in the mirror. Idly she fondled her prick whilst swaying slightly from side to side, arching her back to emphasise the roundness of her backside.

At that instant Mistress entered the room. Jaki stood up straight, embarrassed by her actions. Her heart was beating wildly, and she felt short of breath.

'Hello, Jaki,' Mistress said firmly, walking around her in a full circle, eyeing her up and down critically. She held out her hand and Jaki took it nervously and kissed it, hoping it was the right thing to do. 'Good.' Mistress took her hand away. She wore a simple white blouse, the dark nipples clearly visible against the crisp white cotton. She also wore a pleated grey skirt and the same black heels that J.K. had previously kissed so lovingly.

'Is there anything I can do for Mistress?' Jaki asked gently, uncertain as to the correct form of words to use.

'There is nothing that Mistress desires at present,' she replied, casually walking to the window and pulling the net curtains apart. She peered out for a second at the quiet suburban scene, then turned back. 'You've been a naughty girl, haven't you Jaki?' she declared suddenly.

'No, Mistress,' Jaki replied, desperately trying to think which rule she may have broken. Mistress had spoken of rules before, but Jaki felt that she knew so little.

'Do not lie, girl!' Mistress scolded angrily. 'You've got make-up on. Where did you get it?'

'I'm sorry,' Jaki whimpered, trembling.

'Come here, girl,' Mistress commanded as she sat on the edge of the bed. Jaki approached at once, afraid to resist, afraid to comply. Mistress reached up and pulled her down into a kneeling position.

'You will be punished. Bad girls need to be chastised

regularly, otherwise they forget who they are.' She leaned forward and gave Jaki a passionate kiss. Jaki closed her eyes, and responded. She tasted the smearing of the lipstick, and flicked her tongue into Mistress's mouth.

Mistress leant across from the bed and retrieved a large hairbrush from the dressing table. 'Bend over,' she said harshly, holding the hairbrush tightly in her right hand.

Jaki obeyed and bent over Mistress's lap. Her skirt was pulled up, high over her waist. Her knickers were pulled down, over her pulsing rod, and halfway down her thighs, exposing her bottom completely. Her back was pressed down with one hand so that her arse stuck out, the arse-cheeks slightly splayed to display the short dark hairs around her arsehole. She felt completely under Mistress's command; the steadying arm kept her in place, and forced her to adopt the required position of vulnerability.

Mistress raised her arm and brought it down ferociously, first on one buttock and then the next, pausing between each stroke to admire her handiwork. The buttocks were marked a deep red, the weals bearing the distinct imprint of the flat side of the brush.

Jaki winced and cried out with each stroke, struggling fitfully to escape the perfectly aimed blows. She bit her lip and tried to stifle the cries, but the pain was excruciating. Her bottom seemed to be burning; it felt red hot. At last, after what seemed an age, the beating ceased.

'Stand up now,' Mistress demanded, letting go of Jaki and returning the brush to the dressing table.

Jaki forced herself to her feet. Her body felt on fire as a deep heat spread from her buttocks into her belly. She was surprised to see that her prick was harder than ever. The pain seemed to make it harder, so that it throbbed powerfully, threatening to spill its thick creamy load.

Mistress stood to admire Jaki's crimson arse-cheeks. Silently she made Jaki part her legs so that the thin panties were stretched from knee to knee like black silken bonds. Jaki bent over and caught sight of herself in the mirror. Her buttocks and the tops of her thighs were a beautiful burning red, the suspenders and stocking tops pressed tightly into the pain offering some relief.

'Your derriere was made to be beaten,' Mistress remarked, enjoying the delicious sight. 'Now thank your Mistress.'

'Thank you, Mistress,' Jaki responded. She made to stand but Mistress signalled her to remain bent over.

'After every correction you must thank your Mistress. That is one of the rules.'

'Yes, Mistress.'

'You may go now,' Mistress decided. 'In future you must buy your own cosmetics and jewellery. I hope this has taught you a lesson.'

'Yes, Mistress,' Jaki said, straightening up. She paused for a second to glance at her painful backside before demurely pulling on her panties and lowering her skirt. 'Thank you, Mistress.'

As Jaki left she noticed that Mistress's nipples were erect and jutting against the thin white cotton blouse.. She felt a thrill of delight pulse through her as she realised that her punishment had caused Mistress to become sexually aroused. Jaki knew then that the entire point of her existence was to please Mistress. Life had no greater aim than this.

She retired to the bathroom to change back into J.K., but not before she had studied her aching, burning buttocks in the mirror. The most painful edg ad not yet started to recede, but the pain became pleasure as she started to rub her aching prick into release.

Two days later Jaki was caught trying on some of the discarded clothes. Every evening Mistress cast off the day's clothes, or in the morning tried on and rejected clothes for work, and left them in an untidy bundle by the bed. Jaki liked to try these on, admiring the delicate lacework of the briefs, or the different shades of stocking. Mostly she just liked to feel close to her Mistress, to know that the soiled garments were scented with the heady perfume of her Mistress's perfect body.

Mistress returned unexpectedly and found Jaki lying back on the bed, her skirt pulled up around her waist, barelegged and naked under the skirt. Lately she had begun to shave her legs and they were long and smooth, the thighs milky white, lithe and feminine. Beside her were the thin white briefs that Mistress had worn the day before.

'What have you to say?' Mistress demanded angrily, storming into the room.

'I'm sorry, Mistress,' Jaki cried, jumping out of bed.

'You silly little bitch,' Mistress continued, and dealt Jaki a heavy smack across the face. 'Do you really want to be disciplined again so soon?'

'Please, Mistress, I'm sorry,' whimpered Jaki, backing away.

Mistress grabbed her by the arms and forced her to the ground, on to her hands and knees. Jaki was vulnerable, her backside bare under the short skirt, and the faint marks from her first beating had yet to clear completely. She feared that she would again have to endure the exquisite pain of chastisement, and she dreaded the sharp spasms of hurt across her rear.

Mistress sat on the vanity chair and spread her legs, motioning to Jaki to crawl towards her. Mistress pulled Jaki on to her lap and across her knee. Jaki had her skirt pulled up high, and realised that her prick was pressing on the warm flesh of Mistress's thigh. She tried not to press her hardness against the softly yielding ebony flesh, afraid that she would break another of the rules and have to be doubly punished.

'This is what you deserve!' Mistress declared as she raised her hand and began to spank Jaki's bare bottom.

Jaki managed to muffle her cries of pain as blow after blow fell upon her backside. Mistress directed her hard resounding smacks first across the buttocks, then to the upper thighs. The sharp slapping sound filled the room with a taut regular rhythm. Jaki lost count of the number of smacks, her whole being concentrated on her inflamed backside. Mistress used her left arm to press hard into Jaki's back so that the back was arched and the posterior stretched into tight round globes that burned deep crimson.

Jaki felt lost in the pleasure-pain of her spanking, in the steady rhythm of hurt that descended on to her raised behind. The fire burned deep into her belly, into her balls and the base of the tight hard prick.

Mistress switched targets: her last few blows were directed at the deep deft between the burning cheeks. The unexpected blows intensified the pain and Jaki began to let out short gasping breaths. The blows stopped as suddenly as they had begun, just as Jaki let out a sigh and spurted her creamy white spunk over Mistress's thigh.

'You filthy little bitch!' Mistress hissed venomously. She pushed Jaki to the. floor with a shove. Jaki felt an instant relief as she pressed her aching backside to the cold varnished floor. She knew that she was in for much worse, but was thankful even for the briefest of respites. Mistress stood up, the spunk trickling slowly down her left thigh. 'Lick it dean,' she ordered.

Jaki reluctantly crawled on all fours towards Mistress, revolted and humiliated, yet strangely attracted by the demand. Mistress pulled her skirt a little higher and Jaki pressed her lips to the warm dark flesh above the knee. She trembled as she planted gentle loving kisses on the soft smooth flesh, and began to work her mouth higher towards the trickles of come.

She closed her eyes as she licked the first globules of her own spunk, tasted the salty jelly on her tongue and swallowed. Opening her eyes she quickly licked up the rest of the spunk, secretly enjoying the sensation of caressing her Mistress with her mouth.

The humiliation of swallowing her sperm was exciting she felt none of the revulsion that she had expected. The experience of showing her utmost devotion to Mistress was worth it. She wanted to prove to Mistress, beyond all doubt, that she was an obedient and loving servant.

'Lie down now, on your back,' Mistress said after Jaki had finished.

'Yes, Mistress,' Jaki responded automatically, and lay down on the cold floor. Her skirt was in disarray and part of her backside, still painfully smarting, was pressed firmly against the cool floor.

Mistress strode across the room and stood over Jaki, one foot on either side of the head. Before Jaki understood what was happening Mistress squatted down and pressed herself on to Jaki's face.

Jaki tried to turn away but was pressed down by the pressure of Mistress's exquisite dusky posterior. The skirt cut off most of the light and she was enveloped by the powerful perfumes from Mistress's private places. It felt like heaven.

'You do not yet understand the absolute difference between Mistress and servant,' Mistress began. 'The servant is submissive in all spheres. That includes sexual satisfaction. The needs of the servant must be subordinate to the needs of the Master or Mistress. If I choose to correct a servant it is because I have decided to do so, either because the servant has transgressed or because I derive pleasure from the punishment. The servant may only derive sexual release at my command. Do you understand?'

'Yes, Mistress,' Jaki managed to reply as Mistress gave her room to answer.

Mistress raised herself slightly and pulled aside the thin gusset of her panties. Jaki could see the prominent pink rosebud set between the dark pussy lips. 'Pleasure me with your mouth,' Mistress ordered, still holding aside the panties with one hand to reveal all of her beautiful dark cunt amid the tight black curls of hair.

Jaki pressed her face into the folds of skin, relishing the salty sweet taste of her Mistress. She played her tongue back and forth, searching for the hard pink clitoris. Mistress pressed down, pushing her opening directly over Jaki's mouth. Jaki found the centre and began to suck and bite and flick it with her tongue, the sweet honey juices that flowed filling her mouth. She swallowed the juices with a shiver of pleasure, and felt her prick harden again.

Mistress began to swivel and ride Jaki's mouth, pressing down here, shifting there, deriving the greatest of pleasure. She arched her back and began to moan blissfully, feeling the hot tongue work deeper and deeper into her. At last she stiffened and let out a single cry of elation as she climaxed, filling Jaki's mouth with wave upon wave of creamy love juices.

Mistress shifted slightly. Jaki relaxed, her face covered in a thin layer of sweat and sex cream. Because she had brought Mistress to climax she was filled with a perverse and satisfying pride.

'Now my bumhole,' Mistress announced; she inched forward, pulled her panties back to reveal the tight arsehole and positioned it above Jaki's mouth.

Jaki could see the puckered nether lips in the shifting light, the inviting anal orifice set between the two hemispheres of Mistress's firm round arse-cheeks. She flicked her tongue across the arsehole, lovingly licking along the anal crease, the sharp little anal hairs tickling her tongue. She pressed the tip of her tongue gingerly into the tight sheaf of muscle and could taste the forbidden sour taste of arsehole. The anus closed around the tip of her tongue and she began slowly to press in and out, each stroke of her tongue probing deeper into Mistress's rear.

Jaki's prick was rock hard again, her balls began to ache slightly and she knew that she had to hold back as she had been commanded. Mistress arched her back, enjoying the slow even entry of tongue up and down her arsehole.

Raising her arms and gently taking hold of Mistress's backside, Jaki very gently splayed the arse-cheeks, gaining deeper entry. At last she managed to raise her head slightly and inserted her tongue as far as she could extend it into the tight little bumhole, lubricating the passage with spit.

She realised she was kissing Mistress from the rear in the same way that they shared a kiss face-to-face; her tongue was pressing in deep and she moved her head from side to side, consumed with the sheer pleasure of the sensation. All thoughts were banished from her mind as her stinging backside became part of a single blissful sensation. Her whole being was focused on the single intense act of sucking from Mistress's beautiful arse.

Mistress reached out, she closed her eyes and took hold of Jaki's tense hardness. She rose and fell gently over the mouth that voraciously explored her anal hole. The sensation was like no other she had ever felt. A second orgasm was building up within her. It was a different sort of feeling, most unlike the feelings she had derived from being pleasured in her vagina. This built up slowly, layer upon layer of sensation that built up into a peak of pleasure, until at last Mistress gained release in a screaming climax, riding wildly on Jaki's face, the tongue deep inside her.

Mistress stood up. She had wanked Jaki as Jaki had tongued her arsehole. Both now felt sated, both elated from the highly charged erotic experience.

'Clean up now,' Mistress said quietly.

'Yes, Mistress,' Jaki responded, the taste of arsehole in her mouth, and as she stood she saw the fingermarks still red against the white flesh of her buttocks. The sight filled her with pride.

Four

J.K. riffled quickly through the pigeonhole. Among the bundle of library messages, student union notices and junk he was surprised to find a personal letter. He grabbed all his post and made his way to the refectory.

He had begun to look on his life as J.K. as shallow and uninteresting. He endured as best he could, longing always to return to Jaki's uniform and to her duties. He used the promise of his second life to drive himself forward, so that he continued to excel at his studies. He rewarded his successes with extended sessions as Jaki, or bought her little presents of clothes and make-up.

The refectory was crowded and noisy. Small groups of students sat or stood around the long tables, sipping coffee, arguing, laughing loudly. He was never part of those tight circles of friends and colleagues. He got himself a coffee and sat by himself in a corner, trying to ignore the commotion that thronged the long smoky canteen.

Previously he had avoided the refectory as much as possible. The sight of so many people together had always emphasised his loneliness. He felt totally cut off from the lively community around him. But now he didn't mind so much. He felt that Mistress was all that he needed; she was enough to fill the vast empty space of which he had been so painfully aware.

Slowly he had begun to relax a little. He still didn't

have any close friends in the class, but he had begun to talk a little more, to emerge slowly from his self-imposed isolation. And, no matter how difficult things were, he would always return to the silence and security of home. He looked forward to ascending the stairs, to donning the pretty blue skirt, the panties, the stockings and the blouse.

He opened the routine mail first, sipping slowly from the steaming cup of coffee. The extensive library messages detailed the passage of books into, and out of, his grasp. He scribbled notes on the computer printouts, eagerly looking forward to receiving the latest books that he had ordered, calculating which volumes to return on which dates. The student union notices he put aside, uninterested in the multitude of activities and events that were on offer. At last he had only the private letter left.

It was a simple handwritten note. Had it not had his name on it he would have been sure that it was a mistake. The note was a request that he be at a certain room at a certain time. It gave no details, except to say that it was important. He was perplexed; the note was signed Laura Stratton, but he knew no such person. He looked around furtively, wondering whether he was not the victim of some practical joke, but he was alone, resolutely ignored by everybody. He pocketed the note, deciding that it would do no harm to satisfy his curiosity.

He spent the next few hours in the library. He worked quietly on an essay, drawing freely from the volumes' around him. But every so often he would reread the note in his pocket, trying hard to imagine what it could possibly relate to. As the appointed hour grew closer he put the books away, and sat back in his seat, watching the world go by.

The room was a small tutorials classroom in the Media Studies department. He knocked timidly and entered.

'Hi, I'm glad you came,' Laura smiled. She jumped down from the desk she was sitting on and shook hands with him. She was dressed in tight black ski-pants and a simple yellow top.

'Hi,' he said simply, unable to think of anything else to say. He smiled shyly in return. It was obvious that she was a student; she was too young to be a lecturer. She had a friendly open face, her smile wide and bright, and put him immediately at ease.

'You're wondering what this is all about, aren't you? Well, I've got a favour to ask you.'

'Sure; what kind of favour?'

'Good. I just knew you'd be willing to help,' she beamed. 'You live in the same house as Simone Shirer, don't you?'

'Yes; how do you know that?' His smile evaporated and he looked at her suspiciously.

'Well,' she said, 'this favour sort of involves her. Do you know anything about the place she works in?'

'How does it involve her?'

'You're her tenant, right? I bet she charges a fortune in rent. Does she?'

'Look,' he said coldly, 'what is this all about?'

'Don't look so worried,' she smiled disarmingly. 'All I want is for you to visit the place she works at. That's not a big deal, is it?'

'What for?'

'Would you do me that favour?' she said coyly, flashing him an open inviting smile.

'Just a visit? What for?' he asked again. His smile returned weakly. Laura was attractive; he liked her. The small button nose gave her a girlish look which was offset by her seductive dark eyes. There was something about her that made him feel comfortable and relaxed. Most attractive women made him feel nervous or on edge, but not Laura.

'I've got a friend who's got a friend at this place

where she works. It's some kind of reform school, isn't it? My friend just wants to get a message in and out of the place. It's not a big deal.'

'I don't know anything about the place. I've never been there before.'

'But she must have talked about her work to you.'

'No. Never.'

Laura sat on the desk in front of him. 'But you know her. You could make up some story and just turn up.'

'I'm sorry, Laura,' he apologised, 'I don't think I can do it. If it was something else I would.'

'Please,' she put her hand on his, 'it's not a big deal, honestly it isn't. It would mean so much to me.'

'I really am sorry,' he repeated. He liked the feel of her soft hand on his, and only this stopped him from leaving.

'Look, I'm a third-year student. I graduate in three months. Then I have to have a job.' Her tone became more serious. 'This friend of mine, she can get me a job, a good job. All I have to do is this simple favour.'

'If it's so simple why can't she write to her friend? They let people get letters in prison. Why go through me?'

'You really don't know about this place?' Laura sounded a little surprised. 'It's not a normal reform school. It's a special sort of place. I don't know all the details myself, but it needs someone to smuggle a message out of the place.'

'Smuggle?' He started to back away nervously, but she took his other hand and held on to him tightly.

'Please. I need this chance. I'll be ever so grateful.' She gazed pleading into his eyes.

'I'm sorry, Laura,' he repeated weakly. He wanted to break free and escape from her. Something was going on, something that he didn't know about, and he doubted that even she knew. His main worry was that his strange relationship with Mistress would be jeopardised. He liked Laura – in any other circumstances he would have done anything that she asked – but now he felt there was no alternative but outright refusal.

'Please. What more can I say?' She let go and stared glumly at the floor. 'My whole future career is in the balance. You're a student; think of all your hard work going to waste.'

'It can't be that bad,' he tried to console her. 'If she's such a friend then she'll understand.'

'It doesn't work like that. And she's not such a great friend. She's a contact, and a very important one. I want to be a journalist, I do stringer work already. This woman can get me into the big time in one fell swoop.'

'I'm sorry, Laura. If there was any other way . . .' He felt sorry but there was nothing else he could do.

'Just think about it,' she suggested, seeing that he was backing slowly out of the room.

'I just can't,' he said, stopping by the door.

'I'll do anything to get that job.' She jumped down from the desk, brushing the hair nervously from her face. 'Anything, anything you want.'

'Please don't make it more difficult,' he pleaded, rooted to the spot.

'This room isn't used very much; we're safe here.' She stepped forward and kissed him, at the same time placing his hands on her breasts. She was desperate, but luckily she found J.K. quite sexy; he had a soft gentle face, and paradoxically his quiet understated demeanour suggested a raging passion under the surface.

He took her in his hands inexpertly, and pulled her closer so that he could breathe her scent and feel the texture of her smooth skin on his cheek. They kissed again, mouths locking in a passionate duel. Her breasts were bare under her top, and he could feel the contours of her body pressing firmly against him.

'Please help,' she begged when they parted for a second. From the look in his eyes she could tell that his adamant refusal still stood.

She fell to her knees before him and pressed her cheek against the stiff rod that bulged in his trousers. 'Do you promise to at least think about it?' she asked.

'I'll do what I can, but no promises,' he finally conceded.

She smiled as she unzipped his fly. She fumbled for a second and then withdrew his stiff cock. For a second she gazed at it lovingly, using her fingers to coax and caress it. She liked the feel of the hardness in her hand. It gave her a sense of power, knowing that she could use his prick to give him that exultant moment of transcendence when he would shoot his seed.

She flicked her tongue over the purple knob, using her tongue to search for the most sensitive spot. She twisted her head so that he could watch her playing her mouth over his prick. He stumbled back on to a desk and she began to take the prick into her mouth. First the head, which she took into her mouth and sucked at, rubbing the inside of her cheek against its smooth glistening surface. She played her fingers up and down his prick, skilfully wanking him.

When she heard his first ecstatic moans she fell fully on to the hardness. She took it into her mouth, sliding her tongue up and down the thick vein on the underside. She rose and fell rhythmically, occasionally letting her teeth graze his rod, other times drawing in her cheeks so that her mouth was warm and tight. He was making sharp upward thrusts and she liked the idea of him fucking her in the mouth. They began to move together, a single unit of motion, engaged in an elaborate duet.

At last he stiffened, grabbed her tightly and pumped spurt after spurt of thick cream into her hot mouth. He relaxed and lay back, overcome by aftershocks of delight as she lapped the last drops of sperm from his still-hard prick.

'You'll do your best?' she asked, standing up. Her

face was flushed pink, and from her expression it was obvious that she had enjoyed the experience.

'Let me think about it,' he agreed, sitting up and gingerly tidying himself up.

J.K. had racked his brains and had been unable to come up with anything to help Laura. The essential element in his life was the relationship with Mistress. Now this had been complicated by the possibility of a further relationship with Laura.

He had enjoyed the feel of ramming his prick into Laura's pretty mouth; he had liked the way she had taken his length and swallowed the creamy emissions without complaint. But, enjoyable as the feelings were, he knew that Laura had been driven to it by her desire to get a job. If that pressure were absent would she even have given him a second look? The look of pleasure on her face had been real enough, he was sure of that. But it was not enough to risk losing Mistress and, more importantly, losing his other self.

Fortunately Laura had not been in touch yet. He felt sorry for her but could not see what he could do to help. It had also occurred to him that perhaps Mistress was in some kind of trouble or danger. If the journalist wanted to smuggle things into and out of the Institute, then plainly something somewhere was wrong. He wanted to tell Mistress, but then he would have to tell her how he came to know about it. He could not see how he could explain to her what had gone on between Laura and himself.

However as Jaki all such thoughts were banished. Jaki was another person, with her own thoughts and her own concerns. When the transformation took place it was as if one person died and another was born. That evening Jaki was fully preoccupied, and she applied herself completely to the task of preparing everything for the arrival of Mistress and a friend. She had cleaned

87

the house from top to bottom, prepared some light refreshments and fixed some drinks.

Jaki waited with the patience that she had only begun to acquire from her ritual punishments and humiliations. She had come to know herself fully, rejoicing in the freedom and certainty only a slave could know. She had complete control of her life and destiny and these she subsumed totally to her Mistress. She yielded to regular painful chastisements and from these derived a bittersweet sexual gratification and the knowledge that the weals raised on her tender skin were the physical evidence of her devotion to Mistress.

She was nervous and for the umpteenth time she strode across the room to check her face in the mirror. Her eyes were lined with thick black pencil, her eyelashes wore a dark mascara, her lips were a deep scarlet and she had gently rouged her cheeks. She straightened her uniform again. Mistress had bought her a new skirt, shorter than the previous one, but still worn with a frilly white apron tied with a bow. The skirt was so short that the tops of her seamed stockings were visible as she walked or when she bent over. The shoes had slightly higher heels, so that as she walked the shape of the buttocks were pressed clearly against the tight-fitting skirt.

At last she heard voices on the stairs and, heart beating wildly, she assumed her position by the sitting-room door.

The door was opened and Mistress entered with the friend with whom she had shared an evening at the theatre. Jaki was trembling with nerves. This was to be her first public appearance, and everything had to go well.

She had poured two glasses of white wine minutes earlier and now, with shaking hands, stepped forward to offer them to Mistress and her friend. Mistress wore a tight off-the-shoulder black latex minidress. It clung to her sensuously, accentuating the contours of her large breasts, the smooth, gently curved belly and the pert round backside. The effect was heightened by knee-length black leather boots finished with shiny spiked heels. Mistress took both glasses of wine and passed one to her friend.

'You may address our guest as Mistress Diana,' she said and handed the second glass of wine to Diana.

Diana offered her hand and Jaki stepped forward and, bowing lightly, kissed it. She took the opportunity to get a good look at Diana. She was young, younger than Jaki had imagined, still in her early or middle twenties. She was fair with blonde hair cut short in a modem geometric style that suited her slightly round face. Her skin was very pale and her blue eyes sparkled. She was dressed in a shiny red slinky low-cut dress that ended several inches above the knee and also presented an enticing view of her full voluptuous breasts. Her legs were bare and her feet were clad in bright red ankle boots to match the dress.

'I didn't think she would be so pretty,' Diana told Mistress with a mischievous smile.

'Pretty and obedient, just as I like my maids,' Mistress answered as Diana stepped closer. Simone took Diana gently by the shoulders and pulled her close, planting soft loving kisses on her mouth and neck. Diana squeezed Simone's rubber-dad breasts softly. gently rubbing her thumbs over the hardening nipples constricted by the smooth pliant skinlike garment.

Jaki stared in amazement. The thought that Diana would be Mistress's lover hadn't occurred to her. The first pangs of jealousy stirred in her heart and she stepped back into the corner of the room, her eyes fixed on the two women caressing and cuddling.

'I like her uniform,' said Diana as they parted for a moment. She picked up her glass of wine and sipped from it.

'Come here,' Mistress ordered Jaki sternly.

'Yes, Mistress.' Jaki obeyed and walked selfconsciously forward. She was turned by Mistress so that her back was to Diana. 'She has delicate white flesh that marks well,' Mistress commented, 'even with the lightest spanking.' She raised Jaki's skirt to show Diana. Jaki blushed a deep red. Humiliated by the manner in which she was being displayed, she averted her eyes in shame.

'Is she spanked often?' Diana asked, stretching a hand to stroke Jaki's thigh, moving up over the stocking tops and caressing her buttocks. They were nearly naked; the silken panties were of the briefest kind and served to display her behind provocatively.

'Not often enough, I think,' Mistress laughed gently, letting the skirt drop.

Mistress motioned her away and so Jaki retreated to the corner of the room to pour more wine. Her mind was a mess of contradictory emotions; the humiliation had begun to arouse her. She felt jealous of the way Mistress kissed Diana, but she had also felt excited by Diana's touch.

Having poured the wine, Jaki stood in the corner, feet together and back straight. Outwardly she was perfectly still, but in reality she strained to catch parts of the conversation taking place between her Mistress and Diana. They had sat down in the two deep leather armchairs that dominated the centre of the large rectangular room. Jaki had hoped that her Mistress would shoot a stray glance in her direction, to acknowledge her existence, or to signal approval that she had performed her tasks properly. Forcing down her disappointment, she waited silently in her corner.

'Bring two brandies,' Mistress commanded after a time, without bothering to glance in Jaki's direction.

'Yes, Mistress.' Jaki, after the strain of being ignored for so long, obeyed at once, animated by an overwhelming desire to please. She went over to the well-stocked bar, selected two crystal brandy glasses and carefully poured from a decanter of fine cognac.

First she served her Mistress, who took the proffered glass without looking up. Jaki stiffened. She realised that it was Diana who should have been served first, but the need for Mistress's approval had caused her to forget all else.

Quickly she offered the second glass on the tray to Diana, who smiled at Jaki serenely. With her right hand Diana took the brandy and slowly ran her left hand up Jaki's thigh. Jaki didn't pull away; as a servant she knew that she was subservient to any placed above her.

Diana stroked the inside of Jaki's thigh, sliding her fingers up over the stocking tops, playing with the suspender straps. All the time she continued her conversation with Simone, who likewise continued to act as if nothing untoward were happening. Slowly Diana began to trace the contours of Jaki's rear; she squeezed the soft flesh just below the balls, traced the shape of the panties then inserted a finger underneath the silky material.

Jaki was aroused, her erection solid against the tight silky material of the panties. Diana contrived to slowly pull down the back of the briefs; the skirt was tight but somehow she managed to pull them down far enough so that Jaki's bottom was bare under the skirt. The hard prick was clearly visible, even from under the apron, bulging plainly against the skirt.

Jaki closed her eyes, her face bright red with embarrassment. She at once enjoyed the touch of Diana's hand against her skin, but was also ashamed at the thought that she was being idly played with, her own pleasure or discomfort of no consequence. Mistress Diana slid her hand down between Jaki's arse-cheeks, using two fingers to spread the globes while, with the middle finger, she explored. Jaki parted her legs somewhat but then stiffened as Diana found the target.

Diana pressed her middle finger against the tight bud of Jaki's anal hole. She felt resistance and began to press further. The back passage was unlubricated and the taut sheaf of muscle closed tightly around her finger. She enjoyed the feel of the servant's tight arsehole, judged that it was still virginal and wondered how Simone had let such a prize go unclaimed.

Diana had shoved a finger deep into Jaki's hole. The sudden sharp pain as the finger penetrated fully into the rear passage was excruciating, and Jaki cried out and pulled away sharply.

'I'm terribly sorry,' Simone cried, jumping up angrily from her seat. She strode across the room and grabbed Jaki by the arms and shook her violently. 'You stupid girl, is this how one behaves?' she demanded.

Jaki fell to the ground, close to tears, trembling with terror, and filled with trepidation at the thought of her inevitable punishment. Fervently she began to kiss Mistress's sharp heel, rubbing her mouth along its cold sharp length, licking wildly towards the pointed toe of the boot that she took eagerly into her mouth.

'Stand up, you grovelling little bitch!' Mistress scolded, pushing Jaki away with her boot, the heel digging sharply into Jaki's chest.

Jaki stood, a look of purest panic on her face, her eyes wide and her mouth opening and closing wordlessly. The room seemed to collapse around her, the world revolved around the three people in the room, and she knew that she was at the absolute mercy of Mistress Shirer and Mistress Diana.

'I think you were right, she isn't spanked often enough,' Diana declared airily. She too stood, and reached out and pressed Jaki's backside over the skirt.

'I really am terribly sorry, Diana,' said Simone, partially regaining her composure. 'You will, of course, punish her in any manner that pleases you.'

'She needs to be strapped. A sound thrashing across

'that pretty little posterior will teach her how to behave,' Diana said with a mock sternness belied by the sparkle in her bright blue eyes.

'Here, or would you prefer to administer punishment upstairs?' Simone asked. 'You can have the pick of any of my selection of implements,' she offered generously, 'and I'm sure you will find one to your taste.'

Jaki dolefully followed the women up the stairs, her heart low and her mind filled with grim foreboding. She sensed that Mistress Diana was altogether different from her own Mistress. Where Mistress Shirer was strict, Mistress Diana seemed needlessly cruel – where Mistress Shirer was sober, Mistress Diana was frivolous.

Jaki hesitated at the entrance to the bedroom. It occurred to her that she could escape. If she ran downstairs she could become J.K. again, shed her second self and revert to the mundane ordinariness from which she had emerged. Her heart pounded wildly: she knew that the most dire physical punishments would be inflicted upon her. It would be her crossing of the Rubicon. If she entered there could be no turning back, ever.

Trembling, she entered the room. The two Mistresses were standing over a silver tray, and a drawer, one that had always been locked, was pulled open.

'Place the chair in the centre of the room, in front of the dressing table,' Mistress Shirer directed, over her shoulder.

Jaki obeyed and pulled the heavy wooden chair to the centre of the room. She positioned it carefully between the bed and the dressing table.

'I admire your taste,' Diana commented, surveying the various instruments of correction laid out before her. She fingered the heavy leather belts, the riding switch, a thick black strap with knotted ribbons of leather at the end. 'I always think,' she continued lightly, 'that the skin should be softened first before applying the real punishment.'

'In that case,' Simone smiled, 'may I suggest that her buttocks are firmly paddled first?' She bent down and unlocked another drawer, pulled it open and selected from it a heavy wooden paddle. Its handle was padded with soft bands of suede, the paddle itself was the size of a man's hand, the surface was as smooth as glass.

Diana took the paddle and weighed it in her hand, it had the right heaviness about it, she brushed her fingers across the surface and smiled sweetly. 'An excellent choice. I think the cane next,' she decided, fishing a long bamboo cane from the drawer.

Jaki looked at the implements of her correction with unconcealed horror. Apart from her hand, Mistress Shirer had only ever used the clothes brush or leather belt to beat her. The various mechanisms of pain that she saw paraded for the first time looked unbearably cruel.

'The paddle and the cane?' Simone asked. She gestured towards the other instruments, offering them all to Diana.

'These will do just fine, thank you,' Diana said declining the other instruments, though she lingered momentarily over the leather strap.

'Put these away, girl,' Mistress Shirer ordered.

'Yes, Mistress,' Jaki responded instantly. She carefully picked up the silver tray, afraid to touch the devices, as if the devices could of themselves cause pain. After replacing the tray in the drawer, which she slid shut wishing never to see it open again, Mistress Shirer handed Jaki the paddle and the cane.

'You may begin whenever you are ready,' Simone remarked to Diana, sharing a smile.

'Come here, girl,' Mistress Diana urged impatiently, and stood waiting by the chair.

Jaki approached anxiously, conscious of the heaviness of the paddle in one hand and the long flexible cane in the other. Diana took the two instruments from her and

94

placed them on the soft leather seat of the chair. She pulled the skirt up over Jaki's waist and secured it with a clip. Expertly she undid the suspenders and let them fall to the floor. The stockings were tight and remained in place as Mistress Diana pulled the panties over the flaccid penis and down to the knees.

'Bend down, across the back of the chair,' Mistress Diana directed eagerly. Jaki did as she as told. The back of the chair pressed into her waist and the tendons in the back of her knees were stretched painfully.

'Would you like to bind her?' Simone asked. She lay back on the bed, her feet drawn up under her, the rubber dress stretched tight and shiny over the fullness of her thighs. Diana declined the offer and instead forced Jaki to bend down further and directed her to hold on to the back legs of the chair, as low as possible.

Jaki was already in pain, the position uncomfortable, the chair biting deep into her and every muscle stretched taut. Her legs were forced apart and positioned parallel to the chair, the thin lustrous panties stretched tight between her knees. She twisted her head back and saw herself displayed prominently in the mirror. Her long, high-heeled legs were tense, the black stockings embellishing the natural shape of the thighs. Her buttocks were positioned beautifully, two perfect white hemispheres separated by a darker crease, the tight anus surrounded by tufts of short spiky hair. She noticed that her position also displayed her heavy ball sac between the creamy tops of her thighs, offset by the deepest black of the stocking tops.

She watched Mistress Diana pick up the paddle and stand in position. Behind her she could see Mistress Shirer sprawled luxuriously on the bed, watching the unfolding ritual with keen interest. Her last thought, before the paddle came down on her proffered rear, was that her Mistress looked more beautiful than ever. The first stroke landed on the left buttock with a loud whack, and she yelped with the suddenness and the intensity of the attack.

'You are right, she does mark beautifully,' Diana remarked, pausing to contemplate the result of her first stroke. She was pleased with the effect of the deep scarlet weal on Jaki's buttock, in sharp contrast to the white sheen of the other, unpunished, arse-cheek.

Jaki felt the stinging pain spread as the distinct impression of the paddle deepened, etched in brilliant red on her skin.

Diana, satisfied that her attack was of the correct intensity, let loose a succession of fierce strokes. She beat Jaki methodically, each buttock in turn, then the top of each thigh and then back to the buttocks. She varied every stroke, never hitting the same place twice and ensuring that the tightened rump was tanned evenly.

Jaki winced and cried out. The heat burned her backside, and each stroke was as acute as the last. She wanted to let go, to release her white-knuckle grip on the chair, but she was locked into place with fear. Tears streamed down her face as she watched herself being beaten.

Diana stopped at last, pleased with the even colour she had brought so painfully to Jaki's rear cheeks.

'Thank Mistress Diana,' Mistress Shirer ordered.

'Thank you, Mistress,' Jaki responded weakly and eased her grip on the chair. She felt her body ache all over, and spasms of pain still shot through her flaming backside. Vaguely she was conscious of the fact that her position, stretched across the back of the chair with her backside blazing, was the station that she aspired to. Despite the smarting, and the humiliation at being handed over to a stranger for correction, she ardently hoped that her Mistress would be pleased.

'I do love the look of a nicely tanned rear,' Diana giggled lightly. She put the paddle down and picked up the thin yellow cane. She flexed it, expertly testing its strength.

The cane whistled through the air and Jaki screamed in agony as it bit deep into her raw red skin. She wept openly, then turned and saw the thin red strip that had cut into her, across both arse-cheeks. The second and third strokes swished loudly on to her behind, leaving equally deep red lines just below, and distinct from, the first. She gritted her teeth and gripped the chair tightly, aware instinctively that if she let go she would collapse in a bundle on the floor.

'And now, madam, I think it's only fair that you take a hand in the correction of this girl,' Diana joked, laughing gaily and offering the cane to Simone, who arose and accepted the cane, kissing Diana gently on the mouth.

Jaki was shaking, her bottom cheeks quivering; it hurt if she moved and it hurt if she didn't. She wore a pale harrowed look, her eyes bloodshot, beads of perspiration trickled down her drawn pale face, her lips trembling uncontrollably.

Mistress raised the cane and dealt a first blow that resounded about the room. Jaki screamed a long wretched wail of desperation as the stroke cut into the taut arse-flesh made tender by the skilled application of the paddle. She breathed fitfully, gasping for air. Automatically she turned her head to see the second stroke slice into her.

For a moment she felt herself blacking out, and as she half-closed her eyes, a strange delirium seized her and pulled her beyond the pain barrier. The strokes fell rhythmically now, a slow and steady whistle of air, a sharp retort and a blast of molten sensation. She fell silent, blocking all extraneous impressions, concentrating instead on the steady beating of her heart and the skilled use of the cane on her raw bottom.

She closed her eyes and felt outside of herself, a

spectator in the ritual of her humiliation. She saw the way that Mistress Diana admired Mistress Shirer's skill with the thin bamboo rod. She saw the arousal evident on Mistress Shirer's face, the look of lust in the dark oval eyes, the delicate pout of the full sensual lips. She realised with a perverse sense of pride that the Mistresses were keenly admiring her aching posterior.

'Hurt me, hurt me,' Jaki whispered hoarsely, forcing her legs to straighten, arching her back as far as possible to raise her bum-cheeks slightly higher. She rode the rhythm of the cane, raising herself to meet the swift downward play of the cane. An electric shock of pleasure greeted each blow, and her prick was a throbbing pole of smooth hard flesh drooling translucent drops of sticky fluid. She turned back to watch herself in the mirror, enjoying the sight of herself stretched over the heavy frame of the chair, a willing sacrifice to her beloved Mistress.

The strokes of the cane ceased and Jaki had lost track of time. She became aware at some point that the two Mistresses were standing over her, quietly looking at the proud arse still offered up pertly. The smooth surface of the buttocks had lost the silky white sheen and the seat was warm and scarlet, the colour a deep even tan down to the soft white flesh that peeped over the dark black band of the stocking tops. The deep red streaks of the thrashing were separate, clearly distinguishable symbols of the devotion Jaki held for Mistress.

'Have you ever used her pussy?' Diana asked, lightly caressing Jaki's distended arsehole. The tight dark button flexed responsively.

'Not yet,' Simone admitted, idly passing her fingers over the chastised rear end, pleased to see that Jaki was still firm to the touch and did not pull away from the pain.

'I enjoy nothing better than to ride a disobedient servant,' Diana admitted. 'I have a beautiful leather dildo specially made for the purpose. You should see the look of terror in their eyes when they see my sleek black prick. I had it hand-made; it has just the right balance of hardness and flexibility. I can take a servant, male or female, and ride him or her to my own gratification and at the same time administer a punishment they never forget.'

'Unfortunately I have nothing of that kind to offer you,' Simone apologised, intrigued by the idea of buggering her servant into submission.

'A pity. This is such an attractive tight pussy imagine how it would it would grip at the base of my weapon,' Diana said wistfully, evidently relishing the idea. To emphasise the point she pressed her middle finger deep into Jaki's rear opening. Simone watched with interest as the hole tightened and relaxed with the slow movement of the finger, in and out.

Diana withdrew her finger and Simone pressed her own finger into the hole as far as it would go, the other fingers pressing firmly on the soft arse-flesh of the buttocks. She found the warmth of the passage and the soft constricting rippling of muscle attractive, and wondered at the possibilities it offered. Having tested her servant's passageway she withdrew her finger, noting the pleasing feel of the tight anus gripping invitingly.

Jaki had at first found the entry of flesh into her behind perverse and unnatural, and had wanted to resist the probing intrusion. But the pain had altered her sensibilities and she now felt an explosion of erotic pleasure at every touch, whether on her aching wounds or into her narrow ring.

Diana leaned forward and pressed her hand towards Jaki's face. 'Lubricate my fingers,' she ordered, inserting her fingers into the soft warm mouth. Jaki sucked at the fingers, flicking spit from her tongue around the long delicate digits. She took the taste of her bumhole into her mouth, swallowed the acrid taste with a thrill of delight, lapping the fingers as if they were coated in honey.

Simone watched, quietly pleased with the behaviour of her servant, as Diana again entered the exquisite rear hole. Jaki again gazed at her reflection in the mirror at the degrading, but inwardly desirable, sight of her debasement at Mistress Diana's adept and delicate hand. The action grew faster and harder, the spit-smeared fingers easing entry deep into the rectum. The ache in Jaki's prick grew ever stronger, charged by the dextrous pumping of flesh into her arsehole, speeding an erotic charge deep inside to fuel a twisting swirl of pent-up energy.

Diana pressed a second finger into play, forcing the ring wider apart, pressing urgently at the walls of the inner passage. The hole alternately tensed and relaxed, the fingers penetrated further and the arse-cheeks rose and fell to meet the escalating thrusts.

Mistress Shirer unexpectedly took Jaki's pulsing cock in her hand and caressed the silky smooth skin deftly, complementing the up-and-down motion of the arse-cheeks and Mistress Diana's skilful frigging.

Jaki could feel the explosion coming – the butterfly feeling in her belly, the flexing of her massive prick and the hot rasping sensation under the balls. She was breathing short gasping breaths and murmuring deliriously. She thrashed her backside wildly, engrossed in the golden feeling of being expertly finger-fucked in the arse.

Jaki ached as she came, ejaculating thick wads of creamy white come on to the seat of the chair. All the pain and humiliation that she had suffered were justified by the most intense orgasm of her life. She had for the first time experienced the fleeting joy of total submission. Her mind burned with the image of the two Mistresses in lustful adoration of her anus.

'Thank Mistress Diana for punishing you,' Mistress Shirer reminded Jaki curtly.

'Thank you, Mistress,' Jaki said immediately, still bent over into her posture of abasement. Mistress Diana took Jaki by the hair and forced her to a crawling position on the floor. Jaki raised her head and took Mistress Diana's outstretched fingers in her mouth and, without prompting, she licked the thin film of spit, sweat and arse-taste clean.

Jaki realised, without rancour, that her own pleasure had been purely incidental, that the two Mistresses were interested in her only as a means to their enjoyment. They had allowed her to gain gratification solely because it suited their purpose. They gave pleasure to emphasise their domination, to prove to Jaki that they had it in their power to give her release at will.

Mistress Diana irritably withdrew her fingers while Jaki was still drawing on them. Jaki stared up at her, crestfallen lest she had somehow caused displeasure, but Diana, showed no interest in her. Jaki realised that the time had come for her to be cast aside again. She was seized with the impetuous desire to throw herself down at the bright red ankle boots so near to her. She wanted to lick the bright red boots, to suck urgently at the heel, to pass her lips over the tight red leather straps that bound the boots so tightly.

Jaki resisted the temptation, mighty as it was. She knew that to give in would be to place her own desire before that of a Mistress, and so to risk punishment again. At once she understood the contradiction at the heart of her condition. Her own pleasure was intricately wound up with being humiliated and disciplined, as she had so forcefully experienced. However, to deliberately invoke punishment would mean to actively seek pleasure, in which case it would not be punishment but purely pain. The very essence of punishment lay in its arbitrary use as a method for the imposition of

101

Mistress's will. The perverse pleasure that she experienced lay as much in submission and shame as in the depth of pain.

Simone took Diana by the hand and led her towards the bed. The two women kissed ecstatically. Simone stepped back the instant they parted and with a quick motion unzipped her latex dress. The dress fell to the floor to reveal the totally naked body underneath. Jaki, still on her hands and knees, stared at the divine body. She ached with renewed desire at the sight of the firm full breasts, the darker nipples standing out enticingly. A neat dark bush surrounded the slightly fleshy opening to the prominent pink bud that was barely visible. The boots, the surface a glossy black sheen, seemed to merge with the long lithe thighs.

Diana also divested herself of her dress, letting it drop and stepping out of it. She wore delicate pink and white panties and a matching open-nippled half-cut bra that raised the two firm white globes so that they were displayed appealingly.

Again the two women embraced, locking mouths and using their hands to slowly examine each other's body. Simone slid her hands down Diana's smooth white back, drinking in the aroma of her perfume.

Jaki stood up quietly. Longingly she gazed at the two women, uncertain what action to take. She watched as Mistress Shirer slowly pulled Diana's knickers down, revealing two immaculate bottom-cheeks, and her long elegant fingers pulled the arse-crack gently apart, revealing the sensitive folds of the labia surrounded by a bush of barely visible fair hair.

As the two women moved on to the bed, hands and mouths gently probing still, Mistress Shirer glanced towards Jaki. 'Turn around,' she demanded. Jaki turned away, assuming that she had imposed on their privacy by her yearning gaze. 'Turn fully towards the mirror,' Mistress Shirer instructed. Mistress Diana lifted her mouth from Mistress Shirer's breasts, which she had been softly tonguing, to watch.

Jaki turned and faced the mirror, where she could see the two women clearly, her own lonely reflection an apt symbol of her own imposed detachment.

'See how beautifully her bottom is coloured,' Simone observed, turning back to Diana.

'Press your legs together,' Mistress Diana added, 'and straighten your back. This is how bad girls are displayed after punishment.'

Jaki did as she was told, realising that her posture, aided by the height of her heels, served to fully exhibit her brutally spanked and caned rear. She understood that Mistress Shirer had no concern with any unintended intrusion, because to show concern would be to cast some value on her presence. She was required to attend only for the erotic view that her thrashed posterior afforded – and to emphasise once more her unworthiness.

She watched the two women making love. Mistress Shirer was sliding her fingers into Diana's sweet wet pussy, while Diana was teasing the nipples of the heavy black breasts with her sharp white teeth. Painfully Jaki was aware that she could never be in their position; she would never be able to make love as they did. She would never be able to make love, and would be available only so that others could take their pleasure as they wished.

Simone was mouthing Diana's body, pressing her full luscious lips against the velvety white flesh. With deliberate slowness she edged down, paying close attention to the breasts then down over the belly towards the damp woman-hole that burned with expectation. Diana raised her knees and parted her thighs, opening herself to Simone's penetrating tongue.

Jaki remained in position. Though aroused by the alluring view of her Mistresses, she had begun to accept her role. She was becoming attuned to the idea that her

103

life would be one of selfless devotion, tempered by withering bouts of pain and degradation. There would be no reward; the occasional granting of the joy of sexual relief would be incidental to the greater joy of her Mistress's pleasure.

She watched Mistress Shirer, her ravishing mouth still supping the honey from Diana's dripping hole, as she shifted her body over so that her wet sex was over Diana's mouth.

Diana carefully guided Simone into place and then she too began to use her tongue expertly. She curved her back, thrashing wildly under the skilled onslaught of Simone's darting tongue. The two bodies became entangled, the contrasting tones of dark and white flesh writhing with the pleasure drawn from expert Sapphic caresses. Their mouths met and parted, instruments of exploration; they sucked and licked, tasted each other, occasionally biting savagely, then kissing tenderly. Simone and Diana brought each other to screaming joyful orgasms. Unselfishly and without constraint they shared their bodies totally, giving and taking pleasure in equal measure.

Jaki saw the two women cast occasional lustful glances at her tortured image, finding arousal in the sight of the abused arse and thighs and in the memory of the punishment and degradation they had so recently inflicted.

For a moment she saw herself and her new world through the eyes of her other self. With a shudder she saw the world that J.K. inhabited, saw the future that lay ahead of him, an empty life buried in work, responsibility and the aimless consumption of goods for the sake of it. She saw a world without colour, without depth, without a focus for the love and devotion he was so capable of. Most of all she saw the loneliness, and the pain of knowing that he had only his judgement to guide him through an uncaring dangerous world.

Alarmed by her thoughts, Jaki was suffused with an intense feeling of love and devotion that filled her with an indescribable joy. She loved Mistress Shirer more than anything else in the world, and knew that she would do anything that was asked of her. She longed to be commanded again, to prove time and again her own worthlessness, and to show that she belonged in totality to her Mistress. There could be no greater goal in her life than to subsume her very self in the divine flame of her Mistress's will.

The two Mistresses lay exhausted on the bed, wholly indifferent to Jaki's presence, their bodies hot and tired from their frantic lovemaking. Arms and bodies entwined, they swapped quiet affectionate kisses, delighting in their continuous unhurried sexual explorations.

Simone sat up on her elbow, and rubbed her hand between Diana's thighs, pressing her fingers between the moist pussy lips and round the sweaty arse crack. Idly she played her finger against the closed arsehole that rose and fell with Diana's deep satisfied breathing. 'Turn over,' she said softly, rolling Diana gently on to her belly so that her lovely backside was partially raised. Simone also turned over, pressing her chest low and her head on to the pillow. 'Like this,' she urged Diana, who assumed the same position, knees pulled up towards the breasts and bottoms raised high. They arched their backs so that their bottoms were tight and round and their arseholes distended invitingly.

Jaki admired the two arseholes, one black and the other white, each perfect and each in the centre of stunning bottoms raised seductively.

'Tongue your Mistresses' bum holes,' Mistress Shirer commanded over her back, parting her thighs slightly so that her rear hole was ready for the deepest piercing.

Jaki turned, her arse alive with pain at every motion, and took in the vision before her. Her heart beat with anticipation, the thought of mouthing deep into the two deep anal holes making her head swim with delight. She was already erect as she stepped on to the bed.

For a second her other self emerged again, unbidden. She saw that she was about to degrade herself again by sucking at the arseholes of women who treated her with nothing but contempt. She banished the thought instantly. Her other self was for the outside world, a necessary evil and nothing more.

Jaki, her arse a smarting mess of deep red weals, dressed in the uniform of the lowliest servant girl, her skirt still pulled over her waist, felt herself to be desirable. She bent down and sniffed the deep sexual aroma of Mistress Shirer's arse and pussy, then breathed in the perfume of Mistress Diana's anus and she-hole.

She flicked her tongue over the exquisite bud of Mistress Diana's bumhole, relishing the salty sex taste, then did the same to Mistress Shirer, recognising the tang that she had enjoyed so often before.

Going down deep into an arsehole, she began to lose herself in purest sexual sensation. Her last thought, before giving herself fully, was that she could no more revert permanently into her other self than a beautiful butterfly would turn back into a caterpillar.

Five

Three weeks had passed and Lucy had settled in fairly comfortably. She was a born survivor and had adapted very quickly to the strange and unorthodox regime. There was much that was still new – every day was different and every situation presented a new set of challenges. Many of her assumptions about herself and the world around her had been challenged and found wanting. It was a difficult and testing time, but she found the strength to adapt and to evolve a new and appropriate set of responses.

She was surprised most of all by her own emerging sexuality. Her resolute refusal to previously acknowledge her attraction to her own sex had been swept away in a rush of ardent desire. It was not that she no longer wanted men. Far from it. She fantasised frequently about all the men that she had enjoyed, and all that she would enjoy again. just the memory of the feel of a stiff prick inside her could make her damp and breathless with wanting. But now she had discovered another world, where women were attractive and desirable partners, another route to heaven.

Lucy's first impression of the Institute, that it was a place of constant perverse pleasure and pain, had been shown to be largely false. Punishment was no doubt central to the whole idea of the Institute, but in fact it was rarely used. Its value lay as an ultimate sanction, a threat and a deterrent. In three weeks Lucy had only witnessed two or three instances of girls being punished, and only in Jenny's case had the punishment inflicted been severe.

Her other first impression, and one that had initially filled her with undisguised horror, was that lesbianism was rampant. Many of the young women did make love with each other, Lucy now included. But it was not as open as it had first appeared. There were a number of girls that seemed to be permanently on heat, swapping partners with shameless regularity. But the vast majority were either celibate or quietly discreet in their relationships.

Jenny had initiated Lucy, teaching her how to give and take pleasure from another woman's body. Lucy had responded passionately, instinctively. It now seemed so natural and beautiful that she could hardly remember her previous revulsion An emotional bond between them had developed very early on, and when Jenny had left the Institute, two weeks after Lucy's arrival, Lucy had become sad and withdrawn.

Lucy no longer had a roommate, and nor did she want one particularly. She was in no hurry to plunge into another relationship, and, certain now of her feelings, she knew that such a relationship would be inevitable with any roommate. Instead she turned her attention to what was going on at the Institute.

Anne Young had been right – there was definitely something extraordinary going on. Lucy did not feel that it was wrong exactly. Her own feelings were ambivalent. She had found arousal and pleasure in punishment, she had found pleasure in sex with another woman, and she had actively sought her own humiliation. Without the Institute she would have never explored these facets of her personality. She fully accepted that the Institute had begun to teach her about herself, to give her a greater depth of understanding about her innermost motivations.

But despite this she remained unsure as to the true purpose of the Institute. The programme was itself an odd mixture. There were vocational classes of various sorts, preparing people for life on the outside. But these classes coexisted with the study of philosophy and psychology, of politics and religion. Lucy had seen girls who were practically illiterate involved in intricate discussions on economic and biological determinism. Theory and practice were constantly examined, the women always searching for a way to explain both their own motivations and their responses. Along with the taught classes there was an active body of sociological research taking place.

The central aim was always to turn the attention towards the complexity inherent in the world, from the complexity of a single individual to the many-layered and almost indescribable complexity of the outside world. Yet this high-level philosophy was in parallel to the imposed hierarchy of power, complete with punishments and humiliations.

Lucy retained her suspicions; she couldn't shake off the feeling that what was going on was somehow wrong. Nor could she close herself off from her previous life. She carried about her a lifetime of disappointment and cynicism. The thought of the money she could earn by telling the truth seemed more immediate and more real then all the promises of self-fulfilment and inner knowledge.

She had not started to write yet. She was afraid that her notes would be discovered if there were another room search. Nor did she have access to a tape recorder on which to record her daily observations. But she had a strong memory and mentally kept track of times and dates, memorising every incident that came to her attention, ready for the moment when she could put it all down and pass it on.

She had started to think about the contact very soon

after Jenny left. Of all the possible places for making contact she had decided that the library was the most likely. It was a central meeting place, with people free to come and go as they pleased. There were lots of quiet corners to meet in, away from the prying eyes of Prefects and staff.

She soon staked out a place for herself, and took to spending as much of her free time there as possible. Her place was at a table by the main desk, under the eye of the librarians. From here she could see all who came and went, and, more importantly, they could see her. She scrutinised everyone, looking for the faintest glimmer of recognition. She waited for hours, hoping to hear the magic word, but to no avail.

When the word was eventually uttered it took her by surprise. She was seated by the main desk, flicking idly through a magazine, thoroughly bored and depressed. She had given up hope, thinking that perhaps she ought to look for another meeting place. Only the dull thud of the librarians stamping the books marked the slow drag of time. She no longer bothered to search each new face for signs of acknowledgment. The words were spoken quietly, and did not sink in immediately. But suddenly the disconnected sounds seemed to click and she sat bolt upright.

'Yes, that's right, Conrad,' one of the librarians was saying.

'Where's that?' a young-looking woman asked quietly, brushing her long golden hair with her hand absently.

'Twentieth-century literature,' the librarian replied, and pointed across to the other side of the library.

The girl smiled her thanks and walked towards the section she had been pointed to. Lucy watched her go, hoping that the girl would recognise her; she tried to catch her eye but the girl didn't even glance in her direction. She watched the girl for a second, then followed.

Lucy pretended to scour the same shelves, glancing at the girl continually, but she was ignored completely. Finally the girl found what she was looking for, retrieved a single slim volume from the shelf and walked off quickly, wrapped up in herself and oblivious to the eager look on Lucy's face.

Lucy hesitated – she had been sure that the girl was the contact, but had expected her to make the first move. When the girl had failed to make any response she had hesitated and missed her chance. Crestfallen, she wondered whether she had let the opportunity pass through her fingers. Before she could decide what to do the girl had gone.

In desperation it occurred to her that a message may have been left on the shelves. She brightened up when she found a set of books by Joseph Conrad. Things seemed to make sense, especially when she found the book called *The Secret Agent*. Anne Young's words came flooding back to her. She flicked through a number of volumes quickly but found nothing, not even in *The Secret Agent*.

The twin sisters, Tiffany and Chantel, had been sitting in that section of the library. Lucy knew them vaguely and had spoken to the more extrovert sister, Tiffany, on a number of occasions. 'Did you see the girl that just went past?' she asked them anxiously.

'Long blonde hair?' Tiffany asked.

'That's right.' Lucy smiled hopefully.

'Her name's Ruth; she's due out soon,' she replied.

'Any idea where I can find her?'

'What d'you want her for?'

'Well,' Lucy hesitated, 'it's sort of personal.'

'I see,' Tiffany smiled knowingly. 'She likes to hang around the gym.'

'Thanks.'

Lucy spent the rest of the day searching for Ruth but was unable to find her. She had nothing but the name and description to go on, and though a number of girls said they had seen her, none knew her room number. She tried the library again, but by late afternoon she gave up for the day.

The fact that Ruth was due for release convinced Lucy that Ruth was definitely the contact. It could hardly be a coincidence: Conrad, *The Secret Agent* and her scheduled release. Lucy cursed herself for not making the first contact, for not seizing the chance with both hands. It would have been so easy to whisper 'Conrad' and to exchange a smile of complicity.

That night Lucy sat up and scribbled notes, piecing together her own story with that of the Institute. Her hand ached from the strain of writing, but she wanted to miss nothing, to leave out no detail that could possibly have a bearing on the story. When she finished she read through the pages and made rough and ready corrections, adding bits that she had left out, expanding on details where necessary.

When she was satisfied with the finished notes she turned her attention to a hiding place. She quickly discounted all the obvious places, her years of experience of being spied on having taught her well. She cannibalised a plastic carrier bag, wrapping the pages in a thin polythene envelope. Carefully she opened her window a few inches and then taped the tight bundle to the outside of the frame. The room was high up and she was certain that it would be safe there.

Her mind raced with plans and ideas, her first task to make contact and then to pass the story on. She slept uneasily, waking every so often, feverish with excitement.

Ruth stood in the draughty lobby at the foot of the concrete stairs that led to the changing rooms, and peered through the glass door into the gym. All around her were the sights and sounds of the sports hall, people coming and going, dressed in uniform or kitted out for various sports. She ignored the distant piercing shriek of a referee's whistle, and the excited calls and shouts of the girls playing netball or volleyball.

Instead she reserved all her attention for a single figure inside the gym. Her heart beat faster and she felt a knot of anxiety in her belly as she studied the agile and attractive Mistress who was coaching a group of girls in netball. Mistress Diana seemed to be barely older than the girls in her charge. Her short blonde hair and fair skin combined to give her a girlish look, which was matched by her open and vivacious manner.

Ruth envied the other girls for being so close to her, close enough to gaze into her sparkling blue eyes and listen to her bright enthusiastic voice. Diana was dressed in a tight red cotton T-shirt that clung to her full pointed breasts, and a short white tennis skirt. She was relatively new at the Institute and had yet to acquire the characteristics of the other staff. She had none of the dark severity of Mistress Shirer, nor the threatening glamour of the other Mistresses.

Ruth's heart was pounding and her stomach was all butterflies as she watched her showing the girls how to net the ball. As Diana leapt up into the air, to skilfully make a throw, her short skirt flared up to reveal fully her long smooth thighs and tightly curved bottom. Ruth was seized with a painful and desperate longing to be with her. She realised that the most notable difference between Mistress Diana and the other staff was in the fact that she still smiled at the girls, laughing gaily and chatting amiably. It wasn't that she didn't perform her duties as Mistress – Ruth was well aware that Mistress Diana could be remorseless in administering punishment – she simply didn't feel the need to constantly remind the girls of her position.

As Mistress Diana continued her lithe and agile movements Ruth had the opportunity to appreciate the

113

full beauty of the long and elegant thighs, and to admire the way the light pink lace panties showed off the firm young backside to best effect. She felt an intense attraction to the young Mistress that was more than purely physical, though the sexual element was undeniably very strong. Ruth wanted to share more than her body with Mistress Diana – she wanted affection and closeness. She wanted an emotional intimacy that would complement any sexual relationship. It was love.

'You there, what are you doing?' a Prefect asked Ruth loudly.

'Nothing, Mistress,' Ruth lied, averting her eyes both as an appropriate gesture of humility and to avoid any questioning stare.

'Take this note to Mistress Diana.' The Prefect handed a small white envelope to Ruth. 'Then get to where you should be, instead of hanging around. Understood?'

'Yes, Mistress,' Ruth replied brightly, overjoyed at her good fortune at being given a legitimate reason to approach Mistress Diana. The Prefect turned away and Ruth quickly readied herself, passing her hand through her long hair and straightening her skirt. Finally she pinched her nipples between her thumb and fingers, squeezing till it hurt so that the nipples were hard and pointed, jutting prominently against the thin white shirt.

She entered the gym nervously and walked down to the end, near the goal area, where the girls were practising to shoot at goal from outside the area. She stood meekly just off the pitch until one of the girls pointed her out to Mistress Diana.

The Mistress smiled when she saw Ruth, then told the girls to carry on and jogged lightly off the pitch. Her breasts swayed sexily in the tight red shirt, the darker area around the nipples clearly visible underneath the thin cotton shirt.

'Not you again,' she sighed patiently. Her face was slightly flushed and she seemed to be glowing a healthy vigorous pink.

'I have a note for you,' Ruth smiled back happily, waving the letter in front of her to justify the intrusion. She lightly caressed Diana's hand when she handed the letter over, a light, almost imperceptible caress.

While she read the letter Ruth stood close, breathing in Diana's light scent and basking in the reflected glory of the Mistress. She playfully pressed herself on to the Mistress, rubbing her chest coquettishly against her bare arm.

'You can go now,' Diana said, screwing the letter up and turning away.

'Is there anything you would like, Mistress?' Ruth asked, her tone faintly pleading. She gazed lovingly into Diana's sparkling clear blue eyes, fully aware that her inviting look was thoroughly and openly sexual.

'That isn't the way to look at your Mistress,' Diana told her softly but firmly. She knew that Ruth had a crush on her, as did a number of other girls, but she was willing to let things go only so far before asserting her authority.

Ruth turned away, uncertain how to interpret the delicate tone of voice. She was aware that any other Mistress would have punished her for the wanton and inviting look, but Mistress Diana was different. She thought she detected a hesitation as Diana started to turn away and suddenly felt certain that Diana also felt an attraction between them.

Ruth reached out, her eyes half closed with trepidation, and touched Mistress Diana very gently on the back of the thigh.

'Get out now,' Mistress Diana ordered coldly, turning back to face Ruth. 'This is the only warning you'll ever get,' she glared, 'but if you do that again I'll have you thrashed and displayed in front of the whole class.'

'Yes, Mistress,' Ruth managed to say, her bottom lip trembling and her eyes wet with tears. Her heart felt heavy and the whole world seemed to have collapsed. She watched Diana flounce back to the game, not even glancing back to see the effect of her harsh words.

Miserably Ruth turned and dragged herself out of the gym the laughs and squeals of the girls confirming her in her isolation and sudden despair. She stood in the lobby and the cold draught made her feel even colder; she shivered and hunched herself up, trying to block out the icy atmosphere. She felt small and alone, drowning in an ocean of cold indifference.

Instinctively she turned to take one last look into the gym, planning to return to her lonely and empty room. However, the moment she saw Mistress Diana laughing along with the other girls she changed her mind . just the sight of the Mistress was enough to start to lift her mood. 'She only acts that way because she has to,' Ruth reasoned, unable to reconcile the frivolous pretty young woman in the gym with the harsh and cruel reprimand she had just been given. Though it was only the lightest of caresses, she felt certain that Diana had hesitated and responded positively in some way.

She decided to stay a little longer, unwilling to believe that Mistress Diana had meant all that had been said. She stood outside the gym, staring longingly at Diana, trying desperately to think of some way of making contact again. Her mind was filled with pleasant daydreams, as she imagined being in Diana's arms, touching and kissing, holding hands, showing the rest of the girls that they were lovers.

Lucy found Ruth outside the gym staring in forlornly through the window. She hesitated: now that she had found her she was overtaken by a tremendous doubt. For some reason Ruth didn't look like the contact. It was an intangible feeling, but she could not, by any stretch of the imagination, connect Ruth with Anne Young.

116

'She's nice, isn't she?' Lucy commented, hoping that Ruth would make the contact, mutter the single word that would banish all the doubts.

' Yes, she is,' Ruth replied wistfully, turning to find Lucy by her side, also peering into the gym. Ruth knew that she could only be referring to Diana: the girls in the gym were easily outshone by the attractive young Mistress.

'Hasn't she got gorgeous tits?' Lucy observed, eyeing Diana's firm round breasts, their shape displayed completely by the skintight shirt.

'Yes,' murmured Ruth, slightly jealous that another girl was admiring her unattainable and beautiful Mistress.

'I bet she's a great fuck,' Lucy continued in the same leering manner.

'Don't talk about her like that,' Ruth chided, affronted that anyone should speak so coarsely of Diana.

'Like what?' Lucy demanded, turning to face Ruth. Her doubts were confirmed. Ruth was not the contact that she had been so assiduously seeking.

'Like that,' Ruth repeated angrily.

'Oh,' Lucy sneered, 'you mean "a great fuck"? What should I say, I bet she's a wonderful loving person?'

'Go away,' Ruth said weakly, turning back to study the object of her deepest desire.

'It's like that, is it? It's true love.'

'No, it's not,' Ruth denied vehemently, embarrassed.

'You'll never have her,' Lucy continued, ignoring the obviously untruthful denial. Her voice lost its sarcastic edge, and she sounded genuinely sad. Ruth's obvious loneliness reminded her so much of her own position.

'How can you be so sure?'

'Because she's a Mistress and you're nothing,' she paused, 'just like me.'

Ruth smiled at Lucy; she was certain that she would

117

succeed where all others had failed or given up hope. It could only be a matter of time; her selfless devotion could not go unnoticed forever. She felt certain that the day would come when she and Diana would be inseparable.

Lucy brushed her long straight hair from her face. She took a step closer to Ruth and awkwardly took her hand in a strangely childish gesture of friendship. 'You're like me, just a nothing,' she told Ruth sympathetically.

'I don't accept any of that,' Ruth responded emphatically. 'We're all somebody.'

'I'm Lucy. What's your name?

'Ruth.'

Lucy turned her back to the gym and faced Ruth squarely, smiling a friendly open smile that brightened her plain looks. Keeping hold of Ruth's hand she nervously reached out with her other hand and stroked her thigh just above the knee. There was a hint of uncertainty in Ruth's eyes but Lucy carried on, slowly working her hand higher, enjoying the feel of the soft flesh under the skirt.

'Do you like it?' Lucy whispered, her eyes scanning the lobby in case somebody else came in. It was the first time she had ever tried to seduce another woman and she was unsure that her actions were having the desired effect.

'Yes,' Ruth admitted quietly, keeping her eyes firmly fixed on Mistress Diana.

Lucy squeezed Ruth's hand reassuringly, at the same time passing her fingers delicately over Ruth's panties, feeling the soft folds of skin and the curly bush at the mouth of the sex. She tried to pull the panties down slightly but found instead that she could easily slip her fingers under the thin cotton briefs. She felt Ruth catch her breath when she slipped a finger between the velvety folds of skin and into the warmth of her opening.

118

'Not here,' Ruth told her, alarmed by Lucy's caress She was stimulated by the gently feminine touch – her pussy crack was damp and her breathing came deeper. It had been a long time since she had allowed another woman to touch her, and she had forgotten how good it could feel.

'Come back to my room,' Lucy suggested, reluctantly removing her wet fingers from under Ruth's skirt.

'No.' Ruth shook her head, unwilling to end her lonely vigil outside the gym.

'Please, it'll just be the two of us,' said Lucy persuasively. 'No Mistresses, no domination, just the two of us making love.'

'I can't,' Ruth apologised, sorry now that she had allowed Lucy to go so far. She wanted to go, she enjoyed the way Lucy touched her, but she felt that she had to stay.

'Why? Don't you want to share?'

'Yes, but not sex,' Ruth tried to explain. 'I want more than sex.'

'Please. We can have normal sex, no punishments, no submission.'

'No.' Ruth shook her head slowly. 'I want love and affection and everything.'

'We can have that,' said Lucy softly, and pressed her lips on to Ruth's. Ruth returned the kiss a little breathlessly, and seemed reluctant to let go when Lucy pulled back a few seconds later. 'We can have love and affection,' Lucy affirmed. She meant it. Without Jenny she felt empty and alone; for a brief moment she had found someone to share with and now she felt the loss every moment of the day. She liked Ruth, and felt attracted to the innocence and passion that Ruth displayed.

'No, I'm sorry,' Ruth repeated. 'It just doesn't feel right.'

'Why?' Lucy demanded plaintively. 'Don't you like me?'

'It's hard to explain,' Ruth admitted. 'You said that we're nothing, the both of us . . .'

'So?'

'Don't you see? By the two of us making love you're just confirming that we're both nothing. And if you do that then that means we are stuck in our places at the bottom. I want more than that.'

'You're wrong,' Lucy said sadly. She raised her hands and began to softly massage Ruth's breasts, rubbing her fingers lingeringly over the nipples. She was confused by the contradictory signals; Ruth's body was soft and responsive, and she had returned the kiss eagerly, yet there was a hard stubborn overriding refusal from the heart.

'Besides,' Ruth turned to her, 'you might go around saying I was a great fuck.'

'I only said that because I thought you were like the others,' Lucy said defensively. She continued to massage Ruth's breasts with both hands, hoping to make her change her mind, hoping that Ruth's obvious desire would prevail over her inexplicable devotion to the fantasy of making love to a Mistress.

Ruth turned back to the gym and found Mistress Diana staring straight back at her, smiling benignly. She was startled and caught her breath, blushing deep red with shame, embarrassed to be caught being fondled so openly by another girl. Suddenly all the anger and disappointments of the day swelled up in a great surge of panic. She stepped back and violently swung her arm with great force at Lucy.

The blow caught Lucy in the face with a loud and painful smack. She cried out and clutched at her face. Open-mouthed she gazed at Ruth, her expression one of shock and horror and disappointment. She wanted to cry, stung by the violent rejection as much as by the blow. Her instinct would normally have been to hit back, but the disappointment that Ruth was not the contact had been compounded by the vicious rejection of affection. She could only stand, rooted to the spot, drained of all responses.

Diana barked an order over her shoulder to the girls and then made for the door, livid. For a moment she had thought that Ruth had got over her ridiculous infatuation. She had even hoped that Ruth was ready to begin a relationship with one of the other girls, a necessary part of the process of learning. However, it was now clear that Ruth's infatuation was still dangerously strong, and that only a heavy dose of correction would cure her of her youthful and selfish idealism.

Totally overwhelmed with panic, Ruth turned and ran blindly up the stairs. She was shaking and could no longer think straight. The whole world seemed to be collapsing irrevocably about her.

She reached the top of the stairs and stopped, unable to decide what to do, turning first one way and then another. It was only the sound of approaching footsteps that spurred her on. She blundered into the first changing room she found.

The wooden benches were strewn with bundles of clothes and towels, and shoes and socks were placed neatly on the floor next to them. The room was claustrophobic with the stale odour of sweat and chlorine. Turning back, Ruth saw Mistress Diana following, and so she fled further back into the room and finally into the cold darkness of the silent showers.

Her own breathing seemed deafening as she stood in the darkness, hiding. The tiled floor of the showers was cold and dry and started to freeze her feet through her thin canvas shoes. She hardly dared to move, hoping beyond all reason that Mistress Diana would turn back, that all would be forgotten and that everything would be right with the world.

Mistress Diana threw the light-switch and illuminated

the showers with a harsh electric glare. Ruth remained still, hidden behind a partition. There was a moment of silent apprehension and then Ruth screamed as she was hit by a dozen icy blasts of water. She stumbled and fell, stung by the force of the powerful jets of frosty water. She crawled out of the shower on her hands and knees, a freezing soaking wreck. Every part of her body had been soaked by the jets that squirted from shower heads arranged every two feet on either side of the partition. Her long bedraggled hair, which had been washed by the first torrents, fell across her face.

It seemed to take forever for Ruth to emerge, crawling painfully along the floor through the water that bubbled along the tiles and into discreetly positioned drains. Her teeth were chattering uncontrollably and her body was cold and numb. She was crying miserably, the warm salty tears lost in the water that poured from her and on to the floor of the locker room.

'Stand up, girl,' Mistress ordered curtly, turning the water valve off and silencing the hissing jets of water.

Ruth pulled herself up with an effort. Her clothes were soaked through and clung to the skin, the cold water dripping into a puddle at her feet. Drops of water trickled down her face, merging with the warm and bitter tears. Several shirt buttons had become undone, exposing the valley between her breasts which was glossy with trickles of water dripping down from her face and hair. The shirt was translucent and revealed sharp erect nipples and the fullness of the breasts.

Diana looked at the pitiful face, the wet pouting red lips pulled slightly apart invitingly, and at the little rivers of water which ran down all over the cold soft skin, glistening seductively. 'What is wrong with you, girl?' she wondered, admiring the sensual sight of the drenched and vulnerable girl. 'What do you want?'

'I want love,' Ruth sobbed, abandoning all hope of ever loving or being loved like a normal human being.

She shivered from the cold, the water dripping down her back and down her thighs making her hair stand on end.

'You don't even know what that is,' Diana told her gently, feeling pity for the poor naive girl.

'Then show me. Love me,' Ruth pleaded, trying unsuccessfully to fight back her bitter tears.

'What do you think love is?'

'It just is. There's none of this,' Ruth gestured vaguely with her hand, 'none of this Mistress and servant stuff.'

'You poor ignorant girl.' Diana shook her head sadly. 'There is a master and servant in every relationship. Out there it's well hidden, so well hidden that thousands believe it doesn't exist. But it does. We only make explicit what is implicit. Every marriage, every love affair contains the same relationship. One person yields to the other.'

'That's not true,' Ruth snivelled.

'It is true and you know it,' Diana told her harshly. 'There is more hardship and pain in any emotional relationship than anything you will experience here. At least here you have the privilege of knowing completely where everyone stands. Out there you're blind.'

'Why can't we be normal?'

'Normal?' Diana laughed sarcastically. 'You mean normal in the way that two lesbians are normal? Is that the sort of normal you want? Or is it another kind?'

'Please,' Ruth begged Diana, 'I only want to be loved. Hold me. Kiss me. Love me.'

Diana took Ruth under the chin and kissed her, pressing her tongue deep into the other's cold accepting mouth. Ruth's head swam, as if Diana were breathing life back into her. Diana pulled back a little and Ruth stood on tiptoes, arms at her side and feet squelching in the puddle. They seemed to kiss for ages, searching each other's mouths eagerly and passionately. Diana placed one hand over Ruth's breast, savouring the feel of the wet material clinging sexily to the cold bare flesh underneath.

Ruth felt safe again; there was a warm glow inside her that fought the icy cold on the surface. She closed her eyes, trying to blot out everything but that moment, wanting to capture it forever.

'I have to punish you,' Diana said at last, gently letting Ruth go. She wiped the droplets of water from her face with her fingers.

'Why does it have to be like this?' Ruth asked quietly. The instant of elation had passed. She had known that it would prove illusory, but with it had gone all her strength and power of will. She wore the tired and indifferent look of the defeated.

'Because that's how we are defined,' Diana replied simply.

Other girls began to stream into the locker room, their joking and laughing silenced by the sight of the wet girl shivering miserably. Diana waited until the entire class had assembled before ordering Ruth to face the wall. Ruth obeyed silently and turned to let Diana unbutton the drenched skirt which fell to the floor with a faint splash. The white panties were also sopping wet and they too had become see-through, revealing the dark line between Ruth's round, girlish bottom cheeks. Little drops of water dripped suggestively from between her legs and ran down her glistening wet thighs.

'Drop your knickers,' Diana ordered.

'Yes, Mistress,' said Ruth mechanically, letting the panties fall to her ankles.

'Part your legs and touch the floor.'

Ruth parted her legs, stepping out of the panties and the skirt, and then bent over fully, keeping her knees locked straight. The muscles in her thighs were pulled tight so that the firm shape was displayed in full glistening detail under the brilliant white lights. Her bottom was exhibited completely, the arse-cheeks pulled apart to reveal the soft pink rosebud flesh buried in the bushy mound and the tight folds of the arsehole higher up. The arse-cheeks had an alluring sheen from the thin layer of water that had yet to dry completely, still refreshed by several rivulets of water running down over the buttocks and down the arse-crease from the sopping T-shirt.

'Amanda,' Diana ordered one of the girls, 'you'll find what I want on my desk in the staff office. Fetch it now.'

While they waited for the girl, Diana stroked the inside of Ruth's leg, sliding the palm of her hand smoothly over the flexed muscles of the upper thigh, enjoying the cool sensation of wet skin under her fingertips.

'Isn't this an exquisite backside?' she asked the other girls, who were admiring the spectacle of the soaking girl displaying her most private places for all to see.

Ruth closed her eyes, ashamed to find that she thrilled to the silky touch of the Mistress, and desperately hoping that the Mistress would go further: yet torn by an abject disgust at finding herself so degraded. Diana dallied, brushing her fingers tantalisingly over the wet labia, seductively teasing the delicate folds of skin.

Ruth couldn't see what was happening, and simply heard the girl returning hurriedly.

'All you girls have to learn your place,' Mistress Diana told them all.

Ruth clenched her buttocks, but the first blow made her yelp sharply. She wiggled to one side and saw Mistress Diana wielding a round flat object, which looked like a table-tennis bat, having the same wooden handle and a round flat surface.

'It's a paddle,' Diana explained to her gleefully. 'Perfect for tanning recalcitrant young girls' backsides.'

The blows came down repeatedly and rapidly. Each blow was short and sharp. The water seemed to react with the paddle, making the sting that much more painful. Ruth could feel her arse-cheeks quickly turning a blazing red, the smarting pain spreading an intense heat through her body. Blow after blow landed on the quivering tightly stretched arse-cheeks, each stroke expertly placed to inflict a regular and even pattern of punishment on the naked wet buttocks.

She bit her lip to stop herself crying out in pain. The heat seeped from her arse-cheeks and the tops of her thighs into the provocatively parted quim. Little by little she was becoming sexually excited by the steady, constant infliction of pain on her behind. Somehow she began to lose herself in the heat and suffering; all else seemed to slip away, everything stripped down to the essentials of the situation. The only thing that retained meaning and significance was her sexually open position and the beautiful Mistress administering the chastisement.

She began to breathe more rapidly. Her pussy was aching with desire, each spank from the paddle sending another spasm of sensation pulsing through her sex. She felt herself building up to orgasm, could feel the erotic tension mounting up and waiting for release. She didn't care any more about the degradation and humiliation. She didn't even care about love any more. The naked erotic energy surging through her body was like nothing she had ever experienced before. No other spanking or punishment had ever had this electric effect on her.

At some point the punishment stopped. Ruth was aware vaguely that the rain of blows had ceased. She was teetering on the edge of an orgasm, and felt several explosions of bliss inside her sopping pussy, the thick creamy juices mixing with the water trickling from her wet shirt and running down her thighs.

'You can clean this mess after everyone has left,' Diana told her calmly, then turned and left, not even glancing back over her shoulder at Ruth.

Ruth remained in position, unable and unwilling to

move. Her arse was smarting with a scalding, searing ache. She could feel that the redness had spread, or had been applied, all over her buttocks, the tops of her thighs, deep into the arse-deft and even between the thighs. She felt disappointed and was confused as to whether she wanted the punishment to continue or not. She had become engrossed in the rhythm of correction, raising her arse-cheeks to meet the downward stroke of the paddle, feeding on the abrupt pain of impact to swell the torrent of sexual pleasure pulsing through her. Each stroke had been a fleeting moment of contact, each spasm of pain a distorted link to her Mistress.

The girls took their time getting dressed, staring lustfully at Ruth, their eyes feasting on the glistening red arse-cheeks and the open, desirable sex. Ruth remained defiantly bent over, ignoring their blunt and coarse remarks, feeling the bittersweet pleasure-pain of the abused martyr. It was a delicious feeling and she savoured it as she savoured the sexy tingling of her behind.

When alone she stood up and looked around in a daze. It dawned on her eventually that this was her changing room as well. She bent down and picked up her wet things, her arse still blazing. She half walked and half staggered to the bench where she had left her things early that morning. She sat down on the cold bench, but her arse hurt too much, so she laid out her wet skirt and sat on that. The cold wet garment provided a modicum of relief, though she felt no real lessening of the tension still tight in her belly.

Though she had experienced several waves of blissful experience she still felt unsatisfied. She massaged her cold breasts, playing with the nipples through the wetness of the clinging shirt. She raised both feet and sat along the length of the bench, her knees pulled up and spread apart. Lovingly she brushed her hand through the damp pussy hairs, closing her eyes as a wave of pleasure engulfed her. Her fingers were pleasantly icy inside the heat of her yearning sex. She began to frig herself slowly, revelling in the feel of the icy fingers deep inside her. But pleasant as the feeling was, it was still not enough to bring the complete satisfaction that she needed.

She stopped suddenly and searched through her bag which lay on the floor beside her. From the bag she withdrew a long thin chocolate bar that she carefully unwrapped, thin flakes of chocolate falling about her. She used the fingers of one hand to pull the cunt lips apart to reveal the damp humid flesh within, then shivered with pleasure as she slid the dark chocolate deep inside with one long sensual movement.

She began to cry softly, her body aching with pain and desire. She used the long cool chocolate to explore her pussy, searching for the hot red bud at the epicentre. She pressed the chocolate in and out, faster and faster, driving herself to a fever pitch of excitement. Looking down she could see the chocolate wet with the thick white cream of her sex, and her cunt was smeared liberally with chocolatey love honey.

She masturbated more urgently, bucking her hips in short jagged movements, gasping for breath and moaning wildly. She was pressing the melting chocolate deeper and deeper, charging it at her pleasure-spot for maximum bliss. Tears of pleasure and pain and unfulfilled desire streamed down her face.

At last she let out a long strangled cry and tensed with the onrush of the climax that she had longed for. She sat back, still gasping for breath. Her fingers were sticky from the mixture of the chocolate and her juices that covered the mouth, and the interior, of her sex.

Gingerly she withdrew the chocolate from inside her. It had begun to crumble even before the orgasm had almost broken it in half. It glistened with its strange milky coating, strands of chocolate caught in the thick creamy sex juice. She looked at it closely, the instrument that had brought her satisfaction and relief. She realised that it had begun to crumble even as it brought her to climax.

Very slowly and deliberately she brought it to her mouth. Closing her eyes she touched it with her tongue, tasting herself and the rich velvety sweetness of the chocolate. She shivered with desire once more. Her bare arse still blazed uncomfortably, a testament to the degree of punishment that Diana had so lovingly inflicted.

Ruth had been frustrated in her desire. And she had been humiliated in front of the class; the punishment, so publicly displayed, would scar her backside for days to come. Yet she felt a strange sense of happiness come over her. She closed her eyes dreamily, savouring the forbidden taste of her own body as she ate the chocolate and dreamed of Diana's sweet, cool mouth.

Six

'I've been looking for you everywhere,' Laura told J.K. breathlessly, sliding into the seat opposite him.

'I looked for notes in my post,' he explained, rather startled, and anxious to avoid the accusation that he had been avoiding her. The sun was shining brightly, and he was blinded by the glare from the white tabletops arranged in rows in the refectory.

'Well?' she asked brightly, a look of hope in her soft brown eyes.

'Sorry,' he apologised dolefully. 'I just can't come up with anything.'

She looked at him sadly, her bright smile deflated by the disappointment. 'I can't tell her that,' she said at last, almost whispering to herself.

'I wish it could be different, I really do.'

'I just don't understand you,' she admitted. 'What is the big deal? Why can't you help me?'

'I just can't,' he told her. He felt sorry for her, but was unwilling to put his relationship with Mistress on the line. He turned away from her, hoping that she would admit defeat and leave.

'After what I did for you, that's all I get?' she demanded indignantly.

'Not so loud,' he said, afraid that they would be overheard.

'Why should I be quiet?'

'I thought you enjoyed it,' he whispered, slightly embarrassed even to be talking about it. The memory of her soft mouth on his prick softened his attitude. He looked at her guiltily.

'I did enjoy it, every minute of it. But that was a present, that was my way of thanking you in advance for the help I thought you were going to give me.'

'I'm glad we both enjoyed it,' he smiled. 'What if I meet this person you want the favour done for?' he suggested.

'Yes, yes,' she repeated happily, seizing the suggestion. The smile returned to her face and the light to her eyes – she was clearly relieved that some way out of the impasse had been found. Her efforts would not be entirely to waste.

'I could explain to her that you did your best, but I can't do it.'

'Wait here,' she said excitedly. 'Let me call her and see what we can do.' She leaned across the table and kissed him affectionately on the lips.

He watched her weave her way across the refectory towards the public telephones. He felt happy for her, glad that her despondent mood had lifted. In any other circumstances, he realised, he would have done anything to be her lover. She was bright, attractive, intelligent and sexy. He could see other students eyeing her jealously as she squeezed through the tightly packed tables. He felt a pang of sorrow that things were so complicated.

She was on the phone for only a minute, and from the look of relief on her face he could tell that the call had been at least partially successful. He sat back in his seat and watched her wind her way back to him. She was wearing jeans and a simple white T-shirt; her breasts swung gently as she edged her way back and he longed to cup them again in his hands.

'We can go round to her flat in an hour,' she told him triumphantly.

'Good. I'm sure this will all turn out fine.' He shifted in his seat, making room for her to take the seat next to him.

'I'm sorry if I snapped earlier,' she apologised, squeezing in beside him.

'It's OK.' He slid his arm behind her gingerly. 'I know it means a lot to you.'

'If this works out,' she said, 'I'll take you out to dinner.'

'I'll remember that,' he laughed. For a minute he felt totally at ease. It was an odd feeling and he drew back from it. He wondered what would go wrong, unwilling to believe that anything in his life could go right. The only time things were all right was when he was Jaki, and then there could be no wrong.

'God, I hope this goes well.' Laura became anxious again, as if his negative attitude were catching.

'Don't worry,' he heard himself saying. 'I'll make sure everything works out just the way you want it.' He pulled her closer and put his arm around her protectively. She smiled and cuddled up, enjoying the warmth and tenderness of the moment.

The hour seemed to go so quickly. They had sat together in the refectory, basking in the sunshine and in each other's company. They had spoken little but had communicated much simply by the way they sat so close and gazed at each other with longing and desire.

The traffic moved lethargically through the city. The hot summer sunshine meant that the city was stifling, and the grime and pollution seemed much worse. Laura's car was small and cramped and they were soon caught up in the snarling snake of cars headed out of the city. She drove impatiently, zooming into spaces and trying desperately to escape to the breezier streets close to the Thames.

J.K. almost dozed in the oppressive heat, lulled by the rocking of the car. He seemed to be floating in a dream, held aloft by the sparkling rays of sunshine and by the warmth of Laura by his side. The idea came to him that somehow he could have the best of all possible worlds. He fantasised that he could live two totally separate lives, completely in parallel, with no collisions and no conflicts. Jaki could remain Mistress's slave, give herself completely and utterly to her beautiful black goddess. J.K. could live his life with Laura, a different person, with different needs and desires.

His pleasant dreams were interrupted when the car came to a halt and Laura nudged him gently.

'We're here!' she told him excitedly.

The Thames flowed lazily, the sun sparkling on the surface, so that for a moment the murky brown river was a golden bed of ripples. They stood and watched for a moment, captivated by the dancing motes of light. A number of boats were moored there, and, in the brightness of summer, it was difficult to believe that they had not left London altogether.

Anne Young's flat was in a smart new development that overlooked the river. The glass and steel caught the play of light and reflected it back, a startling mirror image. Laura pressed the bell and the door to the block opened an inch.

The lobby was cool and dark. J.K. was impressed by the studied elegance of the space. The steel and glass were complemented by a simple minimalist decoration of grey and white. Vases of vivid yellow flowers provided the only colour, bright splashes that drew the eye instinctively.

Anne lived in one of the penthouse flats, and Laura and J.K. rode up in the lift. The opulent surroundings made them feel a little uncomfortable and unsure of themselves. It seemed an entrance to a world they had only previously seen from afar.

'Hi, come in,' Anne greeted them at the door.

J.K. was a little surprised. He had expected someone

133

much older and certainly not as attractive as Anne. He was instantly struck by her casual self-assurance. There was something predatory about her, the effect heightened by the bright scarlet clothes that she wore.

'The traffic was terrible,' Laura explained as they were led through the house and out onto the balcony.

'You can cool off up here,' Anne told them. She sat down at the table, and poured three glasses of chilled champagne.

'What a great view,' J.K. said, looking out across the river and down into the heart of the city. There was a cool breeze and he closed his eyes and let the sun suffuse his face with his healthy glow.

'You should see it at night,' Laura said. 'You should see how London lights up.'

'And at dawn, when the sun rises,' Anne added significantly.

J.K. turned and saw the two women exchange a secret smile. He realised immediately that the relationship between the two of them was not as straightforward as he had imagined. The look of complicity unnerved him, and he sat down and took his drink in silence.

'Thank for letting us come round at such short notice,' Laura said, changing the subject.

'It's a pleasure.' Anne looked at J.K. and smiled. 'Laura tells me you're studying computers,' she told him.

'Computer science.'

'I work in television, and you wouldn't believe how much technology's involved nowadays.'

'Anne does a lot of her work from home,' Laura added.

'Yes, I use a couple of computers and a modem and some other bits and pieces.' She paused for a second, gauging whether J.K. was showing any interest.

'It's called telecommuting; that's how most people will be working in the future,' he said at last, though the subject failed to interest him very much.

'Would you like to see where I work?' Anne offered hopefully.

'OK,' he agreed politely, though he would have preferred to sit lazily in the sunshine and enjoy the cool breeze.

'It's just through here.' Anne led the way through a glass door that opened on to the balcony.

'I think this technology's just great,' Laura said brightly.

'Have you considered where you'd like to work when you graduate?' Anne asked him.

'Not really – graduation still seems such a long way off,' he admitted.

The office was brightly lit and well ventilated, offering the same attractive view of the river as the balcony. There were two desks, one for writing and one for the computer. The computer was switched on and its fan hummed noisily.

'I write my scripts and notes on that and then when they're ready I can just dial into the studio and transfer the files across.' Anne pointed out all the relevant bits of hardware.

'What type of processor is it?' J.K. asked, pointing at the computer.

'I've no idea,' Anne admitted. 'You know, television really is an exciting place to be in at the moment, from a technology point of view.'

'Do you use large systems, or lots of distributed processing?' he wanted to know, warming to his theme.

'All types. Apart from this sort of stuff, we've got lots of special computers for video and mixing and that sort of thing.'

'But TV is such a hard area to get into,' Laura mused.

'I can help you if you like,' Anne offered hopefully.

'But you're not on the technical side,' J.K. pointed out sceptically.

'Those barriers aren't so common in television. We're

always looking for especially talented people,' Anne smiled and gently touched J.K.'s hand. 'I can get you in, if you want.'

'If I got into TV as well, we could work together,' Laura suggested, looking hopefully from Anne to J.K. and back again.

'Thanks for the offer,' J.K. said to Anne, 'but I think it's a bit early for me to worry about career plans.'

Anne rubbed his hand softly, not letting the disappointment show. She continued to smile and edged just a bit closer to him so that he was bathed in her perfume and aware of her physical presence. 'What do you think of Simone?' she asked, switching tack rapidly.

'She's my landlady,' J.K. pointed out coolly.

'I know that, but what do you think about her?'

'I don't know,' he mumbled vaguely.

'I've found her to be a very direct sort of person.'

'You've met her?' he asked, rather surprised.

'Very direct and very strong,' Anne continued ingenuously. 'Don't you agree?'

J.K. nodded. All three wandered back into the lounge. J.K. sat down in an armchair, and Laura and Anne sat opposite him. They sipped from their drinks silently for a moment. Laura looked pensive; the smile on her face was growing thin, and her eyes darted back and forth. She knew that the game was between J.K. and Anne; she could only sit and watch. The thought that her future career was at stake made her nervous and she wanted to push everything along, but felt helpless to do so.

'Have you read any of Simone's work?' Anne asked after a while.

'What work?' J.K. asked, wanting to find out more about his Mistress. He looked at Anne. On the one hand he felt very wary of her, but on the other she had a certain very sexy appeal. She was dressed in a short red skirt and a matching red blouse. Several of the buttons down the front of the blouse were undone and when she moved he could see the fullness of her breasts.

'I'm not surprised,' Anne laughed. 'You're studying computers, not sexual motivation, which is what she was working on before. But now I'm not sure what she's working on. Do you?'

He shook his head. 'She never talks about her work,' he said.

'She must be working on something,' Laura pointed out quietly.

'Laura's right. Simone Shirer was a leading researcher in her field. She published quite regularly in scientific journals all over the world. Then she suddenly stopped. It doesn't make any sense.'

'I don't know anything about that,' he said, and shrugged.

'But you must admit it's odd.' Anne moved to the edge of her seat, and her skirt rode up slightly so that an expanse of smooth slightly tanned thigh was visible.

'I'm not sure,' J.K. replied uncomfortably. The sight of Anne's thighs, and the plunging neckline, drew his eyes like a magnet. There was something dangerously alluring about Anne: she smelt of danger and glamour and intrigue. It was a heady and exciting mixture that he fought to resist.

'I think she's involved in something big, something very big,' Anne lowered her voice conspiratorially. 'Whatever it is, it's secret, I mean totally and utterly secret. I think it's some revolutionary discovery that she's made. I think she and her co-workers at the Institute are on to something. But because it's a state-run project she can't publish anything.'

'If that's true,' Laura said, 'then it's a shame. Because she deserves the credit for it. She can't publish in the journals because of some government bureaucracy and so she's losing out on the respect and the glory.'

'I think Laura's right,' Anne said. She smiled her

thanks to Laura, who smiled back happily, assured that she had earned herself a job by her quick thinking.

'But if those are the rules that she has to work under . . .'

'Once the story gets out,' Anne interrupted J.K., 'then she'll be free to publish. She can regain her place at the top of her field.'

'And you want to get the story.' J.K. leaned back in his seat and looked at Anne dispassionately, trying to assess her true motives.

'I'm at the top of my field as well,' Anne admitted blithely. 'And I want to stay there. If I break this story we all do well out of it. Simone Shirer will have the freedom to publish her results, which is the *raison d'etre* of a scientist. I will have the story, which is what drives me. Laura will have a job with me, which is what she wants. What about you?'

J.K. remained silent, unwilling to be drawn any further into the conversation.

'Everybody wins,' Laura added quietly.

'What about you?' Anne looked at him.

'What about me?'

'What drives you? What do you want out of life?'

'I just want to be me,' he shrugged.

'If you help me get the story, not only will you be doing us all a favour, you could also be earning yourself some money. This isn't cheque-book journalism,' Anne laughed in self-deprecation, 'but I see no reason why we couldn't enter into some financial arrangement.'

'I wouldn't do it just for the money.'

'Very commendable. But money does help. I know you'd like to help Laura, wouldn't you?'

'Sure,' he agreed. Laura smiled her thanks but he still didn't feel sure. He was still wavering. Something didn't add up. He could not accept that this was the ideal scenario, where everyone emerged a winner and no one a loser.

'What about Simone? Do you talk? I couldn't imagine

living in the same house as another person and not becoming friends.'

'Are you friends?' Laura asked when J.K. didn't answer.

'Yes,' he admitted, shifting uncomfortably. 'Sort of friends.'

'Close friends?' Anne asked coyly.

'I don't think that's anything to do with you,' he said coldly.

'I didn't think . . .' Laura whispered, looking into her drink. She had assumed that J.K. was uninvolved in any other relationship. He had seemed so shy and inexperienced that she couldn't imagine that he was involved with anyone else, let alone an older woman like Simone Shirer.

'Laura tells me you two are very friendly as well,' Anne told him. His face coloured and he squirmed uncomfortably in his scat. 'That's OK, there's nothing wrong with sharing pleasure with more than one person. But just think, if you help me get the story you can he helping both those people at the same time.'

'I'm sorry.' J.K. got up. He was well aware that he was being manipulated and had had enough. 'I don't want to do it.'

'I bet sex with Simone is great,' Anne continued, a note of desperation creeping into her voice. 'She must know how to make you very happy. I know that sex with her boss, Fiona Schafer, was absolutely terrific.'

'Shall we go?' J.K. asked Laura, turning away from Anne.

'Laura can tell you that I can be very accommodating as well,' Anne said, and gestured to Laura.

Laura stood up. She was tom between leaving with J.K. and going over to Anne. She hesitated for a moment, but was drawn finally by Anne's sheer magnetism. She could feel J.K. looking at her sullenly, a frown of disappointment on his face.

Anne patted the seat of her armchair and Laura sat down there obediently. 'You've done very well,' she told her, stroking Laura's thighs with her elegantly painted hand, a gold bracelet catching the sunlight. She pulled Laura down a bit and kissed her fully on the mouth, a long slow kiss that left a smear of scarlet lipstick on Laura's mouth and gave a slight flush of pleasure and embarrassment to her young face.

J.K. stood and watched. He made no move to leave but remained rooted to the spot, watching the two women kissing passionately. He realised with a slight shudder of excitement that Anne would have made an excellent Mistress. She had the same powerful and dominating sexuality as Simone Shirer. If she were his Mistress he would have walked to the ends of the earth for her; her every wish would have been his command.

'Have you ever made love to two women at once?' Anne asked him, smiling seductively. She was confident now that she had found the key to J.K. It was neither money nor career that drove him, but a more basic, primal drive. Sex.

'No,' J.K. lied, afraid to bring Mistress Diana into the conversation as well.

'I know that you'd like to,' Anne said, her voice slightly breathier. She was becoming aroused herself at the idea of making love with Laura and J.K. She stood up and slowly unbuttoned her blouse, letting it fall carelessly to the floor. She was proud of her body; she kept herself in shape and her tanned skin was still firm and attractive. Her breasts were displayed well in a red lace half-cut bra. She slipped off her skirt and stepped out of it. Through the thin red panties the generous bulge of her sex was clearly visible, surrounded by a soft fair mat of pubic hair.

She turned and pulled Laura's white T-shirt off, leaving her breasts bare. The two women exchanged another kiss and then Laura pulled her jeans off. In a second she was naked, the sun warming her body.

J.K. watched silently. The sight of the two beautiful women had excited him, his prick hot and aching in the tightness of his trousers. He wanted to make love, but not on his hands and knees as a servant. He didn't want to fuck in the way Jaki did. He wanted to enjoy the two women as J.K.

The two women approached him holding hands. They kissed in turn, long slow embraces, J.K. and Laura, J.K. and Anne, Anne and Laura. They explored the different tastes and textures of each other's mouths. Their hands were everywhere, searching, touching, seeking. He had a hand on each woman, roving over their thighs and breasts, pressing firmly at the softly yielding flesh, marvelling that two such beautiful women could feel so different.

Anne dropped down to her knees first, and pulled Laura down a second later. Together they pressed their faces against his fly, pressing the hardness over his trousers. Laura gently undid his fly and pulled his thick hard rod out. She flicked her tongue over it, kissing it softly and lovingly. She used her mouth to pass it over to Anne, who planted a long slow kiss just below the purple dome.

'The bedroom,' Anne whispered. Silent and intent, they walked through together.

The bedroom was airy and light; there was an impression of glass everywhere and they were joined by multiple reflections of themselves. The bed was bathed in a distinct bright rectangle of sunlight. They crossed the room and moved into the rectangle of light.

Anne began to undress J.K. She unbuttoned his shirt and rubbed her hands slowly across his chest. Laura pulled his shoes and socks off, and then began to pull his trousers down. She felt him stiffen, almost resisting. Anne noticed the reluctance as well and she joined in.

J.K. waited a second and then gave up. He lifted himself up and allowed the two women to strip him off completely.

'What the . . .' Laura stared at his smooth shaved legs with a look of disbelief. His long silky thighs had an almost feminine look about them, an effect heightened by the play of light on his soft white skin. There was a tight neatly cut triangle of hair at the base of his prick, the hairs cropped tight, so that his long prick seemed even bigger.

He glanced at Anne and saw the look of recognition in her eyes. 'Is this the game you play with Simone?' she asked quietly.

'I don't understand . . .' Laura continued, rubbing her hands over the luxurious supple flesh. Her initial distaste had given way to an excited fascination. Despite the sexy feminine look his flesh was still muscular and lithely masculine. She began to kiss his thighs, passing her mouth over the flesh and sliding her tongue smoothly upwards towards the hard prick in its neat bed of hair.

'Would you like to try some of my things?' Anne whispered in his ear, careful not to let Laura share in the secret.

'No,' J.K. replied quietly. He pulled her closer and pressed his mouth over her breasts, burying his face deep in the bra. Her scent was overpowering and he licked at her cleavage hungrily. She unclipped her bra and he lunged greedily at her nipples. He sucked deeply at them, and could taste the faint red rouge that she had applied there.

Laura was fascinated by J.K.'s prick. She was a bit surprised that she hadn't noticed anything the first time she had taken the smooth length of hard flesh in her of mouth. But the circumstances had been so unusual that first time, the coupling so hurried, and he had remained fully clothed. She made up for it by using her mouth and tongue to explore the base of his prick. She licked around it and gently massaged his cool heavy testicles with her hand. She began to kiss his balls, finding that even here the hairs had been trimmed short.

Anne cupped her breasts with one hand, feeding her aroused nipples into J.K.'s hungry mouth. He was sucking and biting, sending tingling waves of pleasure through her. With her other hand she was rubbing Laura's back, massaging up and down. She saw Laura shift position, so that she took J.K.'s balls fully into her mouth. With the shift in bodies, Anne was able to begin exploring Laura's bottom. Carefully she slid her fingers between the two arse-cheeks, dallying for a second at the entrance to the tight little arsehole but then edging down a bit, seeking the damp entrance to Laura's sex.

Anne pulled away from J.K.'s mouth. Her nipples were slightly sore, the redness extending fully around each pointed cherry bud. She lay beside Laura and sought her mouth.

J.K. sat up on his elbows to watch the two women kissing and sharing their mouths over his prick. He shivered with pleasure and sighed softly. He could feel the two tongues searching for each other, pressing and rubbing over the glistening head of his cock. It was difficult to tell who was doing what. The two women worked in parallel, and seemed to be pretending that his prick wasn't there, reserving their attention for the play with each other's hot breathy mouth. But instead his prick was central: they lapped at it, licked, bit it gently – he could feel lips and tongues and fingers. There was a glorious confusion of the senses. It was heaven. He could feel the spunk gathering, his belly a tight vortex of tension.

Perhaps they sensed that the constant play on his prick was driving him quickly towards orgasm. Suddenly they ceased and together they edged up to him and the three mouths began to share hot ardent kisses and embraces once more. J.K. pulled them up closer; he had his arms around them and with his fingers he explored their bodies. Laura's sex was tight and hot – she was wet with expectation and she seemed to melt on to him when he pressed his fingers deep inside her. In contrast Anne actively sought his fingers. She was wet too and moved herself into place, parting her thighs fully so that his hand plunged deep into the heart of her.

He frigged them together, finger-fucking them, searching for the keys to unlock their wildest emotions. As he thrust his fingers in and out, the two women used their hands to play with his prick or to massage each other's breasts.

Laura cried out first. She was moaning softly, a sweet singsong of pleasure. Suddenly she rose in a frenzy, and forced his fingers in deeper with her hand. She cried out and gripped him tightly, digging her nails into his flesh. Anne took Laura's nipples into her mouth and sucked the exquisite ripe fruit. Laura froze for a second, then she melted, becoming oblivious, aware only of the long slide into nothingness. Her pussy was bursting, her nipples on fire. She collapsed on to J.K.'s chest, exhausted, a delirious smile on her lips.

Anne lay on her stomach and lifted her bottom up. Her thighs were parted and J.K. was using his fingers to send reamy blissful pulses of sensation deep into her pussy. She began to writhe, rising and falling with the expert thrusts of his fingers. She closed her eyes and let the feeling take hold of her. There was a shadow that blocked the sunlight and she realised that Laura had moved beside her. She felt the fleeting kisses on her neck and shoulder. Then there were two hands playing inside her pussy, two sets of fingers exploring her crack. It was a strange dance, J.K. pressing his two fingers in as Laura pulled hers out. Together there was a rapid thrusting in and out; she raised herself higher, opened herself as far as she could, while her body was attacked with sharp bites and soft kisses on her breasts, thighs, and buttocks.

When it came Anne seemed to become rigid, a look of pain etched on her face, her eyes rolling deliriously. She let out a long slow sigh. Her pussy exploded as her creamy sex juices filled her and coated J.K.'s and Laura's fingers generously. Time disappeared and there was only the timeless and intense moment of orgasm. When she finally looked up she saw that J.K. was lapping the sex cream from both his fingers and from Laura's.

Laura lay back and parted her thighs. She positively ached for J.K.'s rod deep inside her. She pulled him closer, felt his heaviness press down on her. His thick hard prick rubbed against the inside of her thigh and she took it in her hand and guided it towards her pussy.

J.K. waited for a moment, enjoying the feel of his prick pressing at the hungry mouth of Laura's sex. When she reached up to kiss him he thrust deep inside her. She fell back, caught her breath for a second then sighed. He began to pump his hardness into her, seeking the rhythm that would bring her to pleasure. She wrapped her legs around him, lifting herself up to meet his downward stroke.

Anne sat back and watched J.K. fuck Laura. The sight of his clean-shaven legs was a little strange. She looked at his tight masculine backside rising up and down and realised that he looked simply divine. She lazily stroked his back, relishing the rippling young muscle tone, the feeling of energy and power.

'Please, please ...' Laura was moaning, wanting him in entirety, wanting the rush of penetration to last forever. In a frenzy she began to massage her breasts, pinching herself on the nipples, driving herself to greater heights of ecstasy.

'Oh, Jesus ...' J.K. whispered. He forced himself as far as he could, at the same time pulling her on to him, pulling her buttocks apart. He pumped his seed in long slow blissful surges. Laura froze too, wrapped up in the same joyous orgasm.

The three of them lay on the bed silently, their tired bodies warmed by the dying rays of the sun. Over the Thames the sun was slowly disappearing behind the tree line. A cooling breeze was rushing up from the distant mouth of the river, the faintest tang of the sea still in the air.

They remained on the bed until it was almost dark. They spoke little, each of them unwilling to break the spell that had bound them so closely. The bright rectangle of light that had delineated their secret dimension had slowly shifted up the room and had disappeared with the downing of the sun.

'Will you help us?' Anne finally asked. She sat up on one elbow, her pear-shaped breasts tinged with the faintest of colour around the nipples.

'What if I say no?' J.K. asked. He looked across the room at the reflection of their naked bodies.

'Will you say no?' Laura said in turn.

'What if I refuse?' J.K. repeated.

'Don't make me answer that,' Anne replied quietly. 'Please, don't spoil it.'

'If I refuse?'

'Would you want Simone to know what has happened here?' Anne told him reluctantly.

'Isn't that called blackmail?' J.K. said coldly. He looked at Laura, lying naked by his side and wondered how much she had known of Anne's plans.

'And how much do you want Laura to know?'

'Know about what?' Laura demanded, sitting up. The warmth had left the room, and she shivered.

'You're a hard woman,' J.K. told Anne. He didn't know whether he was meant to pity or envy her. She had the ruthlessness that he certainly lacked, but then he wasn't sure that he wanted it.

'I have to be hard, because there's a part of me that doesn't get hard,' Anne replied vehemently. She reached out and took his flaccid prick in her hand.

'Know about what? What is it?' Laura wanted to know.

'Nothing. Nothing important,' J.K. told her softly. He turned and brushed the hair from her face and gazed at her deep dark eyes. There was an anger there, but the anger faded and was replaced by a tender look of concern. He leaned across and kissed her on the forehead, a single chaste kiss.

Anne used her fingers expertly, bringing the soft flesh back to full vigorous life. She rubbed his hardness affectionately, squeezing it lovingly. With her other hand she stroked Laura's thigh, letting her know that everything was all right.

'What do I have to do?' J.K. asked.

'I have a woman already in the Institute. She's getting the story for me. I need you to get the story from the Institute back to me,' Anne explained animatedly.

'But I've never even been there. How can I get in, meet this woman and get out again?'

'You turn up and explain that you live with Simone Shirer and have to see her urgently. Choose a day when you know she's not there. Slip away the first chance you get and try and, make contact with Lucy . . .'

'Where, how?' J.K. demanded. He couldn't see how he could pull it off. There were too many ifs and buts to the whole thing.

'Lucy's a smart girl. The obvious places to try are the recreation areas. The password is Conrad, so try the library, that's the obvious place.'

'OK, I make contact in the library, then what? She's unlikely to carry the story around with her.'

'Make a date and then go back a second time. Same excuse if you like, or think up a better one. It can't be too difficult. Two trips, that's all.'

'It'll mean so much to all of us,' Laura agreed.

'I'll try,' J.K. conceded unhappily.

'That's brilliant!' Laura squealed delightedly. Her whole face lit up, and her happiness seemed to light up the darkened room.

Anne smiled. She bent down and took his stiff rod in her mouth. There was still a faint taste of Laura's pussy on the rod, but she took the prick as far into her mouth as she could. She sucked soothingly on it, relishing the salty taste and the hardness pressing into the back of her throat.

'You know,' Laura told J.K. quietly, whispering softly into his ear, 'I think I love you.'

'I ... I love you too,' J.K. stuttered. He was overwhelmed, happy, confused, proud. It made things so complicated, but he never imagined that anybody could love him. He thought that he was destined only to love others, and never to have the feeling reciprocated.

Anne sat up and smiled at Laura, the two of them sharing an intense feeling of happiness. They could sense that everything was going well, everything was going to work out. Only J.K. held back, a black cloud of apprehension souring his feelings. Things were too complicated, too messy.

Anne leant across and kissed Laura's nipples, delicately flicking her tongue over each nipple in turn. She kissed her briefly, and then kissed J.K. on the lips, a longer, searching kiss. She drew back a second then sat astride his lap. She took his thick cock in her hand and carefully guided it into place. She let herself down on his massive prick, felt it enter deep inside her. She edged down so that it fitted her tightly. The feel of his hardness lodged tightly inside her was delicious; it gave her a thrill of power, knowing that she could ride him at will.

J.K. closed his eyes, Anne sitting warm and tight over his prick. With his hands he reached down and parted her buttocks; the entrance to her pussy was wet, the pussy lips spread tightly around his shaft. Her tight anus was stretched, and he could feel the anal bud reflex instinctively when he pressed his finger on it.

Laura jealously looked at Anne riding J.K.; she too wanted his prick, wanted it to pulse through her again. She thought for a second and then smiled. She stood over J.K. and then sat down slowly over his face, looking down to see him smiling encouragingly. She squatted over his face, using her fingers to open her pussy lips. His breath was hot on the sensitive folds of skin. She giggled when he bit her gently just below the buttock, but the giggle turned into a sigh when his greedy tongue snaked deep into her pussy.

J.K. closed his eyes and let the sensations flood his consciousness. His mouth was supping from Laura's tight wet sex, drinking in her creamy emissions. He could feel her squirming over him, rising and falling in sharp edgy movements. He knew that he could give her so much pleasure with his mouth, and he looked forward to exploring her cute little arsehole with his mouth as well.

Anne was riding him furiously. She rose and fell, moving back and forth, screwing herself around his upright hardness. The feel of his fingers entering the taut ring of muscle in her bumhole spurred her on to greater exertions. She felt as if she was fucking him and he were fucking her, two different sensations, two different pleasures.

As the two women rode J.K., building up to simultaneous orgasms, they leaned across and their mouths joined. They shared the same breath just as they shared J.K.

Seven

The atmosphere at the Institute had become noticeably more tense. Lucy knew that something was going on, the siege mentality was plain for all to see. She was afraid that they were on to her, but time and again her paranoia was shown to be unjustified. She was not treated differently to any one else of the same lowly rank.

The most obvious sign of the cooling of the atmosphere was that the number of punishments was increased. Hardly a day seemed to go by without someone being spanked or caned. The jumpy attitude of the staff was communicated to the Prefects. They didn't know what was going on any more than the others, but they were given a freer hand to punish and to instil a sense of discipline.

Lucy had been most frightened when the room searches took place. It was a concerted effort: all the rooms in the building were subject to close searches twice. She had been in the library the first time and had seen nothing, but when she returned to her room the signs of a thorough search were obvious. Clothes moved, books rifled carelessly, drawers left slightly open. She had immediately panicked, until she found out that all rooms, including the Prefects' rooms, had been similarly treated.

The second time it had happened she had been sitting

on her bed, composing an essay for one of her vocational classes. She kept the fear and the shock from her face. Two Prefects went meticulously over the room, searching all the obvious, and most of the obscure, places. But they lacked the imagination even to look out of the window. Regarding each girl's domain as bordered by the four plain walls of her room, they restricted the scope of the search to the tiny rooms and no further.

The affair with Ruth had been a jolt for Lucy. She became aware of the extent of her increasing loneliness and isolation. It was dangerous to cut herself off from everyone, because she knew that to label herself as odd or different in some way would mean that the finger of suspicion would point to her sooner or later. It also meant that her condition was difficult to take: she couldn't share the daily frustrations with anyone, nor could she find solace in other's arms.

She had asked to be assigned a roommate and had been curtly told that such matters were decided by the Mistresses and no one else.

The rejection by Ruth had been painful. And she soon found comfort in the arms of another couple of girls. She had enjoyed the casual sex, enjoyed the experience of new bodies and new games. But the simple act of sex, joyful and blissful though it was, was not enough. Lucy wanted more. Perhaps it had been the things that Ruth had said, or perhaps it was a sign of growing maturity. Whatever the reason, she wanted a more stable relationship. To make love in the shower with an unknown girl was good, but not the be-all and end-all of a relationship.

Lucy continued to haunt the library. She changed her place and sat in the twentieth-century literature section. Every day she religiously went through the volumes by Conrad, searching for the message that would be the key to her good fortune, and guarantee her a future in the outside world. She briefly considered giving up, but the thought of all the purposeless days ahead made her shudder. She kept her hope, but only just.

Tiffany felt thoroughly bored and out of place in the meditative quiet of the Institute library. She leafed idly through a book on the table in front of her, not even bothering to look at the pages. She was seated at a table in an alcove, surrounded on three sides by high shelves laden with books. From her seat she could stare out at the rest of the large and well-stocked library. She liked to keep an eye out for faces that she recognised, looking for friends to break the monotony and the silence. But the library seemed empty, the other corners and alcoves bare, and a warm enveloping quiet hung over the central concourse.

She looked across the alcove to her twin sister Chantel, her long dark hair cascading loosely over her shoulders, a shaft of light falling across the soft brown skin of her face. She was standing on a footstool and reaching up high to the top shelf, searching for the particular book required for their essay. As it was always she who conscientiously did the work, researching and composing two essays, and then Tiffany would select the best for herself and give the other back to her.

The book was sandwiched tightly between the other volumes, and Chantel reached up on to her toes trying to dislodge it, careful lest the entire shelf of books suddenly come down on her head. Her short skirt was pulled up high, displaying smooth dusky thighs and hinting at the fullness of her round bottom, which was barely covered.

Tiffany could stand the tedium no longer. She jumped up and strode decisively up to her sister.

'It's stuck,' Chantel smiled, surprised and glad that her sister had come to offer help.

'I can see that,' Tiffany snapped. Lazily she ran her

hand over Chantel's gently curved calf and then up higher, up along the warm and silky thigh.

Chantel reddened lightly, a slight pink blush spreading over her light coffee-coloured cheeks. She was always thrilled by her sister's skilful touch, but was embarrassed by the openly sexual manner in which she was embraced in public. Both the girls had a religious upbringing, but only Chantel felt ashamed of the sins that she and her sister committed. 'Have you had any ideas for the essay?' she asked, abandoning her attempt to retrieve the book.

Fuck the essay,' Tiffany replied casually. 'You can finish it later.'

'Shall I get the book?' Chantel asked her, a hint of apprehension in her large black eyes.

'No. But don't get down off that step. We're going to play a game.' Tiffany smiled at her innocently.

'Please, no,' Chantel began to plead quietly. She didn't know the game, but from experience she knew it would lead to trouble. Tiffany's games always led to trouble. It had always been so, ever since the two identical twins were little girls. Tiffany's games had caused them to end up in the Institute, via a long and tortuous sequence of homes and care centres.

'Don't worry,' Tiffany smiled soothingly, giving Chantel another more insistent rub along the inside of the thigh.

'Do we have to?' Chantel asked passively.

'Yes, you have to,' Tiffany answered firmly, gazing sternly into her sister's large placid eyes. She turned Chantel round so that she faced the books again and then passed both hands over the long glossy thighs and up over the firm globed arse-cheeks. She massaged Chantel's bottom momentarily, delighting in kneading the firm fleshy bottom cheeks, and then pulled down the thin white lace panties.

Chantel allowed her sister to pull the panties down

and let them drop in a pretty bundle around her ankles. She looked down and saw Tiffany smile back reassuringly.

'Now pull your skirt up and show everyone what a pretty backside you have,' Tiffany ordered, stepping back to gain a proper view of Chantel balanced precariously on the footstool.

Chantel knew not to argue. She peered out of the alcove anxiously, out into the rest of the library and into other alcoves and reading areas. Luckily it was late afternoon and the library was far quieter than usual. She nervously lifted her skirt, hoping that the library really was deserted. Arguing was pointless really. Tiffany always got her way, and Chantel had resigned herself to obeying her sister's every whim.

Tiffany sat back at the table and admired the sexy view that her sister so reluctantly offered. The skirt was pulled up high, so that a band of white was visible where the shirt was tucked in. The bare backside was beautifully proportioned in comparison to the long straight thighs. The junction between the thighs was darker than the surrounding skin, and a neat black expanse of pubic hair covered the barely concealed pinkness of the vagina. The cheeks were separated by a deep and slightly parted arse-valley that curved suggestively around the tightly puckered ring of the arsehole.

'Stick your arse out a bit,' Tiffany directed from her seat, craning forward to see if anyone was approaching. Chantel held on to the shelves with one hand and with the other held her skirt up. Obediently she bent over and pressed her bottom out. Her knees were bent inwards, so that her bottom cheeks were slightly parted and a faint breath of air grazed the mat of hair between her thighs.

Tiffany smiled. She could now clearly see the dark arse bud displayed in all its glory. She always enjoyed

154

seeing the look of absolute shame and horror on her sister's innocent face. Sometimes Chantel would offer a token of resistance and she relished asserting her dominance, forcing Chantel to back down and to agree to whatever demands were made. But mostly she knew that Chantel would do as she was told, surrendering to whatever indignities were demanded of her.

Chantel gazed imploringly at her sister, waiting anxiously for the moment when she would be allowed to let her skirt down to regain her sense of dignity and decorum. But instead Tiffany gave her a sly smile that told her to remain on display.

The game was a variation of one that they had played a few times before. On one occasion Tiffany had unbuttoned Chantel's shirt and had displayed the upturned fruits to a group of girls. At first the girls watched silently, amused and excited by the sight and by Chantel's obvious deep embarrassment. Goaded by the silence Tiffany had begun to tease her sister's naked breasts, weighing the fullness of each large round orb in her hands, then teasing the chocolate-coloured nipples to make them stand enticingly on end. At last one of the girls made a comment and Tiffany seized on it to start a fight. Chantel remembered vividly that it had ended with all three of them being soundly and publicly caned by Mistress Shirer.

Tiffany was on the verge of giving up when someone eventually came into view. A girl had been on the other side of the shelves searching for a book and, guided by the catalogue numbers, she followed the shelves round into the alcove. She laughed out loud with surprise when she saw Chantel poised on the pedestal, skirt hoisted up and bare posterior exhibited so openly.

'Isn't she lovely?' Tiffany commented to the girl, who hadn't even noticed her sitting excitedly at the table.

'Absolutely,' the girl agreed, a little surprised by Tiffany's presence. She put her bundle of books down

155

on the table beside her and smiled, imagining that she had stumbled into some private joke or game.

'You know the Mistresses love to spank her; they just can't resist the sight of that arse across their laps.'

'Is she being punished now?' the girl asked, not taking her eyes off the ravishing view of Chantel's bare arse-cheeks.

'Not really,' Tiffany admitted, 'it's just that I love the look of her arse so much that I want to share it sometimes.'

'Don't you mind?' the girl asked Chantel, who was hiding her red face under the arm that clutched tightly to the shelves.

'Do you mind?' Tiffany urged Chantel to answer.

Chantel hesitated. She hated being humiliated, but she didn't want to make Tiffany look bad in any way. Her love for her sister was the central element in her life and overpowered every other principle.

'Her arse feels good too,' Tiffany told the girl, noting with annoyance Chantel's unwillingness to answer the question.

'Are you the oldest?' the girl asked Tiffany, intrigued by the strange relationship between the twins.

'What the fuck's that got to do with anything?' Tiffany demanded angrily, standing up threateningly. The question cut her to the quick: it was the one question that she could not and would not endure. When she had arrived at the Institute Mistress Schafer had beaten her with a riding crop for responding to the question in the same way.

'I am,' Chantel answered quietly. 'By three minutes.'

'Shut your mouth,' Tiffany told her truculently. She turned to the girl. 'Do you want to feel her arse?' she demanded.

'Sure,' the girl agreed, somewhat taken aback by the sudden aggression.

Tiffany relaxed slightly, determined to further

156

humiliate Chantel for daring to answer that question when she had refused the first. She walked over to the footstool with the other girl at her side, a cruel and vindictive smile on her pretty face. 'Feel how smooth these thighs are,' she told the girl and began to rub her hand up and down one of the thighs, pressing firmly on the softly yielding flesh.

The girl followed suit; she started down at the ankle and passed her hand firmly upward, over the calf, over the soft area at the back of the knee and then up towards the bum cheeks. She enjoyed the lustrous smooth feel of the warm flesh, noting the contrast between the soft dusky colour of the thigh and her own cool white hand.

Chantel felt her face and neck burning with a raging embarrassment. She tried to fight the feelings of stimulation and excitement, but found instead that this strong sexual response was merged with a sickening guilt and shame. She looked down and saw her sister gazing back at her, smiling, her eyes bright with cruel pleasure and obvious enjoyment. She smiled back weakly, glad that she was pleasing her sister, even if it was in a strange and rather frightening manner that she could not understand.

'Do you fuck her?' the girl asked, sliding her hand up and down the thigh slowly and bringing her palm round to stroke the more sensitive inside of the thigh.

'Wouldn't you if she was your sister?' Tiffany replied nonchalantly, relishing the slight look of shock on the girl's face.

Tiffany turned round and started to go back to the table. She noticed that the girl hesitated. 'You carry on,' she told the girl generously.

'Thanks,' the girl said excitedly, turning back to Chantel. She began to move her fingers over the swell of flesh where the inside of the thigh met the dark triangle of hair and the buttocks jutted so invitingly. She had

157

never realised how much pleasure the Mistresses derived from having power over them. Now that she had a chance to fondle and play with an unwilling but pliant girl, she found herself turned on and aroused by the experience. She carefully parted the dark folds of the pussy lips and admired the entrance to the warm wet flesh inside.

Chantel tried to keep her sex tight, but the awkward position on the footstool meant that the girl easily gained entry to her most secret place. She felt sick with shame. She had jealously guarded her pussy – indeed she had only reluctantly let her sister touch her there when they made love. Now another girl, a complete stranger, was inserting a finger into the entrance of the sex, exploring slowly and relishing the honeylike feel of the first drops of her feminine juices.

'Please . . .' Chantel begged Tiffany quietly, hoping that her sister would show pity and order the girl to stop. But Tifflany seemed to be enjoying the spectacle highly, and had no intention of stopping the girl. The more Chantel squirmed the more she liked it. She was herself becoming excited by the voyeuristic experience of seeing her sister sexually explored by another girl. The further it went, the more excited she was becoming, her heart pounding faster and her cheeks suffused with a pale pink of excitement. Already she had begun to plan on extending the game.

'What's going on here?' a stern voice demanded abruptly. All three girls were startled and looked round with trepidation to the source of the voice.

'I'm doing my essay, Mistress,' Tiffany lied, standing to attention. She sighed with relief that it was only a Prefect and not one of the staff. She assumed the best look of sweet innocence that she could muster and as always it worked: she was a consummate liar and a skilled actress when required.

'You, girl,' the Prefect barked at Chantel. 'Get down from there, now.'

'Yes, Mistress,' Chantel responded fearfully, jumping down from the stool. She felt relief that one ordeal had ended, and dread that another was about to begin.

'Which one are you?' the Prefect demanded, glancing back and forth between the twins.

'Chantel, Mistress.'

'It's always you, isn't it? You'll be punished for this, of course,' the prefect told her harshly, then smiled and admitted, 'I'll enjoy that immensely. What's your name?' she demanded of the other girl, who also looked frightened at what was to come.

'Pauline, Mistress. '

'Well then,' the Prefect turned to Tiffany, 'you will have the pleasure of watching these two naughty girls being punished. And naughty girls have to be punished, don't they?'

All three girls nodded automatically.

'Do I have to get anyone else to watch?' Tiffany volunteered innocently, catching a look of blind hatred from Pauline and abject resignation from her sister.

When the Prefect smiled her assent Tiffany eagerly searched out half a dozen other girls who had been working quietly in different corners of the library. She found Lucy sitting alone, working fitfully through a book, a permanent look of boredom etched on her face.

'Have a look at this,' Tiffany winked to her.

'What?' Lucy rose from her desk, she saw the other young women gathered around her and wondered what was going on.

'Just come on,' Tifflany urged excitedly.

Lucy followed the other girls, glad for the break in her dull routine. She turned into the alcove and was stunned by the scene that greeted her.

'I've not had the pleasure of spanking you yet,' the Prefect told Chantel, 'but I'm glad you've been kind enough to give me the chance to put that right. Pauline first.' She pointed the girl to the table.

Reluctantly Pauline lay across the table, pressing her face and chest flat on to the cold polished surface. The' Prefect pulled the skirt up quickly and efficiently, then pulled Pauline's panties down to the knees. She eyed the bare backside for a second, noting that the arse-cheeks were soft and white and bore no marks of recent punishment. She used two fingers of her hand to massage Pauline between the thighs, pressing her fingers from under the sex right around and up along the arse cleft and over the bumhole. The Prefect made sure that all the girls watching could see the full extent of her close and intimate examination.

Pauline flinched, finding the stroking repulsive and nauseating. There was a sickness in her stomach, a tight swirling ball of nausea. She looked at Tiffany, but the venom and the spite were shrouded by the fear and apprehension in her eyes. The pleasure and arousal caused by her touching of Chantel had dissipated and now there was only the dull fear of pain.

The Prefect raised her hand and brought it down with a loud crack in the centre of the buttocks. Pauline clenched her buttocks, but the blow was well aimed and powerful. Instantly the pure white buttock flesh was well marked with bright red hand prints. Pauline turned round and saw the audience smiling appreciatively. As the Prefect brought down a second blow in the same place, Pauline jumped and tried to move away, but the third blow followed instantly.

Pauline bit her lip, defiantly trying to keep the true extent of the pain from the Prefect and the other girls. But the Prefect had been aiming her smacks squarely between the arse-cheeks, the core of the blow landing on the sensitive nether lips and across the partly shielded arsehole.

Chantel watched wide-eyed, trembling apprehensively. She could see Pauline closing her eyes tightly, clenching and relaxing her buttocks, her thighs tensed so that the muscles stood out firmly. Though Pauline had tormented her, she felt no flush of revenge at the sight. Instead she felt sorry for the poor girl, and painfiffly aware that she was next.

The fourth blow struck home in the same place as the others, and Pauline cried out with the pain of impact. There was a tight zone of red flesh stretching from the arsehole down to the mouth of the sex, in contrast to the general ivory tones of the rest of the buttocks. The last two blows rained down in quick and noisy succession, one for the centre of each buttock. The Prefect stood back and admired the bright scarlet butterfly pattern etched on the quivering arse bent stiffly over the table, the deeper colour in the centre parting and a lighter colour spread over the rest of the buttocks.

'You can stay on exhibit until I've dealt with Chantel,' the Prefect told Pauline casually.

'Thank you, Mistress,' Pauline managed to say hoarsely, adhering to the rules, fearing a second punishment from the zealous and arrogant Prefect.

'As you so enjoy exhibiting your lovely rear end,' the Prefect smiled cruelly to Chantel, 'I think you deserve to resume your elevated position.'

'I'm sorry, Mistress ...' Chantel whispered, not understanding her instructions.

'Get back on the step!' the Prefect yelled at her. Chantel was startled and jumped quickly back on to the footstool, almost losing her grip in the process.

'They say you've got the loveliest arse in the Institute,' the Prefect sneered. 'Unfortunately I can only spank you with my hand. It's at times like these that I wish I could have a cane or birch. Now pull your skirt up and show the rest of the girls what you were showing Pauline.'

Chantel very slowly gathered up her skirt with one

hand, using the other hand to balance herself as she had earlier. With shame she remembered that she was already naked under the skirt, her panties having fallen to the floor when the Prefect had appeared. She felt a cool breeze caress her naked backside, emphasising the nakedness and the vulnerability of her position.

'Bend over properly,' the Prefect warned, wanting to view the beautiful arse in detail. The swelling of the buttocks at the junction of the thighs clearly delineated the perfect roundness of the light brown globes. The buttocks had a natural deep cleavage, the skin darker between the thighs and covered with a sexy carpet of tight curly black hair. Chantel bent over and the arsehole was fully displayed, the black-petalled arse lips pouting invitingly.

Lucy drew in her breath at the sight. She was instantly attracted to the gentle beauty, and the gorgeous backside made her head swim with desire. But the look of humility, the pure innocence of Chantel's expression, was also deeply attractive. Lucy's heart beat faster. She realised that she wanted Chantel, wanted her completely. The two had exchanged a few brief words in the past, but now it was as if Lucy had only just set eyes on her. Standing on the stool, her bared bottom pressed out for punishment, she was a vision of loveliness that took Lucy's breath away.

Pauline looked round from her position across the, table. For a moment she forgot about her own painful bum-cheeks and prone position and marvelled again at Chantel's dark beauty. She had been punished before but, she realised, in this case it had almost been worth the pain to have touched and played with Chantel's gloriously tight pussy.

Chantel cried out with the first loud stroke that burned her left buttock. She turned and saw that all eyes were fixed firmly on her backside. Tiffany smiled back reassuringly.

'You mark beautifully,' the prefect complimented her, massaging the red-brown skin softly with her fingertips. She rubbed her fingers indecently over Chantel just as she had done with Pauline, relishing the intimate feel on her fingers. She smiled cruelly at the look of horror and humiliation evident in Chantel's soft dark eyes.

The Prefect rubbed back and forth slowly several times and then sniffed the deep bouquet on her fingers, savouring the pungent smell of Chantel's pussy and arsehole.

Chantel shut her eyes tightly, shocked and sickened by the perverse and degrading gesture, preferring instead the wicked pain of the spanking. The Prefect had made her feel unclean, and she longed for the moment she could wash away the feeling of guilt and revulsion.

Tiffany watched the Prefect with a new-found respect, impressed by the strangeness of the act and excited by the humiliating effect it had on Chantel. She was becoming aroused by the sight of her sister's abasement, finding that the humiliation was as exciting as the view of her sister being spanked and lusted after by the other girls.

The Prefect returned to the spanking, having succeeded in causing Chantel even more shame than a plain and ruthless spanking ever could. She was allowed only six strokes with the hand so she ensured that each smack was firm and on target. She noted that Chantel did not try to clench her lovely buttock muscles, or seek to avoid the just reward for her transgression. Instead Chantel meekly accepted each withering stroke on her smooth dark skin which, as a consequence, burned an attractive deep red.

Chantel held back her tears as best she could; she wanted to cry out with pain and hurt but she forced it all back. She knew that Tiffany would scold her for breaking down and the thought was unbearable to her.

Her buttocks were alive with a stinging aching pain, waves of red heat seemed to send ripples of sensation from the sites of punishment deep into her secret self. She hated it, and fought against it with all her conscious will, but she was becoming sexually excited by the pain and disgrace. It was the worst element of it all. She was always racked with guilt afterwards, but there seemed to be nothing she could do to prevent it. The space between her legs was wet again, a great hunger, paradoxically fired by the pain and degradation of chastisement, growing inside.

The last stroke felt as strong and as sharp as the first. The Prefect had used the flat of her hand as the focus to each blow, letting the fingers land a millisecond later. In this way the maximum power was given to each blow and was not dissipated in burning her own fingers. She paused to adore the object of chastisement, the perfectly rounded and scarlet-patterned backside. She gently parted Chantel's cunt lips and saw the golden honey oozing in her hole, hot and aching for release.

'Aren't you ashamed?' the Prefect mocked wickedly. 'You've made yourself wet, girl. Aren't you a slut?'

'Yes, Mistress,' Chantel whispered, hiding her face against the books on the shelves.

'Tell your sister what you are,' the Prefect ordered.

'I'm a slut,' Chantel whimpered, crushed by the shame of having her guilty secret revealed to all.

'You deserve to be punished more severely,' the Prefect told her, unwilling to let the opportunity to degrade and punish her pass so quickly.

'Yes, Mistress,' Chantel repeated. She tried to squeeze her legs together, trying to hide the telltale signs of her arousal, but she could feel the dewdrops of love juice start to trickle down her thigh.

'Stop that!' the Prefect shouted, mistaking the guilty squirming as an attempt to extract further pleasure. 'I can't punish you further,' she acknowledged, 'but I

164

think your sister deserves some reward for her behaviour. And some compensation for the shame you've obviously caused her.'

Tiffany looked questioningly at the Prefect, who motioned for her to approach. She felt slightly nervous, a little afraid that she too would be punished in some way. She looked back and saw that the rest of the girls were silent and were watching expectantly.

'I think you should give your slut of a sister six strokes with your hand,' the Prefect told Tiffany calmly. 'We'll ask your sister to see if she agrees, shall we?' she added, noting the look of hesitation in Tiffany's eyes.

'Do you agree?' the Prefect demanded threateningly, though she knew that strictly speaking she too was breaking the rules, and as such liable to punishment herself. However, her desire to see Chantel properly punished and the sexual pleasure derived from the girl's abasement were overpowering.

'If you want to,' Chantel replied meekly, hoping that Tiffany would refuse and rescue her from the undignified and shameful predicament. She turned slightly and gazed imploringly into her sister's dark blazing eyes.

'You have broken the rules,' Tiffany mused out loud, and then watched as the Prefect again parted the cunny lips to reveal the wet pink inner folds of Chantel's aroused sex.

'Six strokes,' the Prefect reminded Tiffany, stepping back to get a proper view of the spectacle.

Chantel seemed to lose all her strength. She clung on to the shelves, hardly able to keep herself balanced.

Tiffany had never spanked Chantel before, though she had often caused her to be spanked and caned. She had always enjoyed watching her sister suffer the various forms of correction employed at the Institute, being aroused and stimulated by the sight. However it had never occurred to her to inflict the same kind of punishment herself. Nor had she realised that her sister was aroused in some way by the punishment.

'No,' Lucy hissed, unable to believe that one sister could humiliate the other so completely. It was not something she would do to an enemy, let alone someone she loved. She had been aroused by the punishment – she felt hot and breathless, a little wet between the thighs. But she wanted it to stop. She wanted to rescue Chantel, to bathe her punished arse, to smother her with kisses and tender loving caresses.

Tiffany ignored Lucy. She raised her hand high and brought it down with a resounding smack on . . .Chantel's already smarting buttock. She felt her own fingers stinging slightly and saw their imprint firmly placed on the buttock-flesh. The experience was immensely satisfying and she felt a distinctly erotic thrill pulse through her body. The second slap she aimed at the other buttock, the *smack!* gratifyingly loud. She paused to admire the sexiness of her sister's punished behind, the red heat smeared all over the buttock-flesh and even into the arse-cleft and most definitely around the dark wet pussy lips at the mouth of the sex.

Chantel let out a soft wordless moan, half pleasure and half pain. Her head was swimming and she felt overwhelmed by the dissonance of sensations. Waves of pleasure merged with equally powerful waves of disgust. The knowledge that it was Tiffany applying the barbed spasms of pain added an edge to the mixed emotions. She felt an odd satisfaction in yielding to her sister. It seemed to be the definitive pleasure, a strange mix of sexual and filial pleasure.

There was a moment of silence after the punishment had ended. The alcove was charged with sexual energy and tension. Chantel, on the verge of collapse and orgasm, was allowed down from the footstool, and reluctantly the Prefect allowed Tiffany to lead her sister out of the library.

Tiffany could hardly wait to get back to their room. Her mind was alive with the possibilities and she could hardly wait it to make love to her sister. Spanking Chantel had given Tiffany an incredible thrill, a feeling of power, a feeling of domination.

Lucy watched them go, silently vowing to rescue Chantel from the unjust tyranny of her sister's control. Another section had to be added to the story she was writing, another incident to record for Anne. But it would be for the best. She let herself dream of escape, with Chantel at her side.

Eight

The only way to Chantel, Lucy soon discovered, was through her identical twin. She recognised much of herself in Tiffany; she recognised the defiance, the rebelliousness, even the same sly deviousness. It was like looking into a mirror and seeing herself reflected as she had been, before arriving at the Institute. But whilst Lucy knew herself to be changed, and was still in the process of change, Tiffany retained all of her old attitudes.

Lucy guessed that the two sisters formed a closed community, a relationship so tight that not even the Institute could penetrate the outer shell. As long as Chantel and Tiffany remained together, they would remain impervious to outside influences. But she felt an aching desire burning inside her. She wanted Chantel – she wanted to free her, to liberate her from Tiffany's evil influence. And when Chantel was free, she had no doubt the two of them could build their own unique relationship.

Days after the incident in the library, Lucy heard that Tiffany was organising a poker game in the room she and Chantel shared. In the tense atmosphere of the Institute such an act was so foolhardy as to be suicidal. Tiffany took a lot of trouble organising the game, but the response was largely disappointing. The fear of capture and punishment was enough to put almost everyone off. Lucy however, seized the chance. She went out of her way to ingratiate herself with Tiffany, and gladly accepted the invitation when it came.

Chantel looked up from her book and across to the four girls seated on the floor, in the centre of the room. There was a heated argument going on and the hoarse whispers were becoming dangerously loud. Tiffany had lost again. In the pale light of the reading lamp, the only illumination in the room, Chantel watched her sister throw her cards down petulantly. She felt sorry for Tiffany, who had never been good at cards, and hoped that she would not be a bad loser and start a fight.

The four girls were seated on a blanket spread out on the cold varnished floor, between the two beds. There was a faint haze of silver-grey cigarette smoke swirling above them as they played. Each girl kept an untidy pile of coins and cigarettes by her side, though Tiffany was down to her last few coins. They kept up a barrage of more or less good-natured banter as the cards were dealt and played, and money was thrown noisily and extravagantly into the pot.

Chantel tried to concentrate on her book but her attention was repeatedly drawn to the boisterous card game. Things had changed in the last few days, and Tiffany had become much more demanding in their relationship. She seemed always to be testing, pushing at the edges to see what would happen. Chantel was feeling a little lost in the maelstrom of emotion, always aware of the strange and contradictory pull between her guilty self-disgust and involuntary sexual responses. Tiffany had begun to spank her regularly, fascinated by the arousal this caused and also savouring the feeling of power it gave her. With this in mind Chantel had looked forward to the card game with nothing but apprehension; she felt that Tiffany would use the occasion to try some perverse new game, to test once more the limits of their relationship.

The girls were all in various states of undress, having sneaked across from their own rooms to join in the illicit game. Tiffany who was naturally the centre of the gathering, wore only her white panties and a cut-down T-shirt that barely covered her full pear-shaped breasts. The other girls were dressed in T-shirts or robes, revealing long lithe thighs and occasional enticing glimpses of their breasts.

'Fuck!' Tiffany cursed, and threw her cards down in disarray.

'Run out of cash?' one of the girls teased, knowing full well that Tiffany had lost all of her own money, as well as the money that Chantel had given her.

'Never mind, Tiff,' one of the others laughed. 'Unlucky at cards, lucky in love.'

'Bollocks,' Tiffany replied blithely. 'Lend me some money?' she asked the three of them.

'No IOUs and no lending money. They're the rules, Tiff,' the first girl told her.

'Oh come on, Lisa,' Tiffany appealed to her. 'They're my rules, and that means I can change them.'

'Rules are rules,' Lucy told her firmly.

'Be like that,' Tiffany sneered, unwilling to argue the point with all three. Her good humour was beginning to wear a little thin now that she faced being pushed out of the game.

'So it's down to three of us,' said Lisa, picking up the loose cards and shuffling the deck inexpertly.

'Not yet it ain't,' Tiffany interrupted. She stood up and padded over to Chantel's bed. 'Have you got any money left?' she asked her quietly.

'I gave you all that I had,' Chantel told her, looking up from the book and gazing lovingly into Tiffany's dark brooding eyes.

'Everything?' Tiffany repeated incredulously.

'Every penny. All my allowance goes on books,' she explained quietly.

'What am I going to do?' Tiffany pondered, looking back at the tight huddle of girls on the floor. To bow out now was unthinkable.

'In or out?' Lisa challenged impatiently.

'What about if we play for something else, not money?' Tiffany suggested, trying to buy time to come up with some way of avoiding the ignominy of exclusion from the game that she had so patiently organised.

'Like what?' Lucy wanted to know sceptically. She didn't want the game to end so quickly. The whole point of the game was to allow her to get close to Chantel, but she had been unable to exchange more than a polite greeting with her. If the game broke up, the night would be wasted, for she would have to return to her own room, alone.

'Forfeits,' Tiffany said.

'What's that?' Cathy, the youngest of the girls, asked.

'It's like . . .' Tiffany paused, trying to think '. . . like doing favours and things. You know, if I lose I do all your coursework for a week, that sort of thing.'

'But you get Chantel to do all your homework,' Cathy pointed out, not grasping fully the point that Tiffany was trying to make. The two other girls also looked distinctly unimpressed.

'Not that exactly,' Tiffany agreed. 'But Chantel can do other things as well,' she added, smiling suggestively.

'Yes?' Lisa urged. She knew Tiffany well enough to recognise the wicked grin on her face.

'Stand up,' Tiffany ordered Chantel suddenly.

Chantel looked at the other girls and then at Tiffany. She knew that it was beginning. She felt a pang of fear in her stomach, a sick, tight feeling of dread.

Tiffany stood her by the bed and turned her to face the other girls squarely. Chantel looked down at her feet, and the first slight blush of shame started to touch her light brown skin. She wore a long white shirt, the tail reaching down to her knees, the sleeves rolled up to

171

her elbows. Tiffany began to unbutton the shirt from the top, slowly undoing each button in turn, all the time smiling at the other girls. She stopped when she reached Chantel's bellybutton.

'Aren't these lovely?' Tiffany asked, pulling the shirt open to display her sister's ample breasts. The others looked on excitedly, enjoying the view of the shapely and firm breasts, the large dark nipples puckering seductively. Chantel stood impassively, eyes averted with shame, and let Tiffany openly exhibit her.

'You're saying that you're going to bet Chantel's favours?' Lisa finally asked, clearly intrigued by the idea.

'Is it up to you? What's Chantel say about it?' Lucy wanted to know, concerned that Chantel was going to be forced to act against her will. She could hardly keep her eyes off Chantel; the more of her she saw the more she desired her. But she always felt disgusted by Tiffany's behaviour, by the callous disregard for her sister's feelings.

'She'll do what I say,' Tiffany answered, annoyed that her total mastery over Chantel was being questioned. 'On your hands and knees,' she ordered curtly.

Chantel dropped obediently on to all fours, neither questioning the command nor showing any outward sign of dissent. Tiffany mounted her immediately, sitting triumphantly on her back. Chantel was taken by surprise, almost buckling under the unexpected burden, but she managed to hold on and to take the full weight of her sister. Her hands and knees took the strain and her back sagged a little; she could even feel the warmth between Tiffany's thighs on her back.

'Yeah!' Tiffany cried out, bucking her knees together and pulling at a clutch of Chantel's hair.

Lisa and the others watched with utter amazement as Tiffany started to ride Chantel about the room, whooping and yelping like a deranged cowboy. Cathy sat up on her knees, giggling, anxious not to miss any of the fun.

Chantel could hardly carry Tiffany: she moved stiffly and in short steps across the cold floor, on the verge of buckling into a heap. She drew short hard breaths, panting under the strain. Yet she made no complaint or reproach, her eyes fixed firmly on the floor, her cheeks suffused with a red blush of shame. Her generous breasts swayed as she moved, her chocolate-drop nipples pointing directly at the ground, tracing tight ovals with each shuddering step.

'Ride her, cowboy!' Cathy joined in excitedly.

Tiffany forced Chantel towards the centre of the room then turned her back again, using two handfuls of long frizzy hair as reins, tugging sharply to indicate where Chantel should and shouldn't go. She waited until Chantel was heading back to the bed, then pulled her to a sudden halt.

'Look at this lovely arse,' Tiffany leered, still seated comfortably. She pulled the shirt tail up and showed off Chantel's bottom, the panties pulled tight over the arse-cheeks which were fully stretched by her sagging back.

'We can't see it properly,' Lisa complained, laughing.

'How's this?' Tiffany asked, pulling the panties up tightly. The thin white gusset was pulled up tight into Chantel's anal cleavage, and contrasted strongly with the dark silky skin. The fullness of the round buttocks was fully displayed, the flawless expanse of dark flesh made more enticing by the sliver of material that obscured the entrance to the sex, but which cleaved the buttocks, alluding to the treasure within.

'It's fine by me,' Lisa decided, unable to keep her eyes off the lovely sight. 'I'll play for Chantel's favours.'

'Me as well,' Cathy concurred.

'All right,' Lucy agreed, though with less alacrity than the other two. She was afraid to stand up openly and

173

challenge Tiffany. In that kind of situation she had no doubt that the sisters would close ranks. Chantel remained utterly loyal, and it was that loyalty that Lucy knew she had to crack.

'Of course,' Tiffany laughed. 'Don't think you're going to win.' She stood up, leaving Chantel on her hands and knees. With a momentary pang of guilt, she patted Chantel affectionately on the bottom before returning to the card game.

Chantel's heart fluttered. Aching slightly she stood up; though she had been shown up in front of the other girls she did not feel bitter or angry. The pat on the bottom was all she wanted, a simple and unforced affirmation of her sister's love. She buttoned up her shirt and returned to her bed and book, forgetting momentarily that Tiffany was to stake her favours on the outcome of the cards.

'You know,' Cathy told Tiffany as the cards were being dealt, 'to ride your sister properly you really need a nice big prick,' and let out a loud raucous laugh. Tiffany smiled in response, not finding the joke especially amusing, and perhaps finding a grain of truth in the ribald comment.

'How are we going to do this?' Lucy wanted to know. Though it was difficult to keep the note of anger from her voice, she judiciously avoided all eye contact with Tiffany.

'Well, say I think up some forfeit. I can say that it's worth a couple of quid, if you all agree then that's my stake for that hand,' Tiffany explained.

'What if we come up with something?' Lisa asked.

'Same thing, we just agree a price that's all. I've already thought of one,' she announced.

'What is it?' Cathy asked delightedly, finding that the heady atmosphere was making her feel slightly giddy. She had been excited by the sight of Tiffany astride her sister and by the view of Chantel's divine backside. She no longer felt very interested in cards, but more in the larger, and more devious, game between the two sisters.

'Let's play this one blind,' Tiffany declared mysteriously, moistening her full dark lips with the tip of her tongue.

The cards were dealt quickly and Tiffany played deliberately to lose, excited by the forfeit that she had devised. None of the others seemed particularly interested in prolonging the hand either, and it was over in seconds.

'What do I win?' Lisa wanted to know, gazing eagerly at Chantel, who had her head in a book again.

'You get the most sexy display anyone's ever seen,' Tiffany promised.

'But I thought the prize would be for me,' Lisa complained disappointedly.

'But it's in your honour,' Tiffany explained ingenuously. 'Chantel, stand up and turn around. Good girl. Now lift your shirt, right up. Drop your panties to the floor.'

Chantel followed every direction meekly, standing with her back to the card players and showing them her bare backside. They all watched her silently, fascinated as much by the display of complete submission as by the innocent beauty of her exquisite body.

'Now squat down,' Tiffany continued, gauging the effect by the looks on her friends' faces. 'Now, Chantel, I want you to press your middle finger into that lovely tight arsehole.'

'You cow,' Lucy whispered to Tiffany, appalled by the demand, but loath to turn away from the erotic display.

Chantel was shocked by the request. She stared open-mouthed into space, her face and the back of her neck burning with a deep red of embarrassment. She felt sick and wanted to cry; her eyes were suddenly wet with tears. She dared not turn round to face her audience,

175

afraid to meet Tiffany's stern and demanding look. There was a moment of hesitation that seemed to last an age. But she knew that she could not let Tiffany down. That alone was more important than her own pride and false vanity.

Gingerly she stretched the middle finger of her right hand and then slowly began to gently touch herself between the bum cheeks. She searched for, and found, her tightly puckered arsehole. She touched the entrance to the hole and felt the tight sheaf of muscle immediately contract. Very gently she began to press the finger into the arsehole, feeling the ring of muscle tighten over her finger, trying to force it out. It was painful and uncomfortable; she managed to get her finger in as far as the first knuckle and then stopped, the dryness and the tightness causing her a burning, wincing pain.

Tiffany was aroused by the view Chantel presented, her finger pressed perversely into her own anal hole. She was also aroused by the captivated looks of desire on Lisa's and the other's faces. She was always excited when other women were turned on by the various poses she forced Chantel to adopt.

'Wet your finger,' Tiffany told Chantel when she noticed that the Chantel had stopped.

Chantel turned slightly to look back. She watched Tiffany show her how, taking her own finger deep into her mouth and sucking it and flicking at it with her tongue. Chantel followed the instructions, pulling her finger from her arsehole slowly, relaxing slightly when the pressure was removed. Still facing the other girls she closed her eyes and took the finger into her mouth. She gagged at the acrid taste, but persisted and sucked the finger deeply, swallowing the strong taste of arsehole and lubricating the finger with a generous layer of spit.

'That's sick,' Lisa commented admiringly, becoming

slightly wet between the thighs and gazing at Chantel with unconcealed lust.

Chantel began to press her finger back in. She felt a sharp pain, an urgent desire to expel the intruder. She bit her lip and shoved the finger in with a hard forceful thrust. The lubricated finger went in as deep as it could go, further than the second knuckle and only slightly less than the full length of the long elegant digit. She paused, trying to relax a little; now that the finger was fully inserted, the sharp jabbing pain ceased. The tight muscle at the entrance clenched pleasantly around the base of the finger, a warm and tactile embrace. She peered down between her thighs and saw that she was becoming wet, her pussy lips slightly puffy and her belly a tight pit of desire.

No matter how hard she tried, she could not deny the fact that she felt sick with embarrassment at the things that Tiffany asked her to do, and at the same time was forced into a state of heightened arousal.

'OK, that's enough,' Tiffany declared arbitrarily, satisfied that Chantel had abased herself to the right degree, and that the other girls had seen enough of the lascivious display for the time being.

'I'm not playing any more,' Lucy told them quietly.

'What's your problem?' Tiffany asked menacingly, aware that Lucy disapproved of the way Chantel was treated, though she had noticed that Lucy had watched with the same look of sick fascination and open desire as Lisa and Cathy.

'Nothing,' Lucy mumbled uncomfortably. 'I just don't want to play.'

'If you leave now you've got to buy your way out,' Cathy reminded her.

'Take it. Split it between you,' she said, pushing her pile of coins into the centre of the blanket, and standing up.

'You're getting soft,' Tiffany told her, splitting the

money equally. 'Me and Chantel are fine. Don't go sticking your nose in, OK?'

Lucy ignored the threat, and Tiffany's frigid glare, and walked over and sat on the edge of Chantel's bed. Chantel quickly checked that her shirt was fully buttoned up, smiling shyly when she saw that Lucy noticed the modest gesture.

'Why do you put up with it?' Lucy asked her quietly, unable to understand why Chantel suffered her ordeal in silence.

'Because she's my sister,' Chantel said and shrugged, her voice a barely audible whisper. She was unwilling to discuss her relationship with Tiffany with anyone. She and Tiffany were the only constant in a shifting and unpredictable world. It was the only thing that had survived; everything else had collapsed or let them down.

'I know you're twins, but just because she's a few seconds older than you, that doesn't mean you should let her dominate you like that.'

'I'm the eldest,' Chantel corrected, reconciled to the fact that most people imagined Tiffany to be the elder.

'Then why let her do it?' Lucy said, finding the relationship even more difficult to understand. She wanted to touch Chantel, to rub her hand over the soft brown skin, but held back, afraid that the direct approach would backfire.

'Because she's better than me,' Chantel replied unwillingly. She found the questioning uncomfortable.

'How can you say that?' Lucy demanded. 'You're cleverer than she is, you're nicer . . .'

'No,' Chantel interrupted, upset to hear Tiffany being criticised in even the mildest of terms. 'Tiffany is much smarter than I am, and she's stronger. I'm nothing compared to her. Look at her,' she looked across to the card game. 'The whole world revolves around her.'

'I think you're wrong,' Lucy told her gently, though

she could see that Tiffany occupied the centre of attention, and that she had a strength of personality that few could ever hope to attain. 'Do you ever think about the future?'

'Sometimes,' Chantel smiled, glad to leave the difficult questions behind.

'When I get out of this place I've got a nice little nestegg to look forward to. What about you?'

'Tiffany and I will get ourselves a flat,' Chantel replied wistfully, a distant look in her tired eyes, 'and we'll work hard. Maybe even go on holiday. Somewhere nice.'

'Where will you get the money to get a flat? What jobs can you get?' Lucy challenged her gently, hoping to inject an element of realism into the conversation.

'We will . . .'

'Listen. I've got a journalist friend,' Lucy almost choked on the word, 'she's going to pay me a fortune for the story of this place. I mean it. An absolute fortune. Join me. When we get out we can get a place. A real place, not some dream. We can get jobs and go on holiday.'

'No.' Chantel shook her head adamantly. She looked a little shocked by the suggestion.

'I won't treat you badly. I'll love you.' Lucy could feel her voice cracking. She looked at Chantel and knew it was futile.

'Tiffany loves me,' Chantel affirmed. Her voice was clear and without reservation, and even her eyes betrayed no hint of doubt.

'How can you say that?' Lucy whispered. She felt sick. She had made a massive miscalculation. Chantel would remain an unattainable prize, bound forever to Tiffany by ties of sex, blood and history.

'You don't understand,' Chantel said, shaking her head sadly. 'Tiffany is my sister. That's all there is to it.'

'But why let her hurt you like that?'

179

'Don't you believe in God?' Chantel asked, gazing deeply into Lucy's eyes, as if to fathom the answer from their depths alone.

'What's God got to do with it?' asked Lucy, nonplussed by the strange question.

'We're fallen, all of us. We're guilty and must be punished,' Chantel said.

Lucy looked askance, suddenly struck by Chantel's otherworldliness, a strangeness that had never been apparent before. She realised that there was no way into the complex relationship between the two sisters. Both of them were connected by a peculiar and alien set of bonds that were impenetrable to everyone else.

'I just don't understand,' Lucy admitted. She felt an intense loneliness, aware that she could never know someone as well, and be drawn into such a tight and intricate web of emotions, as the two beautiful sisters.

Tiffany had played her cards quite recklessly, finding the game rather boring after the earlier excitement. Lisa and Cathy shared the feeling, dealing the cards quickly and reducing conversation to the barest minimum. It didn't take long for Tiffany to lose her money again, partly because she was a poor card player but in the main because she didn't want to end the night playing cards, a poor anticlimax following Chantel's earlier exhibition.

'Play for Chantel?' Lisa suggested hopefully, when Tiffany lost the last of her money.

'Yes,' Cathy urged, 'let's add some spice to the game.'

'Well, all right. Why not?' Tiffany agreed happily.

'I've got a forfeit!' Cathy cried at once, jumping up and down excitedly, so that her small pointed breasts jiggled up and down freely. 'If you lose, Chantel has to kiss your thing.'

Tiffany laughed, quite taken by the idea. It was, in its way, quite an innocent request, and Tiffany realised that Cathy was still a young and naive girl, hardly touched

180

by the corrupting influence of the Institute. The cards were dealt rapidly. They went through the motions – Cathy and Lucy threw a handful of coins into the pot and they played their hands. The ritual ended with Tiffany losing, a big smile on her face and a wicked glint in her eye.

'Chantel,' Tiffany called, 'come here.'

'Aren't you going to say, "Yes, Mistress"?' Lucy mocked softly. Chantel ignored the barbed comment and walked barefoot over to the card game.

Tiffany used her left hand to pull her own panties deep into her crutch. Her pussy-bulge was uncovered, a soft mat of curly hair leading down towards the mouth of her sex. The thin nylon material was stretched into a thin sliver of white pulled between the darker brown flesh of the pussy lips. It was an arresting and alluring sight, Tiffany brazenly displaying her barely covered sex to Cathy and Lisa.

'Kiss me,' Tiffany told Chantel, 'here.' She used her finger to rouse her sex, pressing the lips apart so that the glistening flesh inside could be glimpsed.

Chantel, wearing her unintentionally seductive look of horror and shame, got down on her hands and knees. Tiffany sat back to make more room, parting her thighs to expose herself more fully. Chantel began by brushing her full dark lips over the pussy bulge, pressing soft chaste kisses against the dark triangle of pubic hair. Slowly she began to work her way down, following the thin line of the panties, slipping her tongue out and caressing the fleshy pussy lips. Her kisses began to become more passionate, as she alternately pressed her lips fully against Tiffany's sex or slipped her tongue into the damp entrance to heaven.

Lucy rejoined the group and watched Chantel expertly use her mouth on her sister's irresistible pussy. It was clear that she had used her mouth in the same way before: the way she used her tongue to prise the

181

nether lips apart before swooping deep into the glistening folds was proof enough. Lucy was immensely excited by the sight, much more than by the earlier view of Chantel's gorgeous backside.

'That's incest!' Cathy cried, fascinated and excited by the bizarre behaviour of the sisters. She felt a thrill of vicarious pleasure at the forbidden actions, a thrill tinged with a little disgust. She felt herself becoming hot and restless, her pussy tingling deliciously.

'That's not incest,' Tiffany laughed breathlessly, pulling the panties fully aside so that Chantel could suck deeper. She found that being sucked off in public had its own secret pleasure, and she wanted Chantel to continue, to bring her fully to climax in full view of Lucy, Lisa and Cathy.

Chantel found Tiffany's bud and flicked it with her tongue, teasing it wickedly. She sucked the creamy juices into her mouth, swallowing them as if they were the sweetest honey. She forgot about the audience, oblivious to everyone else; her whole being was concentrated on the single glorious task of bringing pleasure to Tiffany. She could hardly breathe, but she worked deeper and deeper into her sister, using her tongue to brush the walls of the sex, then switching to attack the engorged clitoris.

Tiffany leant back and began to lift herself up. She pulled herself away with one hand pressed Chantel's head down, clamping her into position over the raw aching pussy.

The other girls watched wide-eyed and open-mouthed, jealously excited by the pleasure that Tiffany was so obviously enjoying. Tiffany bucked suddenly and they saw her clawing at Chantel as she plunged down into a long, ecstatic orgasm. Chantel continued to use her mouth, twisting her head back and forth, giving her tongue fully to Tiffany's soaking vagina.

'This is incest,' Tiffany said, breaking the silence

afterwards. She pulled Chantel up gently, gazed for a second into her warm loving eyes and then kissed her fully on the mouth.

Chantel almost swooned with pleasure. She returned the kiss, using her tongue to explore Tiffany's sweet cool mouth, brushing over the smooth perfect teeth.

Tiffany sucked at Chantel's hot breath. She could taste the sweet musky taste of sex on her tongue. They kissed like lovers for what seemed an age. She wanted to see the look of shock on the other's faces, to parade her incestuous behaviour openly, and to prove once more her total mastery of her sister.

Chantel was wet. She felt alive again as her sister seemed to blow life into her. All sins were forgiven in that instant of mutual delight. Her nipples were sharp, sensitive points of bliss pressing against the shirt. She wanted Tiffany to touch her, wanted her to make love, to block out all else and to join together as a single fused unit of flesh and blood.

'*That's* incest,' Tiffany told Cathy, letting Chantel go. 'You can go now,' she dismissed Chantel casually.

Chantel cast her eyes down, avoiding the looks of desire etched on the faces of the other girls. She felt a little crestfallen, her own desire frustrated again, but for a fleeting instant she and Tiffany had shared mouths, had shared a long passionate embrace. There had been nothing but shared pleasure in that evanescent moment. They had been sisters. She stood behind Tiffany with an almost Eastern serenity: quiet, impassive, yet capable of the highest peaks of intensity.

'I want her to suck my tits,' Lisa announced.

'Me too,' Cathy agreed quickly.

'Why play cards for it?' Lucy asked rhetorically. 'Why not auction her?'

'I'll pay!' Cathy agreed enthusiastically.

'I was being sarcastic,' Lucy explained, dampening Cathy's enthusiasm only temporarily.

'All right. We'll play for that,' Tiffany agreed, making herself comfortable once more.

This time they played cards with more interest, each of the players anxious to claim the prize. Tiffany played with cool deliberation, trying her best to win.

'I win!' Lisa cried triumphantly, laying her cards on the table. Tiffany smiled indulgently. She had played to win but was not especially upset at losing; the thought of watching her sister give pleasure to another was not an unappealing one.

'Chantel . . .' Tiffany pointed her to Lisa, who had disrobed, revealing firm high breasts, the small round nipples already sharp pointed buttons.

Chantel, keeping her eyes averted as much possible, walked round to Lisa and knelt beside her. Lisa touched Chantel's face affectionately and swept back her long dark tresses so that her face would be fully visible.

Reluctantly Chantel stooped down and took the small breasts in her hand. She squeezed them considerably so that the nipples were enticing, open targets. She closed her eyes, avoiding Lisa's excited and adoring gaze, and began to kiss the warm heaving breasts. She lapped her tongue over each of the nipples in turn and then began to smother the smooth white skin around the nipples with delicate kisses, pressing her full dark lips firmly against the malleable breast flesh.

Lisa kept stroking Chantel's face, deriving pleasure from the rapt look on Chantel's pretty face and from the loving caresses showered on her breasts. She felt surges of pleasure emanate from her nipples when Chantel began to suck them fully, taking each erect button into her mouth and playing her tongue over the most tender point while sucking hard. In the pale light of the reading lamp the nipples glistened seductively, appetising bullets of red moist flesh. With rising desperation she tried to take Chantel's hand and force it down but Chantel resisted, concentrating purely on the perfectly formed breasts.

Chantel tried hard not to think about what she was doing. Instead she tried to focus purely on the sensations in her mouth – the taste of the nipples being drawn deep into her mouth, the feel of the extended nipples on her tongue. She felt excited by it all: her panties were damp and her own nipples fully erect. The only way she could assuage the guilt – and the guilt was there, a dark cloud over her head – was to imagine that she was sucking at Tiffany's nipples. But it was a difficult illusion to keep up. The taste of the two girls was different, the texture of the skin different. Lisa had tight, firm small-nippled breasts, while Tiffany's were large and rounded and her nipples were large ripe cherries that seemed to fill Chantel's mouth.

'Go down! Into my pussy,' Lisa began to urge imploringly, her body aflame with an urgent ecstatic desire. Chantel was sending her into a raging frenzy of arousal, and her pussy was aching with a deep compelling want.

'That's enough,' Tiffany intervened, pulling Chantel away. She was pleased to see that Chantel had given herself fully, so fully in fact that Lisa was dying for the fire in her belly to be put out.

'Let me have her,' Lisa begged Tiffany, not bothering to cover her glistening erect nipples, moistened completely by Chantel's skilful tongue.

'What do you mean?' Tiffany said innocently.

'Let me have her for the night,' Lisa pleaded.

'To do what?' Tiffany demanded, realising that she now had an element of power over Lisa as well.

'To have sex with her. I want her in my cunt, to do what she did to you.'

'No,' Cathy declared firmly. 'I want her as well. We have to play cards for her.'

'We don't have to do anything,' Tiffany retorted. 'I say we play for forfeits, not for her completely.'

'Please,' Lisa looked at Tiffany beseechingly, 'my pussy's soaking because of her. Let her finish me.'

'No, only for forfeits,' she decided firmly, alarmed by the frank and urgent desire for Chantel. She suddenly felt vulnerable, jealous and a little afraid at the way that Chantel had responded to the other girl's breasts. She wondered whether Chantel had enjoyed sucking Lisa's tits, whether Chantel would enjoy sucking from Lisa's virginally white pussy.

'OK. She sucks the pussy of the winner,' Cathy suggested, hoping to salvage some pleasure from the game.

'No,' Tiffany disagreed peremptorily. 'She sucks the winner's bumhole.' Her suggestion was greeted with a stunned and sickened silence. It seemed that she was intent only on subjecting Chantel to the most degrading of acts, and had no interest in allowing the other girls to share in the pleasure that Chantel could give them.

'You really are sick,' Lucy told her, breaking the silence with her cold and angry remark.

'I don't see you turning away when Chantel's on show,' Tiffany retorted. Lucy was stung by the truth of the accusation and fell silent, slightly ashamed of herself.

'Do you play or what?' Tiffany urged impatiently.

'OK,' Lisa agreed quietly.

Cathy simply nodded, finding the idea perversely attractive. The thought of having Chantel's skilful and expert tongue anywhere on her body was attractive.

Chantel caught her breath. She felt totally sickened by the idea. She had never done such a thing before, not even to Tiffany. She hoped, without hope, that Tiffany would suddenly back down and change her mind. She watched the cards being shuffled. and dealt and, although she didn't understand the game or how it was played, she hoped to glean some understanding of what was to come.

The game was played with quiet intensity, the coins and notes piling up in the pot as each girl tried to raise the stakes.

'That's all my money,' Cathy murmured, staking the last of her cash.

They all turned their cards over together. Chantel saw that they all looked up at Lisa, and knew that she had won.

Silently Lisa got up on to her hands and knees and turned around. She looked back and smiled sweetly.

Chantel looked down at Tiffany, her dark eyes wide with a wordless imploring look of desperation. Tiffany looked back coldly, glad to see that Chantel wore her look of humiliation and disgust.

Chantel dropped down on all fours, trembling slightly. She crawled slowly towards Lisa, her stomach churning nervously. Lisa's panties were stretched tight over her fair white buttocks, the material pulled higher on one side so that the full shape of one of her buttocks was displayed. Her cotton panties had a darker wet patch between the thighs, the creamy evidence of her arousal obvious for all to see.

Lisa pulled the panties down herself, eager now for the experience to begin. Chantel turned back to Tiffany and halted for a second, waiting for a last-minute reprieve.

'Use your tongue properly,' Tiffany cautioned her.

Chantel pulled Lisa's panties down fully, and looked at the smooth white buttocks that were spread shamelessly for her. The pussy was oozing golden drops of cream and the pink clitoris was visible between the parted pussy lips. Lisa pushed her bum higher so that the arse-cheeks were spread apart and the buttocks curved to their full extent. Chantel followed the line up from the pink flesh up between the arse-cheeks to the taut round bud of the anus.

Chantel went down slowly, breathing in the scent of Lisa's aching sex. She gingerly touched her tongue on one side of the arse-cheek, feeling the tight anal bud tense momentarily. She passed her tongue back and forth over the arsebud, exploring the pouting arsehole with the very tip of her pink tongue. A wave of revulsion overcame her when she swallowed the taste of arsehole from her tongue; it was an unnatural and different taste. But she persisted, drawing her tongue on a tight circuit around the entrance to the nether hole. She summoned up her courage and plunged her tongue a little way in. Lisa moaned softly, a little cry of pleasure and surprise. Chantel drew her tongue in and out, finding that the sheath of muscle gripped at her tongue engagingly.

'That's it,' Lisa told her, surprised to find the sensation pleasurable. The feel of the tongue forcing itself into her arse was sending bizarre spasms of sexual pleasure throbbing into her belly. Her pussy was wet still, but was now feeding off the waves of bliss that Chantel was pressing into her arsehole.

Chantel found that once her initial revulsion passed the feel of her tongue exploring Lisa's bumhole was immensely satisfying. She pressed deeper, her tongue enclosed by the warm smooth walls of the arse. When she closed her eyes she imagined that she was sucking at Tiffany's arsehole and was filled with delight at the thought. Her shame was still strong, but it had become another element in the contradictory weave of emotions that was at her core. It was always the same mix of elements: guilt, shame, pleasure and pain. It was a strange blend and only Tiffany seemed to be able to play off the opposing components, so that Chantel was forever at her mercy.

Lisa was panting sharply, her body pulsing with wave after wave of bliss from her invaded anus. She could feel Chantel passing her tongue in and out, sometimes with long slow languorous movements, and other times with sharp hard thrusts of the tongue. She pulled her own arsecheeks apart, wanting Chantel to bury herself deep into the burning hole.

'She's really being fucked,' Lucy commented, dismayed by the sight of Chantel greedily eating from Lisa's backside.

'Fuck me . . . Fuck me . . .' Lisa repeated deliriously, and she seemed to freeze, arching her back as her pussy exploded into orgasm. She fell to the floor, completely satisfied, her body tingling with an ecstatic afterglow.

Chantel smiled weakly at Tiffany, ashamed that she had taken so much pleasure from the degrading and servile task of sucking Lisa's arsehole.

Tiffany was astounded. She realised that far from punishing Lisa and Chantel, she had rewarded them both. She looked blankly at her sister, realising yet again that Chantel had found pleasure in punishment, just as she had with the spankings and canings. Yet the astonishment was tempered with pride that her sister had performed so well, had accepted her submissive task without complaint and had done exactly as asked, even to the extent that she ignored her own evident initial abhorrence. She knew that Chantel was a creature of her own making, that Chantel's desires and emotions had been moulded by many years of her bidding. Tiffany was mistress of her sister more completely than anyone else could ever be.

'It's just you and Lisa,' Cathy reminded Tiffany, eager for the game to continue. She had failed to win any of Chantel's favours, but the sight of Chantel sucking Lisa's enticingly offered backside had wound her up to such a degree of arousal that she felt herself to be on the verge of orgasm. Her fingers had been secretly rubbing against the outside of her panties; she felt the damp patch grow and ached with the desire to frig herself fully.

'I'll play you for her,' Lisa offered, standing up to remove her knickers completely.

'No,' Tiffany said.

'Every penny I've got,' Lisa proposed, pushing the large pile of coins and notes to the centre of the blanket.

Tiffany eyed the money keenly. It was more money than she had had for a long time. She was tempted by the offer, and turned to Chantel who had resumed her position behind her.

Chantel was shocked by idea. She looked at Tiffany and realised with horror that her sister was on the verge of agreeing.

'Please, no,' Chantel whispered, afraid to openly refuse her sister, but even more unwilling to be passed over to someone else like a prized possession.

'But I want you to,' Tiffany replied sweetly, her face drawn with a most innocent and moving smile. The very fact that Chantel had taken the unusual step of openly questioning her order was enough to convince her to play.

'You don't have to,' Lucy urged her, glad that Chantel had at last decided to make a stand against the vindictive domination of her sister.

Chantel meekly nodded her assent, driven by her sister's will and by Lucy's counterproductive urging. She knew that she could not resist without publicly rupturing her relationship with Tiffany. And to resist and lose would be to make Tiffany look bad and herself look weak.

'Why bother with cards?' Tiffany asked Lisa, scooping up the cash with an exaggerated gesture.

'It's all yours,' Lisa agreed. She put her robe on to cover her nakedness and walked over to Chantel. She took her by the hand and pulled her along to the door.

Chantel glanced back and saw that Tiffany had her arm around Cathy and was whispering into her ear and laughing.

'It's OK,' Cathy called to Lisa, 'you don't have to worry about being disturbed. I'm spending the night here.'

Chantel felt a lump in her throat and her eyes filled with tears. She didn't want to make love to another girl;

she had never made love to anyone but Tiffany. Neither did she want someone else sharing Tiffany, exploring her smooth brown body, giving and taking pleasure.

Yet she went along reluctantly, pulled eagerly by Lisa. Already she could feel the same sick arousal flickering inside her. Her nipples were hard and her sex was humid and damp with expectation.

Nine

Chantel entered her room and found Tiffany deep in conversation with another young woman. They looked up at her and fell silent.

'Hello,' Chantel said brightly, hurrying into the sunlit room.

'This is Jessica,' Tiffany said, introducing the sleek fair-haired girl at her side.

'Hi,' Jessica smiled. She had an oval face, with full red lips, a small pointed nose and large blue eyes that sparkled.

'Are you new at the Institute?' Chantel inquired politely, going to the chest of drawers to put away the clothes that she had just ironed.

'No, not new,' Tiffany replied for Jessica rather coldly. Chantel caught the slightly agitated tone of voice and fell silent.

For some days Tiffany had been restless, and Chantel had come to recognise the times she needed silence. Tiffany had been making ever more outrageous and humiliating demands, and the more Chantel submitted, the more dissatisfied Tiffany seemed to become.

Chantel had been forced to stop wearing panties so that she went about the building aware at all times of her nakedness under her skirt. Tiffany would take every opportunity to flaunt Chantel's state of undress by lifting the skirt and showing complete strangers

Chantel's backside or the bulge of her sex. Chantel had even been caught once by a Prefect and had been soundly spanked for being out of uniform.

Following the card game Tiffany had forced Chantel to engage in sordid acts for money. She had been forced on to her hands and knees and made to pleasure girls in the front or rear with her mouth. On every occasion Tiffany had watched with unconcealed pleasure, and had then brought Chantel back to the room where she soundly spanked her before sitting astride her mouth and riding until overcome by a glorious orgasm.

Chantel had been made to stand at the top of the stairs in the library so that any girl passing by could see up her skirt. Tiffany had watched from a corner, as Chantel acted the complete innocent whilst a number of girls took voyeuristic pleasure in spying up her skirt and gazing at her alluring body.

Now she could feel, from the tense atmosphere in the room, that Tiffany was planning some new act of indignity. She wondered whether Jessica would be buying her mouth or not. She glanced casually in her direction, passing her eyes discreetly over the long lithe body. Tiffany and Jessica were sitting back on the bed, talking in secretive whispers so that Chantel could not overhear.

Chantel shut the drawer; she had washed and ironed all of Tiffany's clothes as well as her own, and had now packed them away neatly. She decided to go to the library rather than stay in the room. Something about Jessica made her nervous.

'Where are you going?' Tiffany asked as, Chantel reached the door.

'I was going to the library,' Chantel explained placidly.

'Is that how you act when we've got a guest in our room?' Tiffany demanded angrily, exchanging a significant glance with Jessica.

'I'm sorry,' Chantel apologised to Jessica, who was looking on indifferently.

'Sorry isn't good enough,' said Tiffany striding over and grabbing Chantel by the hand.

'I'm sorry.' Chantel repeated blankly. She allowed herself to be pushed back on to her bed, and then looked on as Tiffany picked up a slipper from the pair at the foot of the bed.

'I think it only right that you be punished,' Tiffany told her, waving the slipper in the air menacingly. 'Jessica,' she called, 'you're entitled to punish her as well.'

'Thanks,' said Jessica gratefully. She came over and eagerly picked up the other slipper.

Chantel looked up at the two girls standing over her, clutching the rubber-soled slippers. She knew that Tiffany had simply found an excuse to inflict another round of humiliation and pain: any excuse would have done, she realised. Jessica smiled cruelly, her eyes sparkling with anticipation. Absently Chantel noted that Jessica had the same stern look as some of the Mistresses, the same cold austere beauty about the eyes and lips.

Tiffany turned Chantel over and unbuttoned the skirt, letting it slide down around the ankles. Chantel looked back and saw Jessica give an admiring nod at the sight of the bared backside.

'Offer yourself properly,' Tiffany directed.. Chantel obeyed and got on all fours on the bed, parting her legs slightly so that her bottom cheeks were properly splayed. She brought her chest down flat on to the mattress and raised her bottom as high as she could.

'Look, she's embarrassed,' Jessica laughed, finding the pink blush of shame on Chantel's sad face totally captivating.

Tiffany raised the slipper high and brought it down with all her might with a loud satisfying smack. A bright red imprint was burned deeply into Chantel's soft brown arse-flesh. Jessica passed her fingers over it, feeling the heat of the flesh on her cool fingertips. She too raised her slipper and gave Chantel a resounding smack on the other buttock.

No matter how often she was spanked Chantel always found the pain excruciating. Her buttocks were aflame with a bright incandescent pain that stung bitterly. Tiffany and Jessica stood side by side and beat out a steady rhythm on her beautifully proffered posterior. Each girl concentrated on one arse-cheek, carefully spreading the rain of blows over every visible inch of buttock flesh, and down over the tops of the thighs and down towards the knees.

'I told you,' Tiffany remarked jubilantly when she saw the first signs of Chantel's unwanted and uncontrolled arousal.

The spanking stopped but Chantel continued to let out little cries of pleasure and pain. She sighed deeply as the fire spread from her buttocks into the centre of her sex so that she forced her buttocks higher, desperately seeking the source of her pain.

Chantel was turned over roughly. She winced when she was forced to sit on her smarting backside. Silently she watched Tiffany begin to undress, lifting her shirt over her head and letting her skirt fall to the floor. Jessica watched for a second, then turned and went back to the other bed.

Tiffany let her panties fall to the floor and stood proudly in front of Chantel, who gazed back adoringly. Chantel had explored every inch of her sister's body; she knew the effect on it of every caress and every gesture. She knew that Tiffany's nipples were unusually sensitive, that the left side of her pussy was more sensitive than the right; she had even discovered a secret place in her arsehole that caused her to writhe ecstatically when it was tongued or fingered.

195

'You're beautiful,' Jessica told her, coming up from behind and planting a row of soft kisses on her pretty shoulder and neck. Tiffany felt the sun fall across her breasts, increasing the contrast between the darkness of the nipples and the light brown of her skin.

Jessica gave Tiffany a long, brightly coloured makeup bag, and Tiffany opened it excitedly. Chantel saw her withdraw an odd-looking object from the bag. It was a v-shaped piece of rubber or plastic, several inches long and knurled or ribbed on the surface. There was a small ring at the base of the v-shape through which Tiffany carefully threaded some long leather bands.

Chantel, staring wide-eyed at the wicked-looking leather straps, imagined it to be some peculiar instrument of punishment. She pushed herself back, knowing that the straps would bite deeply and painfully into her tender body.

Tiffany took the object in both hands and carefully inserted one of the arms slowly into her pussy. Chantel was open-mouthed, gaping distrustfully as Tiffany pressed the thing deep into her sex. She pressed it in and out several times and Chantel could see it glistening with her sister's creamy emissions. At last Tiffany seemed happy with the position of the thing and, aided by Jessica, she tied the leather straps tightly around her waist.

'Do you like it?' Tiffany asked, posing provocatively with the other arm of the object jutting out like a massive erect penis.

'It looks good enough to eat,' Jessica replied, laughing. As if to show that she meant it she fell to her knees and began to smother the false prick with exaggerated kisses. She then took as much as she could of it into her mouth and began to work her head up and down.

'Oh Jesus,' Tiffany moaned, the other prick inside her playing up and down in her wet sex, pressing wave upon wave of pleasure directly on to her clitoris.

196

'It's great, the only one in the Institute,' Jessica told her proudly, getting up from the floor.

Chantel hadn't immediately comprehended what was going on: she was still shocked by the unnatural sight of the white pseudo-prick emerging threateningly from between Tiffany's light brown thighs.

'Lie back, relax,' Tiffany told her, making her lie across the length of the bed.

Chantel lay back, her head on her pillow, her backside, which was still stinging, pressed flat on the bed and her knees closed tightly together. Tiffany snuggled up next to her, scattering gentle kisses on her frightened face and eyes. Chantel froze when she felt the hardness of the thing press against the warmth of her thigh.

Tiffany continued working with her mouth, showering Chantel with a pattern of sweet loving caresses. She unbuttoned Chantel's shirt and began expertly to massage the gorgeous twin globes of flesh, seeking out the hardened nipples for special attention. Chantel could not resist for long, and soon she was responding to Tiffany's kisses, enjoying the feel of the cool mouth on hers.

Tiffany slid her hand down and pressed questioningly into the damp quim, her finger playing in the viscous honey at the mouth of the sex. Chantel allowed her legs to be parted so that Tiffany could press her fingers deep into the sex, sliding in and out so that she spread her legs further. She wanted Tiffany to go deeper, to play with the fiery rosebud at the centre.

Tiffany seemed to swap position, and suddenly Chantel found that her sister was between her thighs. Tiffany sat up and smiled; she looked down at Chantel's body, spread invitingly before her. She knew that Chantel was still technically a virgin, and that no man had enjoyed her body yet. Lovingly she fondled the hard prick between her legs, smiling when she saw Chantel looking at it with apprehension scored deep in her face.

Tiffany leant forward and guided the rigid tool into the entrance to Chantel's sex. Chantel squirmed uncomfortably, trying desperately to pull back, to pull away from the massive threatening monster at the gates to her special place.

Tiffany lurched forward and the prick was thrust deep into her sister. Chantel screamed with the horror and the momentary pain.

Then Tiffany began to fuck her sister, urgently thrusting the prick in and out. With each thrust a wave of pleasure engulfed the two of them, the passage of the massive hardness deep into the heart of the pussy giving a delicious aching thrill.

Chantel began to move with the rhythmic motion of her sister, pressing herself up to make the most of the downward push of the prick, raising her sore backside to make herself as open as possible. She had never had a man, had never wanted a man, and now she knew that she could never have a man. Tiffany was all that she would ever want.

'Turn over,' Tiffany urged her breathlessly, the first drops of sweat appearing on her forehead and between her large excited breasts.

Chantel turned over and let Tiffany insert the prick into her sex from the rear. It was a different kind of feeling, pressing into her sex from another angle: this time Tiffany could gain deeper access. Chantel was almost sobbing, her face stretched in an expression of pure unbridled bliss. Tiffany was pumping harder and harder, slightly out of breath from the exciting exertion. She could feel the heat of Chantel's backside on the base of her belly whenever she impaled her sister with the long thick instrument.

Chantel turned to one side, unable to catch her breath. She saw Jessica undressing and looking at her eagerly. She realised vaguely that when Tiffany finished, Jessica would take her turn with the prick.

Faster and faster Tiffany fucked, using her hands to force Chantel's bum cheeks apart, so that she could gaze at the delicious arsehole and at the wet prick sliding in and out of Chantel's fiery sex.

'Fuck me . . . Oh, I love you, I love you . . .' Chantel sobbed hysterically.

'I love you too . . .' Tiffany sighed.

Both the sisters seemed to buckle at the same time. They screamed in unison, plunging into a rapturous climax.

They lay side by side, exhausted, covered with a thin film of sweat. Their glazed bodies seemed to glisten in the sunshine, a glowing aura of satisfaction enveloped them.

Tiffany eventually stood up and let Jessica untie the instrument that had brought them so much pleasure.

As Chantel watched Jessica put it on, she smiled at Tiffany, who smiled back. Chantel was seized by an unexpected and overwhelming happiness. Everything was right. Everything was perfect.

'You know,' Chantel said quietly, 'I'll never leave you.'

'I know,' Tiffany replied absently. She was lying naked on her bed, letting the sun warm her. The experience of fucking her sister with a rubber prick had been exhilarating. For a moment she had felt the surge of power and energy that a man would feel. It was as if she had taken possession of her sister for the first time.

'I'll never leave,' Chantel whispered dreamily, 'no matter what anyone tells me.'

'Has anyone said anything?' Tiffany asked, sitting up on one elbow.

'Well,' Chantel hesitated. She was wrapped in a warm glow of satisfaction, and felt herself to be aglow, floating on air.

'Who was it?' Tiffany asked insistently.

'Lucy. On the night of the card game. She was just being silly, I guess.'

'What exactly did she tell? Did she have a dig at me?' Tiffany sat up fully, glaring at Chantel angrily.

'It was just a bit of silliness,' Chantel replied, shrinking back a bit.

'Tell me. Every word.'

'She said that she would have a lot of money when she got out. She had a deal with a reporter. She said that I should leave you and make my life with her. I turned her down, honestly I did. I turned her down flat.'

'What sort of a deal?' Tiffany said, homing in on the only part of the story that had any meaning for her. Of course she knew that Chantel would have rejected the offer. There could be no other possibility.

'Something to do with the story of the Institute.' Chantel relaxed a bit, glad that Tiffany wasn't furious.

'How much money?'

'She didn't say. She said it was a lot. She said we could get a flat and jobs. She said we could go on holidays.'

'Did she now?' Tiffany stood up and began to dress quickly. 'I think our nice little friend deserves a visit.'

'What the fuck are you doing here?' Lucy demanded. She had just finished a class on the ideology of belief, but the quietly contemplative mood it had engendered was shattered when she returned to her room to find Tiffany sprawled casually on the spare bed.

'That's a nice way to talk to your friends,' Tiffany scoffed, remaining comfortably flat on her back.

'How long have you been here?' Lucy flopped down on her own bed and looked suspiciously across at Tiffany.

'Not long; I just thought you'd like a visit, especially as you're so lonely these days.'

'Thanks for the thought,' Lucy told her coldly.

'So lonely in fact,' Tiffany smiled slyly, 'that you'd even try to steal Chantel away from her own dear sister.

The colour drained from Lucy's face. With a terrible sinking feeling she could foresee all that was to come. 'I'd treat her better than you do,' she said at last.

'Don't look so upset, darling,' Tiffany sneered. 'You're not the first little bitch that's tried it on with Chantel. But you see, Chantel worships me and no one else stands a chance. Not even if they offer all the cash in the world.'

'What do you want?' Lucy demanded, irritated by Tiffany's equivocation.

'That's what I like. Be direct. You and me are a lot alike. If you'd asked me I would've slept with you, darling.' Tiffany laughed again, a short scornful laugh of contempt.

'Not as alike as you think,' Lucy said quietly.

'What? If you've got something to say then say it so I can hear it. How much is this fancy deal worth?'

'A grand.'

'I don't believe you, you little bitch.'

'Three grand,' Lucy narrowed her eyes and stared at Tiffany angrily.

'You're cheap, too cheap,' Tiffany decided. 'I would've got more. Ten or fifteen.'

'But you haven't, have you? You're going nowhere after this place. Absolutely nowhere.'

'And how far do you think you'll get on a measly three grand? Any old slut can sell her story to the Sunday papers and get twenty thousand quid. You've got a better story and you've sold it for peanuts.' She shook her head, genuinely amazed that Lucy had secured such an awful deal.

'So why don't you sell it? If you're so smart, why are you still here?'

'Fuck knows.' Tiffany shrugged. 'All I know is that I'm doing all right here. It's better than borstal or prison.'

'So, how much do you want?' Lucy stood up and walked to the window.

201

'None of it, you silly slut. I don't believe in the future. It's going nowhere.'

'So what do you want?' Lucy leant across, pretending to stare down into the square yard, and caught sight of the corner of the sealed package. She felt silently relieved that her tight bundle of notes was still safely bound on the window frame.

'I want my rewards now.' Tiffany stood up and she stepped towards Lucy. When Lucy stepped back she caught her by the arm. 'I ought to make you suck my pussy dry,' she threatened, squeezing Lucy's arm tightly.

For a second Lucy gazed directly into Tiffany's dark eyes. It was only up close that she could tell the sisters apart: Tiffany had a hardness about her eyes, a look of anger and suspicion that was absent from Chantel's. Lucy was transfixed. She wanted to lean across and kiss Tiffany, to taste her mouth, feel the full pouting lips on hers. But she kept back, afraid that another rejection would push her over the edge into the abyss of black despair.

'I've got a job I want you to do for me,' Tiffany said finally, breaking the tense silence. She released Lucy's arm, but stood her ground, secure in the knowledge that Lucy could not resist.

'What sort of job?'

'I was going to give this one to my dearest sister. But I think I'm going to save her for my best customers.' Tiffany smiled deviously. 'You I don't mind using for the rubbish.'

'Don't fuck me about,' Lucy threatened, but she sounded weak and feeble.

'I owe one of the Prefects a big favour. I'm going to pay her back with you. She'll love you – you look like your backside flares a lovely shade of pink.'

'What if I refuse?'

'Don't be silly. How can you refuse? Mistress Schafer wouldn't want you to refuse me this little favour, would

202

she?' She raised her eyebrows mockingly. 'Tomorrow afternoon, just after three, I want you to be in my room. Don't be late.' She brushed arrogantly past Lucy and slammed the door behind her.

Lucy collapsed on to her bed. It was the worst possible situation. She knew that she was trapped and that there was no way out. Tiffany would have the permanent threat of going to Mistress Schafer or Mistress Shirer.

She began to cry softly. Everything had gone wrong. She was alone and isolated, with no one to turn to. It had been a mistake to talk to Chantel. She had allowed her yearning to blind her to the most obvious of facts. Chantel was an utter slave to Tiffany. It was painful to admit, but Lucy knew that she had now placed herself in the same position. She had no choice now: she too would be a slave to Tiffany. But unlike Chantel, there could be no joy in it for her.

She had been unable to sleep. Even at night there had been no escape from the barrage of fears and worries. She felt drained. She had spent the morning in her computer class: she had had to force herself to pay even the slightest attention. All the time there was the fear of capture in the back of her mind. She dreaded the moment when everything would collapse around her. There was, she was certain, no way that the moment could be avoided. It was an eventuality that was as certain as the rising of the sun or the phases of the moon.

'You're late!' Tiffany scolded when Lucy finally arrived. 'I'm not your slave,' Lucy said bravely. She had deliberately arrived a quarter of an hour late. It was only a gesture, but she wanted to prove a point, if only for the good of her self-respect.

'I forgive you,' Tiffany told her indulgently. 'Sit over there and let Chantel get you ready.'

Chantel was waiting by a chair that had been set in front of the chest of drawers. In her hand she held a flat hairbrush and she had two hairbands over her wrist. Lucy sat down in the chair and looked at Chantel's reflection in the mirror.

'You have to look your best,' Tiffany explained. She sounded happy and excited, secure in the hold she had over Lucy.

Chantel began to brush Lucy's long golden hair, carefully pulling the brush through the flowing golden locks. She smiled sweetly into the mirror.

'Why did you tell her?' Lucy asked quietly. There was no trace of anger or bitterness to her question. She had progressed beyond that stage; she could see the world through Chantel's eyes, and that robbed her of anger and bitterness. It left only sorrow and resignation.

'I had to tell her,' Chantel replied simply.

'But I only wanted to be your friend.'

'No,' Chantel shook her head, 'you wanted to be my sister.'

'Do you know what I have to do now?'

'I'm sorry.' Chantel smiled weakly. 'Tiffany doesn't tell me these things.'

Lucy closed her eyes. The gentle pull of the brush through her hair, the soft touch of Chantel's fingers and the sun falling on her face made her feel dreamy and relaxed. The dread at what was to come was displaced by a melancholy consideration of what might have been. Chantel, with the sun falling like a golden glow on her softly dark skin, her long frizzy tresses falling over her shoulders, looked more beautiful and desirable than ever. Lucy forgave the betrayal. It was Chantel's nature to be innocent and naive, and perhaps innocence is the greatest betrayer of all.

'You've got one thing to remember,' Tiffany interrupted Lucy's contemplative daydream. 'Always call her Mummy. Just remember that and everything will be fine.'

'Call who Mummy?' Lucy opened her eyes and found that her hair had been parted down the centre, and that Chantel was carefully plaiting it into two long ponytails.

'It's a Prefect, I owe her one very big favour. She's a bit sick, this one.' Tiffany snorted derisively. 'She likes to play games, and being Mummy is her favourite game of all.'

'I don't like the sound of this.' Lucy looked around sharply, but Chantel gently turned her back to face the mirror again.

'I did think that Chantel would do this one, or maybe I would have had to do it myself. But when I told her about you she almost wet herself with joy.'

'What did you tell her about me?' Lucy was allowed to stand up and look at herself in the mirror. Chantel had done a good job with the hair, and the long blonde ponytails were finished with pretty pink bows.

'I told her how young looking you are, how sweet and innocent,' Tiffany laughed. 'I told her you were a sweet virgin. Untouched by the filth and depravity of this place.'

'Now this,' Chantel said. She turned Lucy's shirt collar up and threaded a thin striped tie around it. Very slowly, and with an air of subdued concentration, she proceeded to knot the tie, pulling it this way and that.

'What was the favour? What am I worth?'

'The bitch caught me stealing again. I like to keep my hand in, you see.' Tiffany stood by the window, partially obscuring the sun. 'This time I didn't have anyone else to take the blame. Last time I got Jenny to take the blame – do you remember her?'

'You fucking bitch!' Lucy could still vividly see Jenny being beaten by Mistress Shirer, beaten until she pissed herself all over the floor.

'That's right,' Tiffany said. 'Jenny was your roomie, your little lover girl. She was good, wasn't she? Well, poor little Jenny owed me some money, and I made her hide a few things for me in return. Poor cow got caught.'

'You don't belong here,' Lucy hissed angrily.

'Don't give me that "I'm a reformed character" rubbish. I belong here for the same reason you belong here. We're thieves and cheats and no-good rubbish from the city.'

There was a strained silence, Lucy and Tiffany looking daggers at each other. Chantel broke the spell, by gently pressing Lucy back into the chair.

'What are you doing?' Lucy wanted to know. Her shoes were pulled off by Chantel, who had a white pair of socks in her hands.

'You must look nice for Mummy,' Tiffany said mockingly.

At last Lucy was ready. She looked at herself with an expression of utter disdain. She felt ridiculous, a grown woman dressed like an innocent young school girl. There was something odious about the whole thing. Her Institute uniform had been transformed, by the simple addition of a school tie and a pair of white ankle socks, into a school uniform. The ponytails made her look like a young girl barely into her teens.

'You look lovely,' Chantel smiled. She leaned across and kissed Lucy gently on the cheek, a soft sisterly peck of the lips.

'Mummy's going to love you.' Tiffany stood back and admired Chantel's creation. The transformation looked complete: only the hard look in Lucy's dark brown eyes seemed incongruous.

'What do I have to do?' Lucy whispered. She and Tiffany stood outside one of the anonymous blue doors on one of the landings. Lucy had felt embarrassed walking along the corridors dressed as she was. She dreaded capture and punishment by the Prefects or the staff, and sarcasm and ridicule from everyone else.

'I don't know,' Tiffany admitted. 'All I know is that you have to call her Mummy. Just that. So play the game, it can't be that bad.'

'Well, if it's not that bad why don't you do it?'

'Don't be stupid.' Tiffany looked affronted by the suggestion. 'It wouldn't be blackmail if I did the dirty work, would it?' She knocked on the door. 'See you later; be a good girl now.'

Lucy watched her disappear down the stairs. She was alone, her heart beating a rhythm of fear.

'Home from school, darling?' a jaunty voice asked.

Lucy stepped nervously into the room. 'Yes, Mummy,' she said, almost in a whisper. The room was a little larger than her own but the elements were familiar. Two beds, a chest of drawers, a desk, a chair. The desk had been covered with a checked tablecloth, and a bowl of fruit had been arranged in its centre. There were a number of photographs of family in traditional square frames arranged on the chest of drawers.

'I'm just making the tea,' the Prefect told her. She looked much older than the other Prefects. She had shoulder-length brown hair that was swept back and held in place by a red headband. She wore glasses with a thick brown frame, an effect that seemed to add a dozen years to her real age.

'Yes, Mummy,' Lucy repeated. She was at a loss. She stood by the door nervously, fidgeting.

'Come on in dear, come and tell Mummy about school.' Mummy took Lucy by the hand and led her to one of the beds. Her voice was clear and cool, as prim and precise as any of the Mistresses'.

Lucy sat on the edge of the bed and let the Prefect hold her hands. It felt good just to touch someone. The hands were warm and the hold was firm and loving. There was a vague air of threat in the air. The room had been transformed: the Prefect had succeeded in investing her room with a homely atmosphere and it was almost comfortable.

'What did you do today?' Mummy inquired with a friendly open smile. Unlike Lucy, she seemed completely at ease in her self-defined role.

'Writing, and spelling,' Lucy replied, feeling her way into her character.

'Did you do arithmetic as well?'

'Yes, Mummy. We did writing and maths.' Lucy managed a cagey smile.

'I'm sure you did very well.' She almost swooned with pleasure when Lucy called her Mummy. 'And at play-time?'

'We played skipping in the playground,' Lucy improvised.

'Did you play with any boys?' Mummy asked, the faintest hint of suspicion in her voice.

'No, Mummy,' Lucy replied, failing to catch the cloud of doubt in the Prefect's eyes.

'Are you sure? Did you play with those nasty boys?'

'No, no, Mummy.' Confused by the contradictory signals, Lucy couldn't work out what the right answer should be. The Prefect's hold was loving and secure, but the tone of voice was suddenly threatening.

'Liar! You've been a naughty girl, haven't you?'

'Yes,' Lucy agreed, reading from the expression in the other's eyes.

'Did you let the boys touch you?'

'Yes, yes, Mummy.'

'Where did they touch you? Here?' Mummy palmed Lucy's breasts with one hand while with the other she held her hands tightly.

'Yes, Mummy. I wanted to be a good girl but they touched me.'

'And here?' The Prefect put her hand under Lucy's skirt and stroked her hand up and down the thighs. Lucy nodded. 'You bad girl! Did you touch them?'

'No, Mummy, I promise,' Lucy said vehemently. She was beginning to find Mummy's touch, the stroking of her thighs, arousing.

'Liar! You've been a very bad girl.' There was a convincing look of disgust on her face. 'Did you touch their things?'

'No, Mummy, I didn't. Please believe me,' Lucy pleaded.

'I don't believe you. You're a disgusting bad girl, a dirty girl.' Then, almost on the verge of tears, the Prefect said, 'You've broken your mother's heart.'

'I'm sorry, Mummy,' Lucy repeated miserably.

The Prefect rose. She let go of Lucy's hand and went across the room to the chest of drawers. Lucy watched her go, feeling a little sick. The game had become very weird: Lucy felt that it was now out of control. There was a strange logic to it, and this logic was driving it forward inexorably to its conclusion.

'After all I've told you,' Mummy continued disappointedly, 'you've allowed yourself to be used by those dirty boys. Did they press their hard things on you?'

'No, Mummy, no, no.'

The Prefect turned back. She held a wooden spoon in her hand. 'Don't lie to your mother. Don't deny it. Did you enjoy it? Did you like to touch them?'

'Please, Mummy, I was good, honestly, Mummy,' Lucy said, retreating back on to the bed, crawling slowly into the corner as the Prefect approached.

'Come here, you filthy child,' the Prefect said sternly.

Reluctantly Lucy drew closer to the Prefect and allowed herself to be turned over on to her stomach. Her skirt was pulled up and her cotton briefs were pulled down to her knees. She looked up at the Prefect, her eyes wide with fear and pleading. 'Please, Mummy, I'll be a good girl. I'll do everything you tell me, please.'

'You've broken my heart, you unclean girl.' She

shook her head sadly. She hated to do it, but she knew that cruelty and kindness were one and the same thing.

The first blow from the wooden spoon sounded a sharp little smack around the room. Lucy yelped, the pain a tight ball of heat on her backside. She felt with her hand, and could feel the flesh raised in bas relief on her soft white buttock. She remained flat on her stomach, driving herself into the unyielding bed. The blows that followed were concentrated on the centre of her buttocks, discreet individual imprints of punishment.

The Prefect pulled her up and made her stand with her skirt pulled up and her briefs around her ankles. The blows continued, this time aimed at the tops of her thighs.

'You bad, bad girl,' Mummy muttered, wielding the spoon with determination. She held Lucy with one hand and used the spoon with the other. Her face was a mixture of sorrow and desire. The sight of Lucy's skin being tanned and of the delicious view of pink buttocks was intensely erotic.

Lucy could not resist the flame as it spread. Her thighs and her backside were burning, the lava flowing down between her thighs and into her sex. She caught her breath with each impact and felt a dagger penetrate her sex. She moaned, overcome with the pain and pleasure and guilt.

The Prefect pushed Lucy back on all fours on to the bed. Her bare backside was blushing scarlet and the buttocks were parted enticingly. The pussy was wet, the pink bud peering through the puffy pussy lips, and the lovely nether anal lips were pouted. There was to be no let-up: the wooden spoon continued to be applied. There could be no mercy.

'Please Mummy, it hurts ...' Lucy moaned. Her ankles were bound by the stretched white knickers, her arse raised higher and higher. There was no doubt any more – her pussy was afire. The sexual potency of the punishment was working its magic.

The punishment stopped. Its job done, the wooden spoon was cast aside. Lucy was turned on to her bottom. She winced but was forced to sit on the edge of the bed.

'Did Mummy hurt her little girl?' Mummy said and sat next to Lucy.

'Yes, Mummy, you hurt me,' Lucy agreed. Her hair had worked loose and the tidy ponytails were now a mess. Her arse and pussy were alive with a smarting sensation, her nipples hard berries poking against the thin white shirt.

'My poor girl, poor child.' She brushed Lucy's hair from her face. She leaned closer and, almost by accident, brushed her lips against Lucy. 'Let Mummy look after you,' she whispered, her breath hot on Lucy's face.

'Yes, Mummy,' Lucy said, transfixed. When the two mouths met they locked savagely. She closed her eyes, and used her tongue to explore the other's mouth. It seemed somehow wrong, to share mouths with someone she called Mummy. But there was also something attractive and alluring about it. Perhaps it was the idea of breaking the taboo, the pulling away from the imposed rules and mores of society, that added the spice to the game.

'Let Mummy teach you, let Mummy look after you,' Mummy whispered. She stood up and undressed slowly. Her breasts were large globes with strong erect nipples. She had a round belly with a dark mound of hair around her pussy. When she was naked she knelt down in front of Lucy and kissed her again.

Lucy sucked anxiously from the Prefect's mouth. It felt so good, as if a thirst had been slaked by the purest sweetest water. All qualms and scruples were dashed against the rocks of pleasure.

'You look lovely, Mummy,' Lucy told her, taking the nipples into her mouth and sucking expertly. She parted her thighs but Mummy refused to touch her there. Lucy ignored the disappointment, concentrating instead on the wonderful taste of breasts in her mouth.

'That's a good girl.' She pulled her nipples out of Lucy's hungry mouth and kissed her again.

'Mummy, Mummy, fuck me,' Lucy pleaded. The intense heat in her cunt was driving her mad with want. She wanted Mummy's mouth or hand, wanted to feel the pleasure of penetration.

'Let Mummy look after you, not those filthy boys,' the Prefect said, getting up. She padded over to the desk. She picked something up, but her back was turned and Lucy could only admire the firm backside. 'I'll teach my little girl,' she continued, returning.

They swapped fervent kisses again. The Prefect knelt by the bed in front of Lucy, who had undone her shirt and was massaging her own breasts impatiently.

'Mummy!' Lucy was shocked. She looked wide-eyed as the Prefect unexpectedly produced a long thick banana. The peel was still green and Lucy could tell that the flesh of the fruit would be hard and firm. Even when it was peeled the banana was longer and thicker than most men. The white flesh was long and straight, curving only at one end where the Prefect held it gingerly.

'Don't be afraid, darling. Mummy wouldn't hurt her little girl.' She kissed Lucy reassuringly. With her hands she parted Lucy's thighs, pulling her up slightly so that Lucy was on her knees

Lucy let out a long low sigh of pleasure as the fruit was pressed fully into her soaking wet sex. She closed her eyes involuntarily. The fruit fitted her tightly, a cool hard presence deep in her sex. She pulled her skirt up and looked down at the whiteness sticking out between her thighs. She shared a smile with the Prefect.

She lay back, parting her thighs as far as she could. Every movement and gesture caused a wave of pleasure to ripple from her pussy.

Very carefully the Prefect began to press the phallic fruit in and out of Lucy's tight wet sex. She began to make the movement more urgent, and brushed Lucy's hair and kissed her on the forehead, a motherly gesture. The more Lucy writhed and moaned, the faster she drove the fruit in and out. The nasty boys couldn't ever give this sort of pleasure, she was sure.

Lucy lifted herself, raising her buttocks higher and her thighs fully apart. The feel of the banana-prick inside her was a cool source of pleasure, and the painful heat on her backside was being doused by the frigging in her cunt. She closed her eyes to block out all sensations but the blissful frigging in her pussy and the smarting of her buttocks.

'Good girl,' the Prefect whispered softly, urgently driving the fruit deep into Lucy's sex. Her eyes shone with pleasure and excitement. There was no doubt of her arousal, the fingers of her other hand busy exploring her own sex.

'Oh God, Mummy, Mummy ...' Lucy writhed deliriously.

Mummy moved on to the bed, squatting between Lucy's thighs. She was herself on the verge of orgasm, but still she used the banana to drive Lucy further into delirium.

Suddenly the mad driving of the hard fruit in and out ceased and was replaced by something different. Lucy opened her eyes for a second to see the Prefect using her mouth to work the fruit whilst finger-fucking herself to climax.

The two seemed to come at once. There was a flash of electricity and a dying sigh. Lucy bucked uncontrollably, froze and then collapsed. For a moment she was at one with the universe. She was nothing, an

213

unimaginable emptiness. There was no body, no soul, only a peak of bliss.

Lucy began to cry, seized by a convulsive sobbing. The tears streamed down her face and on to her chest and the little rivulets of salty water left a glistening trail down to her pink puckered nipples.

'Don't cry, darling. Mummy's here,' the Prefect smiled, overcome by the unexpected display of emotion. She felt moved and excited, aroused by the childish tears.

Lucy tried to control the tears but couldn't. All the complications and the disappointments she'd experienced welled up in her. She felt lonely and cold. The sharing of bodies, the sweetest sharing of climax, only emphasised the barrenness of her emotional life. She had nothing.

The Prefect stroked Lucy's thigh reassuringly. She got down and began to gently kiss her there. She moved her mouth over Lucy's engorged sex. The banana was smeared with a liberal dose of cunt cream, and with a sense of divine delight she began to flick her tongue around the pussy lips and over the tiny piece of the banana still sticking out of the tightly packed sex.

Lucy wiped away her tears. She sat up on one elbow and watched the Prefect sucking the banana into her mouth. She realised that the Prefect was eating the fruit directly from the sex. The feeling of the mouth clamped tightly over her sex, and the drawing of the tightness from within sent Lucy into another paroxysm of pleasure. She could feel herself building up to another orgasm. The experience of being fucked by a woman she called Mummy had forced all the emotions to the surface and with it a force of catharsis. Lucy cried out with the elation of her second orgasm.

Ten

Lucy returned to her room to find Tiffany waiting, eager for the intimate details

'The favour's done, it's over now. I don't owe you anything,' Lucy told her confidently.

'Don't be so bloody stupid,' Tiffany said, irritated. 'The favour's never done. As long as we're both here you do as I say.'

'No. Being punished can't be worse than having to do as you say.'

'You don't mean that . . .' Tiffany looked shocked.

'I've got another job for you to do.'

'I've told you, no more.'

'I want you to get some things for me. 1 know that one of the Prefect's got a bottle of scotch hidden in her room. I want it.'

'Don't you understand?' Lucy cried emphatically. 'It's over. Go away.'

Tiffany stood up angrily, an air of threatening menace about her. She stepped towards Lucy, but stopped when she saw that Lucy had no fear in her eyes. 'You'll regret this. You'll be sorry you were ever born,' she warned, then stormed out of the room, slamming the door behind her dramatically.

That night Lucy slept a peaceful, dreamless sleep. She accepted that she would be caught, that she would suffer pain and punishment. But there was no dishonour in that; there was only dishonour in submitting to Tiffany's unscrupulous domination.

The next morning she was alone in her room when the Prefect came. The Prefect had orders only to escort her to the office, and from the placid look in her eye it was obvious that she knew nothing else. Lucy followed obediently, feeling free at last of the dread that had haunted her. A weight had been lifted from her shoulders.

'Come in, Lucy,' Mistress Schafer smiled. She was seated behind her desk, confident and powerful. Mistress Shirer was seated to her right and on her left was Mistress Diana.

Lucy approached the desk slowly. She had expected anger and threats, but the three Mistresses regarded her with a cool and detached gaze. She stopped in front of the desk, head held high but eyes averted respectfully.

'Is it true?' Mistress Schafer asked simply, leaning back in her seat.

'Yes, Mistress,' Lucy replied without hesitation. She pressed her chest out and her stomach in. It was defiance without challenge.

'But you were doing so well,' Mistress Diana said sadly.

'You don't like it here?' Mistress Shirer asked.

'I agreed to the deal with Anne Young before I even got here,' Lucy explained.

'That doesn't answer my question,' Mistress Shirer pointed out reasonably.

'I do like it here, sort of,' Lucy decided after a moment of thought.

'Why the hesitation? There are some things that you don't like?'

'I'm not sure this place works. I'm not even sure that what you're doing is right. I'm sorry, Mistress, but I'm not even sure that what you're doing is best for us.' Lucy felt a little nervous of talking so openly to the Mistresses. But she had to tell them, had to express

216

herself. She knew she wouldn't be able to stand the pain of punishment if she remained silent.

'Interesting,' Mistress Schafer mused. 'It seems to have worked for you. You're not the same person I met a few weeks ago. Would you agree?'

'Yes, Mistress,' Lucy agreed. All three women smiled. 'But it hasn't worked for everybody. It hasn't worked for Tiffany and Chantel, has it?'

'You're right. But I would say that they are part of a very small minority. But their stay here is to be extended; we have just had agreement from the court. They have a full year left, and this time we'll separate them. That was our mistake.' Mistress Schafer looked to the others for agreement.

'What else?' Mistress Diana asked.

'I'm not sure that all this punishment is right. You're turning us all into perverts. You know that we get to derive pleasure from the spankings and canings,' Lucy said, flushing slightly.

'We know. That's all part of the regime here,' Mistress Schafer said. 'You all have a masochistic side to your personalities. We bring that out, and release you from your self-repression. Some of you also have very strong sado-masochistic urges and we can bring these out by allowing some of you to become Prefects. In every case we liberate you from the self-repression that so affected you before.'

Mistress Shirer took up the explanation. 'In allowing you to come to terms with your own secret desires you become self-aware. You lose all that misdirected anger and hate. You used to steal and fight because you wanted to be caught and punished. But with your new selfknowledge you can enter a mutually rewarding relationship where you can express yourself fully.'

'That's the theory.' Mistress Diana smiled. 'Now tell us – from your own experience, has it worked?'

Yes, Mistress,' Lucy agreed. She could find no fault

217

with the explanation; it accorded completely with her own experience.

'Do you want to see the Institute destroyed?' Mistress Schafer asked coolly.

'No.' Lucy shook her head. 'But why the secrecy, Mistress? If this place works, why pretend that it doesn't exist?'

'There is no if,' Mistress Diana said vehemently. 'Have you ever seen a correctional institute with no guards, no wire fences, no dogs? We've had no suicides or stabbings here. We've never had anyone abscond. This place does work, and it's unique.'

'There needs to be secrecy,' Mistress Shirer explained patiently, 'because sexual medicine is still so misunderstood by the public. You've studied Freud by now; think of the controversy that surrounded his teachings. Imagine the uproar that this place would cause if the story got out. It would mean the end of the Institute and the end of us.'

'Do you intend to sell the story to Anne Young?' Mistress Schafer asked, cutting the conversation dead. There was silence.

'I don't know,' Lucy admitted, It would have been easier to deny it, but the denial would have been plainly false. Everything was stripped down to basics. There was no room for falsehoods any more.

'You understand that we can't let you go back to your room. We can't let you go.' There was a hint of sadness in Mistress Schafer's voice. Lucy felt almost sorry for her. 'We've discussed this and have decided to accelerate your programme. You'll be moving out of the Institute for a while,' Mistress Shirer told her.

'You'll be staying with me,' Mistress. Diana smiled.

'And if I refuse?' Lucy asked, though both she and the Mistresses knew that refusal was out of the question.

'Then there is nothing for us to do,' Mistress Schafer admitted, 'but to hand you back over to the court.'

* * *

The summer had started to fade imperceptibly into autumn. The sky was streaked with grey and there was a slight nip in the air. Lucy found the sullen grey streets of London alien and confusing after the relative solitude of the Institute. She sat silently by Mistress Diana in the car, staring at the streets that she had known so well with a mixture of boredom and distaste.

After the nerveracking tension, after all the fear and trepidation, the showdown had been remarkably subdued and civilised. There had been none of the anger and rage that she had expected. She finally felt able to relax a little, free at last of the fear of capture or betrayal.

She kept glancing at Mistress Diana, trying to gauge what was to come. The Mistresses had talked of special treatment and of an accelerated programme, but it meant nothing to Lucy. She was a little sorry to have to leave the intense atmosphere of the Institute. She had grown accustomed to the strange regime; she had felt secure there, certain of her place in the world and free to discover the secrets locked away in the depths of her soul. All that she lacked was a partner to share in the voyage of discovery, a shoulder to lean on in moments of crisis.

Mistress Diana lived in a small apartment in a quiet block close to the centre of the city. The building was starting to show its age, but the faded grandeur and slightly shabby exterior all added to a general feeling of comfort.

'Strip off, everything. Now!' Mistress Diana barked as soon as she and Lucy entered the flat.

'Yes, Mistress,' Lucy said, dismayed by the sudden order. She removed her clothes in an instant and stood naked in the hallway. It was cool and she shivered slightly, wrapping her arms about her to keep out the cold.

'Things have changed. You are now my sole

responsibility, nothing at all to do with the Institute. From now on you are my personal servant, is that understood?' Mistress Diana faced Lucy squarely. There was a steely coldness in her bright blue eyes, matched by the firm clear voice.

'Yes, Mistress,' Lucy whispered. She lowered her gaze, instinctively.

'On your knees, bitch,' Mistress Diana hissed. 'You'll be severely punished for all transgressions. You will serve me without question. You have no other function in life. No other function at all.'

'Yes, Mistress,' Lucy repeated. She looked up at her Mistress from all fours, a look of fear and perplexity in her eyes. Again all her expectations had been confounded. She realised that she was at the complete mercy of the diminutive but cruel and powerful Mistress. The thought filled her with dread and a sick feeling of excitement.

'Follow!' Mistress Diana turned on her heel and strode into the first room off the hallway. Lucy followed, crawling on her hands and knees, her breasts swinging jerkily, the nipples puckering from the cold.

The room was much smaller than the one at the Institute. There was a single bed in one corner and beside it a small white bedside cabinet. The only window was high above the cabinet and Lucy could see that the sun had set and the first drops of rain had begun to fall. The only other furniture in the room was a large teak wardrobe by the door and a single wooden chair.

'This is where you stay.'

'Thank you, Mistress.' Lucy crawled around into the room and regarded it without emotion. Already she sensed that her personal comfort and convenience were of no value. There were more important things to worry about.

'Open the top drawer, put the things on,' Diana ordered curtly. She crossed her arms impatiently and watched Lucy crawl across the room. She noted that the firm round buttocks were flawlessly white, and it was obvious that it had been some time since a cane or hand had been applied there.

Lucy opened the drawer and found several leather straps and a number of cross-linked chains. She picked them out gingerly and tried to work out what they were. There were four thick leather cuffs with steel studs and heavy straps and buckles. She sat back on her bottom and put one on each ankle, pulling the strap tight so that the cuff was secured tightly and without play. She glanced up at Mistress Diana, hoping to see a sign of approval, but the Mistress glared at her coldly. She bound the other two straps around her wrists, quickly pulling the buckles tight and testing to see that the cuff wouldn't ride up or down. When she finished she sat up on her knees expectantly, quietly pleased with herself that she had managed to work out what to do without prompting.

Diana held back her smile. She unclipped her skirt from behind and let it fall to the floor then pulled her tight blouse over her head. She stood naked except for her silky black stockings, shiny PVC suspender belt and black, patent leather high heels. Her sex was barely covered by a pair of black wet-look panties, and her breasts, tipped with beautiful red nipples, were fully displayed. 'On the bed,' she said motioning with her hand.

Lucy hesitated for a moment, stunned by the angelic beauty of her Mistress. She positively ached with an impulsive and instinctive desire. She felt a tightness in her belly and couldn't tell if it was the fear or the lust or both.

'On the bed!' Diana snapped angrily. She stepped forward and slapped Lucy firmly on the side of the thigh, leaving a scarlet handprint impressed on the soft white flesh.

Lucy cried out with pain and surprise. She fell clumsily on to the bed and looked up open-mouthed at Diana.

Diana picked up the chains from the floor and stepped over to the bed. She passed one end of the largest chain through a gap in the bed's headboard and grabbed one of Lucy's wrists. Very quickly she passed the chain through a ring in the leather cuff and did the same with the other wrist. From the drawer she withdrew a large steel padlock which she used to lock the two ends of the chain together.

Before Lucy had time fully to understand what was happening she found her hands tightly bound to the top of the bed. When the Mistress stepped away she tried to pull free but found that there was no room for manoeuvre. Her hands were pulled high over her head and there was no way she could pull them down again. She yanked at the chain half-heartedly, trying to convince herself that everything was going to be all right and to keep in check the rising feeling of panic.

'The programme begins right now,' Mistress Diana smiled and her adorable face lit up excitedly. Lucy returned the smile, though a shadow of doubt clouded her eyes. 'We wouldn't want to disturb the neighbours, would we?' Diana said quietly. She pulled her panties down, let them fall about her ankles then picked them up.

Lucy couldn't keep her eyes off Diana's body. She stared at the naked sex. The sweetness of the flesh seemed to glisten invitingly between the hairy pussy lips. She opened her mouth and gladly accepted the loving kiss that Diana offered, closed her eyes and swam in the dreamy feel of Diana's sensitive pouting lips. She tried to prolong the kiss when Diana pulled away slowly; she lifted her head up, trying to keep the embrace, wanting to explore her Mistress's mouth for as long as possible. Already she was wet with longing, her heart beating with a steady ache of desire.

Lucy opened her mouth for a second kiss, and closed her eyes again, ready to be swept along on the wave of sensations. But instead of Diana's gentle lips something else pressed against her mouth. She struggled, twisting her face violently back and forth, staring wide-eyed with horror at her Mistress.

Diana had taken her shiny panties and screwed them up into a tight ball and was trying to force the bundle into Lucy's mouth. The struggle was in vain, Lucy was in no position to resist. In seconds her mouth was tightly gagged, the black panties a tight ball in her mouth.

Lucy felt she was going to suffocate. Her mouth was stretched over the warm shiny bundle. She stopped struggling, trying to control her desperate breathing, trying to fight the panic that threatened to overwhelm her. Her mouth was suffused with the cloying taste and smell of her Mistress.

'Now the neighbours won't hear a thing, will they?' Diana laughed. She bent down and kissed Lucy on the forehead, gently brushing the hair from her eyes. She sat on the edge of the bed and with one hand searched the second drawer of the cabinet, while with the other she began to explore Lucy's breasts. She cupped one of the breasts, testing the texture of the flesh, determining the shape and feel of the firm round orb. Already the nipples were hard and erect, but she could not tell whether this was due to the cold or to Lucy's excitement.

After a second or so she found what she was looking for. She pulled out a thick leather belt from the drawer. She stood over Lucy and doubled the belt over, making sure that the full thickness and stiffness of it was apparent. 'This is going to be your faithful friend and teacher,' she said and laughed at the look of abject fear in Lucy's eyes.

Lucy tried to speak, tried to force the gag out of her

mouth. She edged up into the corner of the bed, as far as possible from the evil-looking instrument that Mistress held so lovingly. The cuffs and chains pulled on her hands, stopping her from covering herself.

Diana knelt on the bed. She turned Lucy on to her stomach, slapping her with her hand when she tried to resist. She paused for a second to look at Lucy's soft firm arse-flesh and then the lesson began. She raised her arm high and brought the belt down with all her might. There was a double retort as both halves of the belt made contact, leaving two distinct red weals on the once-perfect flesh. She applied several blows in quick succession, slicing a pattern of thick scarlet lines across the quivering arse-cheeks.

There was no escape. Lucy's cries were muffled effectively by the pantie-gag, and the chains and cuffs bound her into place. She squirmed and wept, bitter tears streaming down her face. Each stroke was a double-edged source of white-hot pain. For a moment she seemed to lose consciousness. A wall of white seemed to hit her with full force. But the blows continued. A percussive rhythm echoed throughout the room, a spiteful dance of chastisement playing on her smarting bum-flesh.

The blows stopped as suddenly as they had begun. Lucy tried to turn over but her arse was too painful. She managed to look round and saw that she was alone in the empty silent room. The beating had stopped but her body was alive with sharp daggers of pain that made her wince. It hurt too much; the pain had withered her. She felt wretched. Her mouth was dry and the gag filled her mouth with pussy taste.

She lost track of time. Her mind was blank; it hurt too much to think. She lay on her stomach in a sort of daze, conscious but unconscious, aware but oblivious to everything. She closed her eyes and drifted into a dreamy state between sleep and wakefulness.

The beating began again, with no warning – the screaming agony returned. She looked at her Mistress through a haze of bitter tears, silently pleading, begging for forgiveness and mercy. But the Mistress continued to apply the belt, beating out stroke after stroke with youthful vigour. She aimed at the buttocks and down over the thighs, spreading the scarlet tan evenly over the silky white, flesh.

The tanning stopped again. Lucy's body seemed to be quivering all over. The fierce heat began to permeate her being. She became aware very slowly that the fire from her arse-cheeks had begun to burn deep into her sex. The desire was still there, the desire with which she had looked at Mistress had not disappeared – it was strong and pure. The lashing only made it stronger. She knew at once that her pussy was oozing golden sex cream. She was hot and wet, aching for fulfilment. She wanted to feel her Mistress in her cunt, wanted her mouth and fingers deep inside her.

She tried to pull her hands down, wanting to frig herself to orgasm. But the bounds were too strong, too tight. She had a raging fire and no means to do anything about it. The more she struggled, the more ardent her desire became, the pull of the chains exciting her more and more. The stinging of her thighs and buttocks was driving her insane with yearning.

When Mistress returned for the third time, Lucy turned over on to her back. She ignored the stinging of her backside and parted her thighs, lifting herself up, offering her sex to her beautiful Mistress. There was an expression of absolute desire on her face.

'Is this what you want?' Diana teased, passing the belt up and down Lucy's thigh, pressing the cold leather up against the humid entrance to her cunt.

Lucy nodded, pathetically eager, urgently seeking relief for the fires stoked in her belly.

'Bitch! Only a Mistress can give you pleasure,' Diana

225

snorted. She climbed on to the bed and sat astride Lucy's face.

Lucy wanted to cry out with frustration. She had Diana's lovely naked backside inches from her face and was unable to do anything. She peered up at the lovely round globes, eyeing hungrily the tight dark arsehole and the glistening folds of flesh at the mouth of the sex. She tried to lift herself up, to press her face against her Mistress's lovely backside, but was held down by the chains and Mistress's glossy black high-heeled shoes.

Diana could feel Lucy struggling and smiled. She parted her arse-cheeks with her hands, and was gratified when the struggling increased. She put the belt down and turned her attention to Lucy's breasts, playing her thumbs and fingers over the erect teats. The struggling reached a fever pitch when she took the nipples in her hands and started to pull hard, forcefully stretching the well-shaped globes. The nipples seemed to glow a bright red as they were stretched and squeezed and abused.

Lucy wanted to scream, to shout, to cry, to explode. Mistress dismounted and wandered off again, leaving her alone and in silence. Her struggles grown to a fever pitch of frenzy. The torment was unbearable, and still her pussy ached and burned. The only thing she wanted in the world at that moment was to find release, to lose herself in that split second of fulfilment.

When dawn broke Mistress returned. She was naked and stood by the window, letting the early morning sun warm her naked breasts. Lucy turned and looked at her, and they both knew that the time had come.

During the long cold night Lucy had found herself. The fear and the anger were gone from her eyes. The frenzied struggling, and the desperation that had driven it, had ceased. In some indescribable way she had come to terms with herself and the world. All the layers of lies and deceit had been stripped away and she was left with the singularity and purity that was her being. Each new experience had taught her something new, and now she had achieved the ultimate state of knowing.

Diana gently worked the damp gag from Lucy's mouth. She held her breath for a second, not entirely certain that she was doing the right thing. She sighed a sigh of relief when she saw that Lucy remained silent, smiling weakly. Leaving the chains and the cuffs in place, she again sat astride Lucy's face.

Lucy lifted her face and with her tongue she pressed at Mistress's tightly puckered arsehole. She planted a kiss there, thankful for the pleasure and the honour that she was being allowed. Slowly, deliberately savouring every moment, she pressed her face into Mistress's backside. She kissed and sucked, exploring every opening, every fold of skin. The contrasting taste of pussy and arsehole, the texture of the arsehole wrapped around her tongue, the heat of the damp pussy-hole – Lucy treasured every sensation.

Diana sat back firmly, pressing herself down on to Lucy's mouth. She was flushed with the pleasure of success; in a single night she had transformed Lucy utterly and completely. Feeling the first signs of impending climax building inside her she fell forward. Keeping herself firmly over Lucy's expert mouth she too began her exploration. She flicked her tongue into Lucy's sopping wet sex and felt the ripple of pleasure reflected back into her cunt by the other's tongue. She knew that when the orgasm came Lucy would be locked into her new self forever.

J.K. cursed his luck. For the first time since he had agreed to try to gain entry into the Institute, Mistress Shirer had not gone into work. It was the opportunity that he had been looking for. He had been working himself up for days, summoning up the courage to commit the most audacious act of his life. In his mind he had acted out all the details, the lies and excuses necessary to get him into and out of the mysterious Institute.

However, on the day that his Mistress had decided not to go in, she had also ordered Jaki to stay at home. He had turned his gaze down, slightly afraid of Mistress, uncertain how to behave when he was J.K. and not Jaki. All night he had wrestled with the idea of standing up to Mistress, of deliberately disobeying an order. The idea was exciting, his backside tingling with the anticipation of a severe spanking, but he knew it could not be done. To deliberately disobey would be to put Jaki's very existence in jeopardy. Not matter how tempting the idea, he could not have a hand in the murder of his other self.

He spoke to Laura on the phone briefly. She was impatient for news and eager to see him, but he lied to her, pretended he had important work to finish, and told her there was no progress with the Institute. The unspoken presence of Anne Young was always in the background, a silent third party to all his conversations with Laura. The pressure was growing by the day, building into an unbearable force that filled every spare moment of the day.

The worries and the doubts were pushed to the back of his mind when he metamorphosed into Jaki. The dull room seemed to be suddenly permeated with a shifting kaleidoscope of colour. Even his body seemed to undergo a change; the masculine hardness of his body seemed to soften, the muscular lines of thigh and bicep imperceptibly became gentle alluring curves. He ran an electric razor over his legs so that the flesh was smooth and silky. He took his stiff cock in one hand and very carefully trimmed the triangle of hair around it.

She knew that a visitor was expected, so she selected her shortest skirt and highest heels. In minutes the transformation was complete. J.K. was nothing but a pile of discarded clothes on the floor and a nagging worry in the back of her mind. She applied a sexy vermilion lipstick to her lips, and a thick black line to her eyes.

'I want you on your best behaviour today; do you understand, girl?' Simone instructed, as soon as Jaki quietly entered the living room.

'Yes, Mistress,' Jaki responded automatically, scanning the room for tasks to perform, noting that her Mistress seemed slightly agitated.

'Something very special is happening at the Institute,' Simone said, speaking to Jaki directly about the place for the first time. 'In two days time there's going to be a kind of ball in honour of some very special guests. I want you to be there. But I must have the highest standards maintained. The absolute highest.'

'Yes, Mistress!' The thought was magical; Jaki squealed delightedly, and could hardly keep still with excitement. 'I'll be very good, Mistress,' she promised, smiling gleefully.

'If you're naughty I'll have you thrashed in front of all the guests,' Simone warned, permitting herself a rueful half smile.

Jaki fell silent. She was dizzy with expectation, imagining the costumes and the lights and the guests. Her natural exhibitionist instincts told her that she would sparkle like a jewel. But in the very back of her mind there was a sense of relief. J.K. realised that he no longer needed an excuse to get into the Institute – heaven had sent him a perfect opportunity. But the thought, and the remnant of her mind that was still J.K., was overwhelmed by Jaki's lightheaded plans.

The door. chimes interrupted Jaki's fanciful daydreams. She skipped down the stairs eagerly, delighting in the sharp clatter of her high heels on the wooden floor. Her short skirt swished about her, bouncing and swinging with every downward step. It was one of her dearest wishes to have a large full-length mirror installed on one of the landings, so that she could admire herself going up and down the stairs, and see herself reflected in the same golden frame as her Mistress.

She opened the door an inch, letting a slice of bright sunlight fall diagonally across the hall. 'Good morning, Mistress,' she said smiling brightly when she saw that it was Mistress Diana. She opened the door fully and stepped back, bowing lightly as she did so.

'Good morning, Jaki. You look lovely today,' Diana said, holding out her hand.

'Thank you, Mistress.' Jaki beamed delightedly. She bent down and kissed Mistress's hand gratefully. The simple compliment filled her with an ecstatic joy that was almost sexual. Her prick was hard already, and twitched and ached with anticipation.

Diana stepped into the hall and it was only then that Jaki saw that she was not alone. Behind Diana, hidden by the doorway, was another young woman. Her hair sparkled in the sun, the long golden locks tied in a single long ponytail that reached down almost to the small of her back. She wore a simple black coat that reached down to her knees and made her look rather dowdy. Only the black studded high heels suggested that there was potentially something more.

Silently, avoiding Jaki's eyes completely, the young woman stepped into the house. Jaki closed the door at a signal from Diana and stepped back hesitantly.

'Take her coat,' Diana ordered. The young woman undid the top button of the coat and turned her back to Jaki, who pulled the coat off.

Jaki looked on open-mouthed, a tinge of jealousy in her heart. The young woman was almost naked underneath the coat. She was dressed simply in a one-piece black latex blousette. The shiny material clung sensuously to her curves, covering her from the waist up to the neck in a glossy second skin. The garment left her

230

arms totally uncovered, but was finished with a tight collar that extended high up to the neck. The bottom of the garment was a single leather strap with a large buckle directly over the crotch. Without pausing, the girl fell to her hands and knees. The strap fitted tightly between her bottom-cheeks, a thick black line separating the two curved globes of buttock flesh.

Diana started up the stairs, casually certain that the other two would follow respectfully. Jaki hesitated. She wanted to be the one directly behind the Mistress, but she also wanted to study this new creature at closer quarters. The young woman had no such hesitations she crawled along behind her Mistress, oblivious to Jaki's presence.

Jaki followed on, eyeing the gorgeous view of the tethered arse as the girl negotiated each step. The buttocks were firm and well shaped, and clenched and relaxed as the girl moved, suggesting that the lithe young body was fit and agile. Jaki even thought that she could detect faint red lines etched across the smoothness of the skin, the dying marks of a ferocious punishment.

'Lucy, greet your Mistress,' Diana ordered after she and Simone had shared an affectionate and close embrace.

Jaki was stunned when Lucy bent down and began to smother Mistress's boots with urgent loving kisses, gliding her unpainted lips over the shiny patent leather. The display filled her with an angry jealousy. She hated the idea that anyone else should display such servile behaviour towards her Mistress. It had never occurred to her before, but she realised then that the bonds of possession could stretch both ways. She longed to be her Mistress's possession, but now she felt that in some way she too possessed her Mistress.

'Enough, girl!' Mistress Shirer snapped after a second, satisfied that Lucy had displayed complete subservience.

Jaki smiled, her anger subsiding with the admonishment. She looked at Lucy, who had sat back on her and saw that the twin points of her breasts were erect against the shiny latex material. The fact that she had been aroused by her exhibition of servility convinced Jaki that the young woman was a true slave. They shared a common vocation, a shared conviction that their lives were of secondary importance beside that of a Mistress. The last vestiges of envy and jealousy were swept away by a sense of solidarity in their self-imposed humiliation.

'Will she be ready for the ball?' Simone asked, taking a seat in one of the armchairs. She looked relaxed, the agitation that had soured her looks earlier seeming to have disappeared. Lucy's conversion seemed genuine enough; the calm and measured look in her eyes and the detached way she held herself testified to her transformation.

Diana also took a seat, pointing to a spot at her feet for Lucy. 'Coffee,' she told Jaki, and then turned back to Simone. 'She's ready now. The panic's over, completely. Fiona made a mistake in talking to her friends at the Ministry; we could have handled it ourselves.'

'Well, in the end it's probably done us a favour.' Simone smiled, showing her fine white teeth. 'We can show them Lucy, an example of what our work can do, even to the most recalcitrant and difficult young women.'

Jaki wanted to stay and listen. It was the first time she had really heard the two Mistresses so openly discussing their work. She was fascinated by it and wanted to learn more, to prise open the secrets of the Institute for herself. But reluctantly she retreated. She had the coffee to make and the thought of disappointing a Mistress was unbearable.

Whilst making the coffee she was seized by a violent and unexpected revelation. Her initial jealous reaction had blinded her to the obvious. The servile young woman in the other room was the Lucy that J.K. had been desperately trying to make contact with. The surprise almost made her spill the coffee. She flopped back into a chair, gasping for breath.

Her two selves were suddenly in conflict. The careful delineation between J.K. and Jaki was blurred by the sudden conflict of interest. In one fell swoop she had the chance to solve all of his problems. But to do so would be to endanger her own position, and also that of the two Mistresses. The thoughts swirled in her mind, raging back and forth with a will of their own.

'I think the time is right,' Mistress Shirer was saying when Jaki returned with the coffees on a tray, 'for us to think about expansion. We've succeeded in our initial studies – we've proved our point beyond all reasonable doubt.'

'I agree, we all do.' Diana paused to take her coffee. 'But we can't open a second unit until we have a sufficiently powerful political lobby.'

'We have enough of that,' Simone asserted, 'but we're not politicians, we're scientists.'

'We say we're scientists,' Diana laughed nervously, 'but that's not how most people would see us.'

Jaki knelt down by the door, her attention wandering between the Mistress's conversation and Lucy. She was transfixed by the sight – it was the first time she had ever set eyes on another slave. Indeed she hadn't been really sure that other slaves even existed, and had thought that perhaps she was unique. It was like looking into a mirror and seeing a distorted reflection. Lucy had the same rapt look of attention in her eyes, alert always to the wishes of her Mistress. But Jaki was aware also that Lucy had large firm breasts and that the latex outfit accentuated her feminine charms. In that respect at least the two servants were different.

'We've got to go now,' Diana apologised. 'I hope you're convinced that Lucy is fully transformed now.'

'I'll let Fiona have the good news immediately.'
Simone smiled. She stood up and kissed Diana on the
cheek, holding her in her arms tenderly.

Jaki crawled forward quickly, absently aware that her
skirt had pulled high and that her thin nylon panties
had stretched up between her arse cheeks. She skimmed
along the floor and stopped, by Lucy. For a moment the
two slaves eyed each other in silence, Lucy staring at
Jaki's stockinged thighs and the smooth flesh that
peeped over the thick black stocking band.

Nervously Jaki plunged forward and pressed her
mouth over Lucy's slightly parted lips. There was an
instant of hesitation as Lucy pulled back, but then the
fascination beat down the rising sense of disgust. She
accepted the kiss, opened her mouth and sucked at
Jaki's breath. They shared their tongues, exploring the
soft recesses of the mouth.

'You filthy bitch!' Mistress Shirer cried angrily. She
grabbed Jaki tightly by the hair and pushed her away
violently.

'Will she be ready?' Diana demanded, unnerved by
the unexpected behaviour. She looked down at Lucy
who had a dazed expression on her face, eyes wide with
fright and confusion.

'She'll suffer for that unforgivable display,' Simone
promised, glaring at Jaki cowering in the corner. 'But
she'll be ready, I guarantee it.'

Lucy was on edge all day. When night fell, and she was
allowed back into her room, she felt she could breathe
again. She curled up into a tight foetal ball on her bed
and spat the pellet from her mouth. Very carefully she
unwound the sellotape and straightened the damp piece
of paper that Jaki had passed into her mouth. She read
the message and then held her face in her hands. It said
Conrad – have the story ready at the party.

234

Eleven

Jaki listened keenly to the steady rhythm of her high heels on the cold marble floor. The sharp crack that followed every step echoed down along the, corridor, a proclamation of her elegant and feminine stride. The rhythm of her steps was in perfect harmony with the equally loud clickclack of Mistress Shirer, who led her along the long dark corridor.

The corridor was cool and dark, and Jaki was disappointed to find that the Institute seemed to be deserted. She strode along, her head held high and her long flowing locks bouncing lightly as she strode on gracefully. She felt herself to be glamorous and attractive, an object of purest love and desire. She knew that she paled into insignificance beside the exquisite but austere Mistress Shirer, but then she knew that no servant could hope to match the blazing glory of a Mistress.

She felt a cool breeze gently touch her body, and shivered with pleasure. She wore a pair of bright red ankle boots, the pointed heel banging loudly on the floor a symphony to her ears. The ankle boots were laced tightly with red leather straps, and the studded heels were decorated with small silver locks so that Mistress Shirer could easily bind her when required.

Her near nakedness was delectable. She wore black net stockings with a thick black seam that ran straight up from the heel to the stocking tops, a perfect line to highlight the perfect curves of calves and thighs. Shiny latex suspenders held the stockings in place and these were matched by shiny latex panties, which were cut high at the front and rear, so that at the back the fullness of the buttocks was embellished by a dark strip of latex pulled snugly into the arse-crease, dividing the arsecheeks fully. At the front the high cut of the garment fully covered her prick, even when it was stiff and aching with a forceful erection. She was almost naked above the waist apart from a number of bands of leather that were stretched across her bare chest and across the shoulders and upper arms.

Most of all Jaki felt desirable because Mistress Shirer had fitted her with a collar and chain. The thick leather collar was adorned with silver studs and fitted tightly around the neck. As Mistress Shirer walked she tugged occasionally at the long silver chain clipped into the collar. Jaki liked to fall behind a little, to feel the sharp pull of the chain, to feel that she was truly Mistress Shirer's servant.

They entered the boardroom through a large oak door that creaked when it was opened. Jaki was naturally curious and gazed around excitedly. There was a low buzz of conversation in the room, which had a warm and relaxed atmosphere heightened by the flickering light of a coal fire at one end. The walls were lined with books and a number of separately lit paintings. There were about twenty or so people in the room, standing around chatting in small groups. They were being served by about five or six girls, all identically dressed in simple uniforms of blue skirt and white shirt. Jaki guessed that they were from the Institute; she saw that they had the stillness and humility that only a true servant can attain.

Mistress Shirer jerked at the chain and Jaki followed, obediently averting her gaze and concentrating her attention on Mistress, trying to block out the feeling of excitement welling up inside her. She had never been to the Institute before, and she was filled with curiosity, wanting to find out and see everything.

'Heel,' Mistress Shirer snapped, and Jaki obeyed, dropping immediately to her hands and knees. The chain was pulled tight as Mistress Shirer wound her way through the room, smiling to the assembled staff and guests. Jaki followed close at heel, shuffling along submissively, eyes fixed firmly on her Mistress's kneelength boots, the sharp steel-tipped heels glinting. The shiny figure-hugging leather seemed to be moulded to Mistress Shirer's calves so that the boots seemed to be a glossy extension of her exquisite ebony body.

Mistress Shirer stopped and Jaki halted too. She sat back on her heels, letting her arms drop to her side and keeping her head bent down a little. She sat as still as she could, wanting to show everyone in the room how completely servile she was, wanting above all to show just how well she had been trained by her Mistress.

'Are you sure this is such a good idea?' Mistress Shirer asked quietly, leaning across to exchange a greeting with an older woman, dressed in a long dark skirt slit down the front to reveal a pair of black thigh-length boots, the dull leather clinging tightly to her shapely thighs.

'Don't worry,' the woman replied coolly. 'Dr Niven reports directly to the Minister. I'm certain that he'll be interested.'

'I'm unconvinced,' Mistress Shirer admitted. Jaki realised that the other woman must be Mistress Schafer.

'I'd like to introduce Simone Shirer,' Mistress Schafer said as a tall middle-aged man approached them.

'Ah, I've heard much about your sterling work.' Dr Niven smiled, tightly clasping Simone's outstretched hand.

Jaki peered up, trying to sneak a look at the

Mistresses and the Master around her. Dr Niven was tall and straight, and looked to be in his late forties, with a smooth cleanshaven face. His voice was clipped and precise, its measured tone in keeping with the tidy and conservative appearance.

'I read your paper on "The sexuality of purity and danger",' Mistress Shirer told him. 'I found the conclusions very stimulating. Quite a difference from the usual wishy-washy opinions on the subject.'

'Thank you,' Dr Niven replied, his eyes studying Simone closely, taking in a cool measure of the woman.

'If you'll excuse me, Dr Niven,' Fiona said hurriedly, 'I must see to some of the other arrangements.'

Dr Niven and Simone watched Fiona go, her long skirt parting fully to reveal her long leather-clad legs. The tops of her thighs were bare, the soft skin made paler by the blackness of the leather and the skirt.

'It's an honour to work with her,' Simone acknowledged. 'She's done so much. The success of the Institute is largely down to her.'

'I think you're being most modest,' Dr Niven responded. 'We are all aware that your own contribution to this project has been immeasurable.'

'Thank you,' Simone replied, a little uneasy with the praise.

'A private indulgence?' Dr Niven asked, nodding down towards Jaki.

'A little bit of homework,' Simone said. There was a nervous edge to her laugh.

'Most interesting,' Dr Niven reflected, dispelling the unease. 'Do you find that he responds differently than the girls?'

'Definitely. Jaki is not my first male slave, but he is entirely typical. The response is much stronger than that from the girls, and the results are more rapid.'

'Yes, I accept that the response may be stronger and quicker,' Dr Niven observed sharply. 'But is it different?'

'Well,' Mistress Shirer hesitated, 'yes. There is a very strong element of fetishism that is almost entirely absent from most of the young women.'

'That's very interesting,' Dr Niven mused. 'We are currently drawing up a theoretical framework for a second Institute, for young men only. Perhaps you ought to have input in that process. Would you mind your name being put forward?'

'No, I'd be glad to help,' Simone smiled. She couldn't help but be flattered by the invitation. 'How far has the work progressed?'

'It's still only at an early stage,' Dr Niven looked around the room. 'John,' he called to a colleague deep in conversation with another of the Mistresses, 'have you got a minute?'

John Hassleby excused himself and joined Simone and Dr Niven. He was a younger man, thin and pale, with a nervous academic air about him, underscored by the anxious way he peered out through wire-framed spectacles. Dr Niven introduced him to Simone, and the two exchanged polite greetings.

'I have just suggested that Miss Shirer have some input into your working party,' Dr Niven explained. 'I think her experience in this area might prove useful at this early stage.'

'Fine, fine,' Hassleby nodded. 'I think that a similar Institute for young men presents us with a new set of parameters to deal with. I tend to see it as a separate project, not a continuation.'

'Yes,' Dr Niven said slowly, sounding a little unsure. 'but that doesn't mean we forget all that we've learnt here. I think that the initial results produced by Fiona Schafer and her team have a significance beyond this one establishment.'

'Are there plans for other similar establishments?' Mistress Shirer asked, concerned that the pioneering work of the Institute was not going to be applied further.

'The Minister has yet to make a decision,' Dr Niven said, the guarded tone suggesting that the subject was closed for further discussion.

The door opened and they all looked round to see Mistress Diana glide into the room, a near-naked girl following quietly behind.

'The servant girl with the Mistress is an interesting case,' Mistress Shirer pointed out. 'She came here with an unenviable record, a reputation for stubborn resistance and petty crime. Yet by the end of the first few days she had changed completely, a total and absolute change.'

Jaki stared across the room at Lucy who seemed to be naked apart from a leather harness that crisscrossed her body and was decorated with silver chains and buckles. Thick leather straps covered her front and rear, the thong biting deep into her backside. Her breasts were bound by more leather straps and chains that somehow cupped the flesh yet constrained it fully. Thin bands of black leather were also wound tightly down the thighs and from the shoulders down to the hands.

Diana spotted Simone and came towards her, smiling affectionately. Lucy, who was seemingly totally ignored, followed silently. Her eyes shone sedately and were fixed firmly on her Mistress.

'Dr Niven, may I introduce Diana French,' Simone turned to Hassleby, 'and John Hassleby, also from the Inspectorate.'

'Hello,' Diana smiled. 'I hope that what you've seen so far meets your approval.' Lucy. dropped down to her knees, her head bowed in an expression of acquiescence.

Dr Niven laughed. 'Let me play devil's advocate for a moment,' he said. 'Look around you; what do you see?'

'A practical experiment in psychosexual relations?' Hassleby offered tentatively.

'Forget that,' Dr Niven urged. 'What do you see?'

'A number of badly adjusted young women receiving unorthodox treatment,' Simone suggested uncertainly.

'A bunch of perverts!' Dr Niven declared firmly, and then laughed loudly.

'A bunch of state-sponsored perverts,' Simone corrected, also laughing.

'Exactly. Imagine what the press would say if this got out. We'd be lynched.'

'Yes,' Hassleby agreed soberly. 'But ever since Freud any kind of psychological approach to sexual relations has been misunderstood.'

'But the press won't find out,' Mistress Diana pointed out. 'Look at our girls. They can escape, they can leave if they want to. The fact that none has ever left must prove that what we're doing is right. This is Lucy,' she patted her on the head, 'the cause of our recent little panic. Using our own methods we've resolved the problem wholly.'

'I agree,' Dr Niven told her. 'But you can see the kind of pressures that we face. This is a minefield and we really do have to mind every step. This time was very close, as I understand it. But will you be so lucky next time?'

They all fell silent, contemplating the truth of Dr Niven's assessment. Hassleby stood around for a second and then excused himself, rejoining the group he was with earlier.

Jaki couldn't take her eyes off Lucy, who was at Mistress Diana's heel. She was fascinated by the arrangement of the harness, the way it seemed to separate the different parts of the girl's slim body so that each part, a buttock or breast or thigh, was a neat and sexy package. The girl's body was straining against the fetters, and Jaki envied the girl the feeling of containment, the feeling of security and bondage.

Dr Niven stepped towards Jaki and looked at her keenly, his eyes glancing admiringly over the whole body. He put out a hand and brushed Jaki's smooth cheek, almost as if checking to see just how feminine the skin would feel. He nodded approvingly to Mistress Shirer. Jaki accepted the rather rough caresses meekly, knowing that to resist would be to invite punishment and, much worse, to cause her Mistress the gravest of embarrassment.

'And he accepts all this naturally,' Dr Niven said quietly, almost to himself.

'Would you like Jaki to perform some service for you?' Simone offered. 'Please feel free to use her as you wish.'

Dr Niven made no response, but turned to face Lucy, kneeling submissively at Mistress Diana's heel. 'She is one of ours?' he asked, seeking confirmation of the fact.

'Yes. Lucy's been with us for just over six weeks,' Mistress Diana confirmed.

'It's so easy for us to forget about them,' Dr Niven admitted. 'We tend to worry about the funding, or the numbers and statistics. The people just get lost in the detail.' He brushed Lucy's face gently, comparing the softness of the skin with Jaki's. As he passed his fingers over her lips, Lucy opened her mouth and flicked her tongue over them. Dr Niven was intrigued. He stretched a finger and pressed it into Lucy's cool accepting mouth.

Lucy took the finger and began to slide her tongue back and forth over it, moving her head round so that the finger could enter deeper. She closed her eyes and began to suck at the finger, letting her tongue caress it lovingly.

Dr Niven withdrew his hand and smiled at the two Mistresses standing on either side of him. He put his drink down and carefully unzipped his fly, rocked back a bit and then pulled his erect prick out from his underclothes. The Mistresses watched approvingly as he motioned for Lucy to come closer.

Jaki watched wide-eyed as Lucy dropped forward on

to her hands and knees and began to plant slow loving kisses on Dr Niven's hard white rod. Jaki had never seen another erect prick before and she was mesmerised by the sight. She couldn't keep her eyes off the long stretched pole of flesh. From her low position the prick seemed to be massive and threatening, the slightly purple head glistening as Lucy lapped her tongue over it.

Lucy pressed her lips firmly to the base of the prick, the sharp mess of pubic hair an unruly forest. She rubbed her lips up and down, working from the base up to the glistening tip. She pressed the tip of her tongue into the opening in Dr Niven's prick so that the gleaming jewel of seminal fluid was drawn into her mouth. She worked efficiently at the prick, so that Dr Niven could feel a tightness in his belly and his cock twitching and flexing with pleasure. At last she took the glans in her mouth, passing her tongue over it and sucking at it gently. Dr Niven quivered with pleasure and urged his prick all the way into the warm embracing mouth.

Lucy took the full length into her mouth and moved up and down it, licking and sucking. Dr Niven closed his eyes and began to pump long movements into her mouth. She moved faster and faster, trying to take the hardness as far as she could, keeping the same rhythm as Dr Niven. She was sucking deeply, her cheeks drawing in over the rigid tool. Finally Dr Niven let out a strangled aching cry and clutched at her head, forcing his pumping spurting prick as far as it could go.

With a sigh of relief and satisfaction, he stepped back. Jaki couldn't help staring at his prick, which was still hard and glistening in the pale light of the fire.

Lucy sat back and opened her mouth, stuck her tongue out and waited. Dr Niven looked down into the girl's mouth and smiled excitedly. 'She didn't learn that here?' he asked distrustfully.

Diana stepped closer and smiled when she saw the thick creamy sperm still on Lucy's outstretched tongue. 'She's just an excellent fellatrice,' she explained. 'Obviously this is the result of previous experience with boys and the training she has received here.'

'You can swallow,' Dr Niven told her, and watched Lucy swallow the white liquid cleanly. 'Most interesting. She deliberately put herself in the degrading, position of having to ask my permission to swallow.'

'Good girl.' Mistress Diana patted Lucy on the head tenderly.

'Thank you, Mistress. Thank you, Master.' Lucy responded automatically, a look of relish in her eyes.

Jaki watched jealously, envious of the praise that Lucy had received, and peculiarly excited by the act that had just been committed. Lucy resumed her position, kneeling submissively by her Mistress's side. The rest of the party had largely ignored the exhibition, instead sipping their drinks amiably or carrying on deep conversation. Jaki was astounded that everyone was so blase and tried to catch Lucy's eye, to exchange a smile, or simply to acknowledge their shared experience of submission. But Lucy remained still, an unmoving statue bound tightly and with her head bowed in an aspect of deepest humility.

Jaki realised that she was letting her own feeling of excitement disturb her normal submissive posture. She glanced up at her Mistress and was pleased to find herself being completely ignored. She forced herself to sit back fully, averting her gaze and trying to compose herself properly. She knew that she had to block out all the intrusions and to concentrate fully on her Mistress's will. She closed her eyes and steadied her breathing, calming herself slowly, trying to achieve a state of complete subjection, just as Lucy had.

She waited nervously for the chance to be alone with Lucy. She wanted to taste her mouth again, or to explore the inviting crease between her lovely round bum-cheeks. The story was important for J.K. but not for Jaki. There was an uneasy peace between the two opposing personalities, an unspoken symbiotic truce. Jaki would get the story and then she could drive J.K. from her mind and enjoy the pleasures of the party.

The conversation resumed again. Niven and the two Mistresses were joined by another of the Inspectorate, a bright woman of about thirty, dressed in a smart business suit of black skirt and jacket, her white shirt open to reveal the deep inviting cleavage of her breasts. She ran her own business and several of the girls who had left the Institute were employed by her as secretaries and clerical workers.

The conversation was interrupted by the sound of breaking glass and a startled cry. The entire party fell silent and looked round to find one of the serving girls nervously sweeping up the glasses that she had accidentally knocked over.

Fiona Schafer strode across the room and took charge with an air of undisputed authority. She ordered two of the other serving girls to clear up the mess and pulled the guilty girl away and into the centre of the room. The two girls hurriedly cleaned up the mess, their short skirts pulling back when they bent over so that their smooth shapely thighs were invitingly displayed for all to see.

The guilty girl was ordered to clear one of the coffee tables that was dotted around the room. She did as she was told, quickly and efficiently moving all the drinks and snacks on to the other tables and then wiping it with a small cloth so that its polished surface shone.

Jaki was too far away to hear what was being said, but peered up sneakily to watch all that was going on. The girl was ordered to get on to the table on her hands and knees. She did so unsteadily and then looked up with fearful eyes. Her long brown hair fell over her face but the look of trepidation was unmistakable. Mistress Schafer pulled the girl's short skirt over and then pulled the white cotton briefs down. Even in the flickering glow of firelight the girl's scarlet blushes were clear as she looked away, down at the polished table and away, from the staring eyes around the room.

Another girl arrived bearing a silver tray which she presented to Mistress Schafer, who in turn had the tray presented to one of the visitors. The visitor, a ruddy-, faced middle-aged man, beamed with gratitude and selected a short, thick leather strap from the tray. The tray was taken away and the man, who held the strap rather inexpertly, positioned himself behind the girl. He admired the naked backside for a second, made as if to touch the silky bottom-cheeks, then changed his mind.

The first smack rang out across the room and the girl winced visibly. Jaki closed her eyes; the sound was cruel and telling, and she knew from experience just how painful and humiliating a strapping could be. The man and seemed to be using all his strength, and a volley of rapid strikes followed, each stroke resounding around the room. The girl wriggled and winced, her face pale and drawn, but she remained in position, fixed on the tabletop. Her buttocks were barred with thick red marks that flawed the otherwise perfect whiteness of her bottom.

'You disapprove?' Dr Niven asked Mistress Shirer, breaking the silence after the punished girl was made to stand in a corner, her burning buttocks on display for all to see and touch.

Jaki glanced up at her Mistress and saw that she was tightlipped, a look of firm disapproval clouding her dark eyes.

'Yes,' she admitted hesitantly, then more confidently, 'I find that kind of action purely vindictive and selfish.'

'If you had punished her, in exactly the same circumstances, would that have been vindictive and selfish?' Dr Niven continued, sounding slightly surprised by her remark.

'We do that kind of thing all the time,' Diana added with consternation.

'We do, every day.' Simone conceded. 'But the difference is that we have built up a complex and rich relationship with the girls. In this case the punishment is from a stranger, for an act that had nothing to do with him.'

'But I am a stranger to this girl here,' Dr Niven pointed to Lucy. 'Surely the same thing should apply. Was my act vindictive?'

'No,' Mistress Shirer shook her head. 'The difference was that there was no element of punishment, only of humiliation.'

'But they're different sides of the same thing,' Diana interjected, confused by her friend's attitude.

'No, I think it's a valid point to differentiate between the two,' Dr Niven agreed. 'But I still can't quite see what you are getting at.'

'Aren't you being a mite squeamish?' the other woman teased gently.

'Perhaps I am,' Simone smiled. 'But I find the idea that the girl was punished purely for a stranger's edification quite unsavoury. Our role is to punish within context. Punishment for its own sake is not part of our agenda.'

'But it's a difficult question,' the other pointed out. 'If the girl had spilt the drink over his trousers then the punishment would have been acceptable. Or if Fiona Schafer had used the strap, then that would have been acceptable as well.'

'It is a minefield,' Dr Niven repeated, shaking his, head a little sadly.

'It is. But that's why we have to be absolutely clear about what it is that we do. And what we don't do,' Mistress Shirer emphasised.

'But what about Jaki?' Diana asked. 'Do the same rules apply?'

'In part. But Jaki has a different relationship with me, one that isn't mediated by the confines of the Institute.'

'Would you have allowed Jaki to be punished like that?' Diana persisted.

'Yes. Jaki is mine to do with as I please,' she said. 'Jaki belongs to me. The girls do not belong to anyone, not even the Institute.'

'I agree,' Dr Niven finally concurred, aware of the delicacy of the situation, though he was unsure that the other girl's punishment had transgressed the unwritten rules of the situation. 'Tell me, Harriet,' he turned to the other woman, who had called over one of the serving girls, 'how do you handle the girls where you are?'

'Of course my situation is completely different. In some ways I am closer to Simone's situation. There is no Institute to provide a structure. The only formal structure is the framework of employment. I am the employer, the girls are my employees.'

'Do you still spank the girls?' Diana asked, wanting to know more about what her charges did after they left the Institute.

Harriet laughed. 'Sometimes. My girls work very hard, and very well. But they all know that they can be punished if they break the rules.'

'And they do break the rules?' Diana guessed mischievously.

'Some more than others. But so far all my girls from the Institute have been spanked by me or one of my assistants. I know that several break the rules quite deliberately. Usually I spank them all the same. Sometimes I deny them the spanking and that serves to enforce the humiliation.'

'The Minister has asked me, "Do these girls ever get to lead a normal life?"' Dr Niven chuckled. 'My answer is that they get jobs, keep out of trouble and so on. But is it a normal life?'

'Ask him to define a normal life first,' Diana laughed.

'Most of these girls would normally drift into violent relationships anyway. The work has A been done in this area,' Simone added soberly. 'Many of them have already been in relationships with violent men; they have been beaten up and seriously abused. We know that many of them will persist in these relationships. They may swap the man but they won't swap the violence. None of these girls are ever really hurt by us; none of them will turn up in hospital casualty departments with bleeding faces or broken limbs.'

'So the Institute takes away the men and replaces one form of violence with another,' Harriet concluded caustically.

'No!' the two Mistresses replied together.

'We replace an unsteady relationship with a stable environment,' Diana said after a short pause.

'And we replace the real violence with a ritual violence that supplies the same adrenalin and kick that they are addicted to, but without the danger,' Simone said.

'This is one of my girls-to-be,' Harriet said, giving the girl with the drinks tray a friendly pat on the bottom.

'When are you leaving, Christine?' Mistress Diana asked the girl, who looked about her nervously.

'Next week, Mistress,' she replied softly.

'We must do a more detailed follow-up study,' Dr Niven told Harriet and the Mistresses, ignoring the nervous and shy girl.

'Our own initial study shows a zero recidivist rate. Not a single girl has been in trouble with the police so far,' Simone told them proudly.

Harriet was about to say something when she let Christine go. The hapless girl turned, eager to make her escape, and tripped and fell headlong to the floor. Her tray fell to the ground with a loud crash and several empty champagne flutes smashed to the ground. She looked up, mouthing words that didn't come out, her eyes filled with tears and her hands shaking. She started to pull herself up when she realised that there was another body beside her. She turned and saw Jaki, looking dazed, also getting up.

'Clear this mess now,' Mistress Shirer ordered curtly, flicking her hand at the smashed glass and spilt drink on the floor. Christine was joined by another girl and they began to pick their way through the broken glass and mop up the fizzing champagne.

Jaki, who had sat back brushing the spots of drink that wet the tops of her thigh and sparkled against her suspender belt, realised with sudden finality that the blame was to fall on her. 'Please Mistress, it wasn't my fault,' she cried desperately, collapsing to the floor in an abject heap. She scrambled along the floor and began urgently to kiss Mistress Shirer's boots, lapping at the cold smooth leather, knowing that it would do no good. but unable to think of anything else to do. She rubbed her lips along the long sharp length of the heel, pressing her tongue on to the cool rigid hardness.

'May I?' Jaki heard Mistress Diana ask.

Jaki continued to pay homage to the shining boots, passing her mouth over the surface of each one in turn, testing the hardness of the heels in her mouth. She wanted to lose herself in the sensation of adulation. She was already erect, excited purely by the act of tonguing her Mistress's boots so passionately. Dimly she was aware of activity around her, the coming and going of the servant girls. An eager silence fell about the room. All eyes were on her, her bottom raised high, the thin slit of material serving only to expose fully the roundness and tightness of her arse-cheeks.

'Enough!' Mistress Shirer decreed, and grabbed a handful of Jaki's long hair and pulled her away. Jaki sat back on to the cold floor, her eyes darting fearfully from Mistress Shirer to Mistress Diana. 'On to the table, girl!'

she was ordered. Not daring to stand, Jaki crawled miserably across the room, followed by the sound of the two Mistresses marching behind her.

Carefully Jaki climbed on to the empty coffee table. On all fours she fitted the tabletop exactly. Her palms were pressed firmly on the cool polished surface. Her knees ached slightly and she could feel her feet reaching the very end of the table. The chain dangled from her collar like a heavy overgrown necklace. As she looked around she realised, with a shiver of pleasure, that she was perfectly displayed, and that all eyes were on her. Her prick was hard and she felt the first drops of sweat appear on her forehead and between her arse-cheeks.

Mistress Shirer came up behind her and pulled Jaki's panties down, carefully releasing the thick hard prick which swung stiffly for a second. Instinctively Jaki forced her stomach down and her bottom up, wanting to display herself to best advantage, hoping that Mistress Shirer would be pleased, or that some of the smiling appreciative audience would congratulate Mistress on the beauty of her servant.

The latex suspenders were pulled tight over the naked arse-cheeks, and pulled the buttocks fully apart. Jaki's heavy ball sac and the deep bush of pubic hair were clearly visible, the space between the arse-cheeks clean and open, and a faint tinge of rouge had been applied around the alluringly tight anal opening.

There was an exchange of whispers and then Diana withdrew, leaving Mistress Shirer to select an implement from those on the tray offered by one of the serving girls. Jaki caught the girl's eye, and the girl allowed herself the merest hint of a smile as she gazed directly at Jaki's hoisted backside, her eyes sparkling with a glitter of excitement.

Mistress Shirer selected a long thin switch which whistled with cruel promise when it was tested through the air. Jaki bit her lip, afraid, desperately afraid of the punishment to come.

There was a hiss and then a snap as the switch was brought down firmly across Jaki's naked and defenceless rear. She screeched a strangled cry and then a sigh: the lash felt like a burning rod applied to the softest flesh of the body. There was a pause, and the audience murmured appreciatively at the sight of the thin red streak marked against the otherwise pale flesh. She felt her prick stiffen impossibly, even as the first terrible blow sent sparks of pleasure-pain pulsing through her body. She hated herself; the searing pain was always unbearable and always exciting.

There was a second and then a third stroke. The three weals marked separately and in parallel on her flesh, perfect lines of punishment and redemption. Mistress Shirer paused to admire the crisp stamps of disapproval marked positively on the gently trembling arse-cheeks. When she resumed her chastisement she aimed the strokes lower, aiming for the area just above the thick black stocking tops.

Jaki cried out with pain when one of the lashes caught her just above the bulging genital sac. There was a red hot searing pain, an intense unbearable moment of hurt that was followed by a pulsating heat diffused over the rounded arse-cheeks. She could feel her spunk swelling in the pit of her belly, the steady hiss and snap of punishment building up to an uncontrollable frenzy of pleasure and pain. Her eyes were closed and an impression of uncontrolled and involuntary delirium was etched on her face.

She raised her arse higher, wanting to meet the switch on its swift journey to administer correction. She was moaning softly, wanting the pain, aching for the biting impact of the black leather switch.

'A beautiful piece of work,' Dr Niven congratulated Mistress Shirer when she finished. Jaki opened her eyes as a light smattering of applause came from the audience. Biting back the pain, Jaki felt a rush of pride. Her bum-cheeks were sore and aflame from top to bottom, and she could feel hot spots of agonising torment raised on her behind. Fingers of jabbing pain still throbbed with a delicious pleasurable rhythm. Through tear-filled eyes she looked with adoration at her stern and demanding Mistress.

The mass of people, still largely silent and gazing with approval at Jaki's punished form, parted suddenly. The murmur of conversation was silenced and replaced with an expectant hush. Mistress Diana strode elegantly through the parting, poised on steel-tipped red ankle boots. She was naked apart from the boots and a stiff leather bra that raised her breasts high on a shelf. The neatly shaved triangle of hair about her sex was naked, and the lips of her other mouth were swollen and slightly parted.

Mistress Diana was followed obediently by one of the serving girls carrying a silver platter. From her low position on the tabletop Jaki was unable to discern what lay on the platter. Instead her eyes were firmly on Mistress Diana, trying to drink in the full picture: the securely laced ankle boots, the spiky heel a shining threat, the long agile legs reaching up to the bare sex, and the full ripe breasts cupped temptingly by the stiff matt leather bra.

Mistress Shirer leant forward and exchanged a light delicate kiss with Diana. It was a lover's kiss, certain, open and filled with the sweetest of promises.

Mistress Diana turned to the silver platter and picked up a number of straps and chains. These were passed to Christine who took them with a shy and grateful smile. She needed no instructions and approached Jaki directly.

Jaki looked around her in confusion and gazed imploringly at the girl, who smiled knowingly. Christine

253

fell to her knees by the side of the coffee table and laid the bundle of straps and clinking chains by her side. Carefully she retrieved a single strap and chain. Jaki watched with rising horror as the girl applied one strap to the table leg, pulling the buckle tight and tugging at it to test it. The strap was connected to a short silver chain which was in turn connected to another strap. The second strap was applied around Jaki's wrist and pulled tight. The bind was adjusted diligently, and Jaki realised that she was firmly tied to the table. The other arm was also attached to a table leg. Jaki tried to pull free, to see how much room she had to manoeuvre, and found that there was none.

Mistress Shirer watched as Jaki's heels were similarly chained to the coffee table. She ignored Jaki's beseeching look, not even deigning to acknowledge the look of horror dawning on her face. Christine bound Jaki's heels in the same way, pausing only to stare for a second at the bulging prick crying a single tear of glistening fluid.

Unable to move, Jaki strained to look back. Her arse was still smarting and alive with an intense tingling ache. She felt hot, her prick aching, and she knew that she could hardly contain herself.

Mistress Diana coolly picked her chosen implement from the platter. It looked a little like the kind of thing that Lucy wore, a complex cradle of straps and chains. However, firmly embedded in the weave was a long black object like an upturned arch. Mistress Diana smiled as she undid the straps and carefully climbed into the costume then slowly pulled it up from the knees. She took the central device in one hand and with the other she parted the opening to her sex. Very slowly she eased one end of the thing deep into herself. There was a delicious thrill of pleasure as she forced the thing into place, forcing it against the walls of her moist pussy and letting it rest against her centre of bliss.

Jaki stared, wide-eyed with disbelief. Mistress Diana proudly showed off the massive false penis that emerged from between her thighs. She held it proudly while Lucy pulled all the straps tight so that the penis was firmly positioned under the thighs and held fast by straps around-the waist and another strap between the buttocks.

The penis was large and thick, much bigger than any man could be. Its matt black surface was smooth, and the end was a hard spherical head that stood out menacingly.

Jaki tried to pull away, frightened by the dangerous looking object, shocked by the size and the obvious look of intent that shone in Mistress Diana's eyes. The chains clinked and the table rocked a little, but Jaki knew that there was no escape.

Lucy crawled forward on her hands and knees, eyeing the false rod with fear and respect. She was handed a tube, and obediently she squeezed out a thick wad of clear translucent jelly on to her tongue. Very slowly she applied the jelly to her tongue; it was cool and tasteless but seemed to glow in the dancing light of the fire. At last, when her tongue was heavy with the thick jelly, she raised herself up and began to smear the jelly over the hard prick jutting proudly from Mistress Diana's engorged sex.

Mistress Diana closed her eyes and enjoyed the reciprocal feel of the pretend prick deep in her sex. Lucy was mouthing it expertly, taking as much as she could into her mouth and using her tongue to spread the jelly over the surface. Lucy squeezed more jelly on to her tongue and then spread it lazily over the hardness, ensuring that every inch of the massive object was wet with a glistening layer of lubricating jelly, from the glistening globe at the head to the very base where the jelly mixed with the first golden drops of juice from Mistress Diana's tightly filled cunt.

Lucy sat back and looked at Jaki, bound tightly on to the table, her arse quivering from the afterburn of punishment. Their eyes met for a second. Jaki nodded hopefully, expectantly. Lucy shook her head. For a second, a half smile flickered on Jaki's pale withered face. They knew then that there was no turning back. Neither Jaki nor Lucy could deliver the story. They were the story, and whilst they were willing to sacrifice themselves for their Mistresses' pleasure, they were unprepared to sacrifice themselves for baser motives.

The audience was silent, stunned by the perversity of the exhibition underway before them. A number of the serving girls were being quietly touched, some by staff, others by the guests and some by other girls. The sexual tension in the room was electric and was centred on the view of Jaki and Mistress Diana.

Jaki wanted to cry out, petrified of the lustrous penis that Mistress Diana sported. It was unnatural and frightening. But Jaki was also filled with an excitement that she could hardly fight; the thing was both a promise and a threat. She knew that Mistress Shirer would expect her to give herself fully, and that was the sole purpose of existence. To resist would be to deny herself and to deny Mistress Shirer.

Mistress Diana took Jaki by the waist. She placed one knee on the edge of the coffee table and positioned herself behind Jaki's tormented and marked backside. With her hand she pressed the head of her prick at the entrance to the jewel that she had wanted from the first.

Jaki gasped when the head of the monster was pressed against her tight anal hole. She held her breath, unable to believe that the thing could enter without tearing her. Mistress Diana leant forward in a single slow movement and somehow Jaki's arsehole opened and took the full circumference of the fully lubricated pole.

Jaki cried out once, a shrill cry of pain as the immense prick was prised into her accommodating rear hole. She wanted to fight the intrusion, to push against the cool shaft that slid deep between the walls of her arse. It took forever to fill her, a single long action deep into her insides. Mistress Diana halted when the thick rod had been pushed as far as it could go. She rested a second, catching her breath, her heart pounding wildly. Every subtle movement in Jaki's bumhole was amplified by the long tool into a delicious pattern on her pussy, the two poles of the tool an integral whole.

Jaki felt as if she had been cleaved in two; her buttocks were spread fully apart, her bumhole gripping tightly around the base of the prick. There was a feeling of discomfort, a pain that wouldn't go away. But this was complimented by the delight of feeling the thick base of the prick wedged firmly into her wide arsehole. She had taken the fullness of the monster without tearing, and the pleasure of acceptance was mixed with a sense of pride.

Mistress Diana began to pump the penis in and out of Jaki's hole, pressing herself back and forth in long slow fluid strokes. She savoured the feel of fucking the servant girl fully in the arse; the pleasure of sodomy had its own special thrill. She could feel Jaki responding under her, trying her best to take the hardness without pain. She began to pump harder, gyrating her pelvis, thrusting the heaviness faster and faster, somehow managing to drive deeper into Jaki's virginal backside.

Jaki turned back and saw Mistress Shirer laughing with Dr Niven, enjoying the view. Jaki closed her eyes and relaxed, secure that her Mistress was happy with the performance. Mistress Diana was thrusting harder and harder, and Jaki could hear her panting and releasing short gasps of delight. Each push lasted an age, the oiled weapon gliding smoothly in and out of her arsehole, which expanded and contracted over the thickness of the beast.

She also began to moan. Each thrust, and they were

becoming rapid, piercing drives, seemed to inject a greater degree of pleasure into her. Her own prick seemed to be directly connected to the force driving pleasurably into her arse-pussy. She realised at last that she was being fucked like a woman, that the thrusting tool in her arse-pussy was pressing against a secret place that caused her so much pleasure. Her buttocks were still painful from the thrashing, but that only added to the excitement and the delight. She suffered her secret joy in public, glad that so many eyes could see her being so expertly buggered by a beautiful Mistress. She wanted the glory to reflect on her Mistress.

Jaki opened her eyes suddenly, disturbed by an unexpected caress on the face. She was surprised to find that a stranger stood before her. He was naked and was holding his strong hard prick in his hand.

For a second Jaki studied the length of flesh that he held for her. She saw that the head was a dark gleaming purple, the length slightly ribbed, and that it was twitching noticeably. Without stopping to think, she passed her tongue over the glans, tasting the salty taste of prick for the first time. She turned to Mistress Shirer who nodded her assent, her eyes glowing with pleasure and, Jaki hoped, pride.

The stranger inched closer. Jaki pressed her lips and tongue over the full length of the warm flesh. She contrasted the cool hardness fucking her in the arse with the more pliant hardness of the real thing. She opened her mouth and took it fully, sucking immediately at the dewdrops of fluid that were dribbling from the eye. The stranger began to move back and forth, and she rose and fell over the prick.

Jaki was overwhelmed with sensations. She was sucking at the prick being forced into her mouth, alive to it's different textures and to its taste filling her mouth. From behind, Mistress Diana was fucking her vigorously, impaling her with the double prick that pleasured them both. She wanted to cry out with pleasure, but her sobs were stifled by the urgent fucking in her mouth.

A great cry silenced the room. Mistress Diana was seized by a wild swirl of bliss. Her soaking pussy exploded with delight, as she climaxed with a headlong rush into the valley of oblivion and elation. At the same instant the stranger took Jaki's head in his hands and forced his prick deep into the back of her throat. She almost gagged as the man began to spurt thick wads of jism. She felt the velvet purity of the come on her tongue and in her mouth, and swallowed it down, feeling the honey glide down her throat smoothly.

She could contain herself no longer. Her mouth was still sucking at the last drops of come from the prick that had fucked her there. Her arsehole was still wedged tightly over the thick rigid pole that had buggered her so well, and had brought Mistress Diana to climax.

She began to sob. Tears streamed down her face. Her prick was pumping thick globules of spunk over her belly and on to the table. She felt that she was falling through space.

She opened her eyes and looked round at her Mistress who gave her the faintest hint of a smile.

Jaki was happy.